## The Monk Series

# Mr. Monk
# Gets
# Even

# MR. MONK
## GETS EVEN

A NOVEL BY

## LEE GOLDBERG
Based on the USA Network
television series created by

## ANDY BRECKMAN

AN OBSIDIAN MYSTERY

OBSIDIAN
Published by New American Library, a division of
Penguin Group (USA) Inc., 375 Hudson Street,
New York, New York 10014, USA
Penguin Group (Canada), 90 Eglinton Avenue East, Suite 700, Toronto,
Ontario M4P 2Y3, Canada (a division of Pearson Penguin Canada Inc.)
Penguin Books Ltd., 80 Strand, London WC2R 0RL, England
Penguin Ireland, 25 St. Stephen's Green, Dublin 2,
Ireland (a division of Penguin Books Ltd.)
Penguin Group (Australia), 250 Camberwell Road, Camberwell, Victoria 3124,
Australia (a division of Pearson Australia Group Pty. Ltd.)
Penguin Books India Pvt. Ltd., 11 Community Centre, Panchsheel Park,
New Delhi - 110 017, India
Penguin Group (NZ), 67 Apollo Drive, Rosedale, Auckland 0632,
New Zealand (a division of Pearson New Zealand Ltd.)
Penguin Books (South Africa) (Pty.) Ltd., 24 Sturdee Avenue,
Rosebank, Johannesburg 2196, South Africa

Penguin Books Ltd., Registered Offices:
80 Strand, London WC2R 0RL, England

First published by Obsidian, an imprint of New American Library,
a division of Penguin Group (USA) Inc.

First Printing, January 2013
10  9  8  7  6  5  4  3  2  1

LIBRARY OF CONGRESS CATALOGING-IN-PUBLICATION DATA:

GOLDBERG, LEE, 1962–
    Mr. Monk gets even: a novel/by Lee Goldberg; based on the USA Network television series
created by Andy Breckman.
    p. cm.
    ISBN 978-0-451-23915-0
    1. Monk, Adrian (Fictitious character)—Fiction. 2. Private investigators—Fiction. 3.
Eccentrics and eccentricities—Fiction. 4. Obsessive-compulsive disorder—Fiction. 5. Murder—
Investigation—Fiction. 6. San Francisco (Calif.)—Fiction. 7. Mystery fiction. I. Breckman, Andy.
II. Title.
    PS3557.O3577M727 2013
    813'.54—dc23          2012031430

Set in ITC New Baskerville

Printed in the United States of America

PUBLISHER'S NOTE
This is a work of fiction. Names, characters, places, and incidents either are the product of the
author's imagination or are used fictitiously, and any resemblance to actual persons, living or
dead, business establishments, events, or locales is entirely coincidental.
    The publisher does not have any control over and does not assume any responsibility for
author or third-party Web sites or their content.

*To Valerie and Madison*

This is the end for me and my long, wonderful association with Adrian Monk. The series of books may continue, but this is my fifteenth and final *Monk* book.

The association began when *Monk* creator Andy Breckman hired me and my then screenwriting and producing partner William Rabkin to write an episode of the TV series titled "Mr. Monk Goes to Mexico," which would end up being the first of three episodes we wrote for the show.

At the time, Bill and I were about to begin writing and producing the Lifetime TV series *Missing* and I was deep into writing the *Diagnosis Murder* novels, which were based on the TV series of the same name that we'd also written and executive produced.

When Andy was approached by NAL about writing the *Monk* novels, he declined the opportunity and recommended that I write them instead.

I took the assignment, which was an insane thing to do, since it would mean writing a new book by night every ninety days, alternating between *Monk* and *Diagnosis Murder*, while also running a TV series during the day.

That's how much I loved Adrian Monk.

I kept up that brutal pace for two years before finally ending the *Diagnosis Murder* book series.

Andy liked my first *Monk* novel, *Mr. Monk Goes to the Firehouse*, so much that he hired Bill and me to adapt it into an episode of the TV show. The episode, titled "Mr. Monk Can't See a Thing," may be the first time in American TV history that a tie-in novel of a TV show has been adapted into an episode of the series . . . and by the author of the book, no less. (If it's ever been done before, we haven't found it. And if it has been done, it's obviously a rare occurrence!)

If it wasn't for Andy's enthusiasm and support, I doubt I would have written so many *Monk* novels or had so much fun doing them. He gave me his trust and the creative freedom to make the book series entirely my own, and for that I will always be grateful.

I want to thank Kerry Donovan, who has been my editor on this series from the very beginning, my agent Gina Maccoby, who put together the deal, and my go-to medical and forensic expert, Dr. D. P. Lyle. I also regularly leaned on my "cop buddies" Paul Bishop, Lee Lofland, and Robin Burcell for their expertise on police matters, and I hope I didn't embarrass them too much with the great liberties I took with the information they gave me.

It's not easy writing two books a year, particularly if you're doing it part-time while making your living in television. I can trace my life in these books, like *Mr. Monk in Outer Space* and *Mr. Monk Goes to Germany*, both of which I wrote while writing, producing, and shooting a movie in Berlin and Cologne. They kept me sane, and out of trouble, while I was far away from home.

For the most part, though, the time I spent on these books was time I didn't spend with my family, particularly on this last one, which required more than a few all-nighters. So, with deep appreciation, I want to thank my wife, Valerie, and my daughter, Madison, for the sacrifices they made during the past seven years while I pretended to be a woman assisting an obsessive-compulsive detective on his investigations.

And finally, I want to thank all of you for being such devoted readers, and for the many e-mails, letters, and kind words you've shared with me over the years about these books. It meant a lot to me.

Lee Goldberg
Los Angeles, California
June 2012

# Mr. Monk
# Gets
# Even

# CHAPTER ONE

# Mr. Monk Is Murder

'd never gone so long without a murder.

Investigating one, that is.

In the six months since I'd moved to Summit, New Jersey, to work as a police officer, I hadn't come across a single homicide.

And for me, that was a major adjustment. That's because for years I was the personal assistant to Adrian Monk, the famous detective and consultant to the San Francisco Police Department, and it seemed like we couldn't go anywhere or do anything without getting involved in a murder investigation.

The man was a murder magnet. It used to drive me crazy (that, and his obsessive-compulsive disorder). It didn't matter whether we were at a family wedding, on a flight to Paris, attending a play, visiting a winery, or shopping for groceries—we'd inevitably find a corpse. He couldn't go two days without ending up in the middle of a homicide investigation.

And now, after all my complaining, I actually found myself missing the murders. Let me qualify that before you write me off as a terrible person. It's not the violent loss of someone's life that I missed, but rather the intensity, complexity, and high stakes of the investigation that often followed.

The crimes I investigated in Summit weren't nearly as interesting, complicated, or important as murder, which I suppose was a good thing—at least for the community I was serving, and for police Chief Randy Disher, who'd recruited me. He was formerly a lieutenant at the SFPD, where he'd been the right-hand man to Captain Leland Stottlemeyer, the guy who Monk worked for.

Disher got to know me well while I was Monk's assistant, but not as well as he got to know Monk's previous assistant, Sharona Fleming. The two of them fell in love and he moved to Summit to be with her.

Disher warned me that things moved a little slower in Summit than they did in San Francisco, and that was true. Except, of course, for the short time Monk was here, when suddenly there was an armed robbery, a firebombing, and a murder all in the space of a couple of days.

Since then, though, the biggest crime I'd had to contend with was one that Monk, with his obsessions for cleanliness and order, would have actually considered truly heinous: I was investigating a string of laundry detergent thefts from area grocery stores, including more than twenty-five thousand dollars' worth from a single store in Summit.

That's what led me to spend my day off in Sharona's old, dented Volvo wagon in the grocery store's parking lot, waiting for the thief to strike again. Since we were only a six-person force, I was doing the stakeout on my own. But I figured that after facing countless murderers I could handle a mere detergent thief by myself, even if he was the Professor Moriarty of his field of crime.

Although life in Summit wasn't particularly exciting, I still enjoyed being a cop. Next to being Monk's assistant, it was by far the best job I'd ever had and the first one I'd earned based on my skills and proven performance rather than being something that I'd just chanced into (like working for Monk) or grabbed out of financial necessity (like every other job I'd ever had).

So I took enormous pride in the badge and gun that I carried and the uniform that I usually wore, even if I was often bored, homesick, and lonely.

I hadn't had a chance to find an apartment in Summit yet, so I was living at a local hotel at a discounted "law enforcement" rate (which meant I was also the unofficial "house detective" for the hotel and got called whenever a guest got rowdy or anything disappeared). So it wasn't as though I was living in solitude.

And I certainly didn't lack dating opportunities. Plenty of men in Summit hit on me—I just wasn't interested in pursuing a relationship. I wasn't missing out on the excitement of life in the big city, either, not with New York just a forty-five-minute train ride away.

What I missed was San Francisco itself and my life there. I missed the fog and sourdough bread, the cable cars and the Golden Gate, the steep hills and bay windows. But most of all, I missed my twenty-year-old daughter, Julie, even though she'd moved away from home to live across the bay and attend UC Berkeley long before I left.

Now she was on summer break and working as Monk's temporary assistant. Julie was living in our house again since we hadn't had any luck renting it out, and she was trying to save what little money she was earning. Nobody would ever get rich working for Adrian Monk.

At first, I'd called her two or three times a week . . . until she stopped answering my calls. I got the subtle hint. So I cut my calls back to once every few weeks so she wouldn't find me quite so needy and irritating.

And as infuriating, demanding, and frustrating as Monk was, I missed him, too. I had known that I would, but I hadn't expected to miss him quite so much.

He'd called me a few times since I'd moved, mostly to talk about Julie. He'd usually start by saying what a great assistant she was, and then complain that her car was a rolling death trap (because the tires on her car were a mix of brands and didn't have matching tread designs) or that she drank smoothies (he was afraid of milk and couldn't stand the idea of various fruits being blended together) or that she expressed a wanton disregard for human decency (for wearing a bracelet on one wrist without a matching one on the other). These were all deficiencies in her character that naturally he attributed to lazy parenting on my part.

You'd think that infuriating diatribes like that would make me thankful that I was a few thousand miles away from him, but the anger and irritation he caused only made me more homesick.

It's crazy, I know.

And I had to keep my craziness a secret from both Julie and Monk.

So I pumped Ellen Morse for information about them during her biweekly trips from San Francisco back to Summit to manage her store, Poop, where she sold products made from excrement, including shampoo, artwork, stationery, incense, and even coffee. She'd opened a second store in San Francisco just to be closer to Monk, who'd improbably and miraculously started a relationship with her during the short time that he was in Summit, despite the fact that he was repulsed by what she did for a living.

But Ellen was slightly obsessive-compulsive herself, at least as far as symmetry and organization went, and loved Monk, though she was frustrated by his crippling fear of intimacy. They hadn't kissed yet and he'd held her hand only once, just long enough to give it a squeeze, and then had immediately slathered his hands with disinfectant cream, which killed not only germs but also the slightest shred of romance.

The way I looked at it, Ellen was lucky he touched her at all, considering she regularly handled poop products—such as fossilized dinosaur dung and greeting cards made from buffalo crap—with her bare hands. She'd repeatedly assured Monk that the products were totally safe and sanitary, but he didn't see how that was possible if they were derived from poop. Intellectually, I knew she was right. But instinctively, even I had to side with Monk.

He was on my mind while I sat on that boring stakeout because of the nature of the crime that I was investigating— detergent thefts—and because in a few short days I would be back in San Francisco, taking an early vacation to attend the wedding of Monk's agoraphobic brother, Ambrose. He was marrying Yuki, his ex-con, biker-chick girlfriend and live-in assistant.

That was bound to be a memorable event.

Before I could give much thought to it, my attention was drawn to a short man in his thirties wearing an untucked red flannel shirt over a gray hoodie. He was rushing out of the grocery store and pushing a cart filled with jugs of Tide detergent.

I was pretty sure he hadn't paid for any of it and that he'd managed to slip past the busy cashiers without being noticed. So I got out of my car and met him just as he popped the trunk on a 2005 Chevy Malibu with badly oxidized blue paint. Monk would have arrested him just for the lousy paint job.

The man was jittery, and all his facial features looked like they were crammed way too close together, as if his head had been scrunched by some heavy object, so he appeared to be wincing even before I pulled out my badge and flashed it at him.

"Excuse me, sir. I'm Natalie Teeger, Summit Police," I said. "What's your name?"

"Jack Badelaire," he said.

"Can I see some ID?"

"What's the problem?" He took out his wallet and handed me his driver's license. He was indeed Jack Badelaire, and a resident of Summit.

"I've never seen anybody buy so much detergent at one time," I said.

He shrugged. "I'm a very clean person."

He obviously didn't know who he was talking to. I got

right in his face. "The hell you are. I spent years working for Adrian Monk, the cleanest man on earth. He wipes his bottles of disinfectant with disinfectant. He cleans his brooms after every use and replaces them weekly. He washes his doorknobs in the dishwasher. Once a year, he removes his flooring and scrubs the concrete foundation underneath. So don't you dare tell me that you're a very clean person, because compared to him, you live in filth."

He looked frightened now, and not because I was a cop who'd caught him committing a crime. He thought he was dealing with an armed lunatic. Perhaps he was.

"I know," he said. "That's why I need detergent."

"All this is for you?"

"I have a big, dirty family."

I nodded. "Can I see your receipt?"

He made an elaborate show of looking through his wallet and his pockets. "I must have lost it."

"No problem. We'll just go back inside the store and find your cashier. I'm sure she'll remember you. It's not often they get a guy buying a dozen jugs of Tide."

"I think she went on break," he said.

"Then we'll ask the manager to call up your transaction on the register."

He licked his lips and shifted his weight. "You know, I am so tired and distracted, it's possible I might have forgotten to pay. It's very hectic in the store today. I can go back inside and pay now."

"Let me tell you what's going to happen, Mr. Badelaire. I'm going to arrest you for shoplifting. Then I'm going to look through weeks of store security footage, and we both know I'll discover that you've forgotten to pay for cartloads of detergent many times, so the charge against you is going to become felony theft, and you'll end up doing hard time in prison. Of course, there's another way we can handle this."

"You can let me off with a stern warning?"

"You can tell me where you were going to deliver the detergent and agree to be a prosecution witness against the others in the ring. You could get off with just restitution and probation, though that will ultimately be up to the DA and the judge."

"What makes you think there's a ring?"

"Well, I sure hope there is, for your sake," I said. "Otherwise you're going straight to prison."

I think he grimaced, but it was hard to tell with that scrunched-up face of his.

"There's a ring," he said.

"I thought there might be," I said.

The U-Store-It facility outside of town was composed of three long, flat-roofed, one-story, cinder-block buildings that contained dozens of individual storage units, each about the size of a single-car garage, with roll-up corrugated-metal doors that were painted orange.

There was a tall fence topped with razor wire around the property and only one gated entryway for cars. The walk-in gate, however, was propped open with a brick, so people like me could get in without having to punch in the required code. That seemed like a mighty big security breach, but there was a reason for it.

An open storage unit at the end of one of the long rows was

attracting a steady flow of people, mostly women. The ones who were leaving the unit carried grocery bags or were pushing shopping carts I recognized as having been borrowed from Costco and several other local big-box stores. The carts and bags were full of diapers, shampoo, and laundry detergent.

I approached the storage unit, looking like a weary, beaten-down single mother without much cash. It wasn't a hard performance for me to pull off. I'd had plenty of experience in that role.

The storage unit was laid out like a mini-mart, with metal shelving along the walls and one freestanding set down the middle. A young Asian woman in a T-shirt and jeans sat on a folding chair behind a card table with a cash register on top. She was reading a tattered Michael Connelly paperback. I wondered whether the book was stolen, too. Behind her, listening to an iPod, stood a big Hispanic guy in a tight tank top that showed off all his muscles and tats. I guess he was there to prevent shoplifting from the shoplifters. I wondered whether he'd paid for the music on his iPod or if it was pirated.

The cashier glanced at me and said, by rote, "Everything is half off the ticketed price."

"Thanks," I said, and went inside.

I browsed the shelves. They sold soap and cleaning supplies, mostly, along with some basic foods such as flour, rice, and breakfast cereal. A refrigerator in the back was filled with jugs of milk. The thieves didn't even bother hiding where their merchandise had come from or what it actually cost. Each item was still marked with the original price stickers from the stores they were stolen from. In fact, the information was a selling point to their cash-strapped clientele.

I knew it was a profitable enterprise. They paid an army of shoplifters twenty percent of the retail price of the items they stole, and then sold the items for half price. It doesn't sound like much, but the profits could really add up. They made five dollars tax free on every fifty-ounce bottle of Tide that they sold.

Part of me felt guilty for what I was about to do. The only reason that this underground market existed and thrived was because so many people in the present economy simply couldn't afford to pay full price for milk, soap, and other basic necessities.

I grabbed a bottle of Tide and took it to the front table. "Do you take credit cards?"

The woman looked up at me from her book and sneered. "Cash only."

"Do you give a law enforcement discount?" I reached into my purse and pulled out my badge.

The woman, and the four other customers in the store, bolted. But the big Hispanic guy was resigned to his fate. He stayed where he was and raised his hands in surrender. He'd probably been in trouble with the law before and didn't want to add resisting arrest to his offenses.

While I read him his rights and handcuffed him, the woman was nabbed by the two uniformed police officers who were waiting at the gate, the only way out of the property. I'd called them in for backup before I'd arrived.

By the time I got to the gate with my prisoner, the cashier was in the backseat of the patrol car and Chief Disher had pulled up in his police-issue SUV.

Disher was in his late forties, but he had a boyish quality

that made him look easily half his age. And when he was dressed in uniform, as he was now, complete with his wide-brimmed ranger-style hat, he looked like a kid in a costume. The big goofy smile on his boyish face only underscored that impression.

"Great work, Natalie," he said. "It wouldn't surprise me if this arrest brings down the entire criminal enterprise."

"Thanks, but it's hardly the French Connection," I said as I put my prisoner in the backseat of the patrol car. "They're selling stolen laundry detergent and low-fat milk, not cocaine and heroin."

"Yeah," said the woman in the backseat. "You should be going after real criminals."

"You are a real criminal, lady," Disher said, then slammed the door and turned to me. "You're not looking at the big picture."

"There's a big picture?"

He led me away from the car. "I'll bet my badge that this isn't the only underground store this ring is operating. We'll cut a deal with the woman you just arrested and she'll sing like Adele and bring down the whole operation to save herself. The Summit Chamber of Commerce and the New Jersey Grocers Association are going to be very grateful to you."

"That's my dream." I gestured to the four frightened customers who were being interviewed by the uniformed officers. "What about them? They are probably working for minimum wage or less. Their only crime is just trying to get by."

Disher glanced at them. "I understand how you feel and you don't have to worry—we're not going to arrest them. But these thefts cost legitimate businesses tens of thousands of dollars, and to make up those losses, they cut back on employees or close stores, putting more people in the same lousy financial situation as those folks are in who were shopping here today."

He had a good point. "I hadn't thought of it that way."

"Not only that, but petty thieves and drug addicts swarm to areas where they know they can make a quick buck selling shoplifted items, and that causes a domino effect in crime. We don't want that element here."

"You've given this a lot of thought," I said.

"That's why I wear the big hat," he said. "This may not be the most exciting investigation you've ever been a part of, and laundry detergent may not be as sexy as recovering blood diamonds, rescuing a kidnapped child, or catching a serial killer, but this is what real, street-level law enforcement is all about. And most impressive of all, you did it on your own time. You should be proud of yourself."

Maybe so, but I wasn't feeling it.

I remembered the satisfaction, the pure adrenaline rush that I felt every single time I helped Monk solve a murder, particularly on those cases that seemed utterly unsolvable.

This felt nothing like it. Nor did any of the other arrests I'd made or crimes that I'd solved since I got to Summit.

I was beginning to wonder if I'd ever feel that way again, or if it was even possible without Monk.

# CHAPTER TWO

# Mr. Monk and His Assistant

**W**hile I was in Summit, hot on the trail of laundry detergent thieves, life was going on as usual for Monk, Julie, and my friends in the San Francisco Police Department.

Which brings me to the story of a BMW 320i parked on a downtown street. The roof was flattened and the windows were shattered. That's what happens when a two-hundred-pound weight is dropped on the ultimate driving machine from seventeen stories up.

But when that two-hundred-pound weight is a human body, it also creates a gory mess that draws a crowd of shocked onlookers and a swarm of crime scene investigators and homicide detectives.

And if it happens in San Francisco, it also draws Adrian Monk.

He was standing still beside the BMW, but his attention wasn't on the corpse. He was staring at a gleaming silver 2004 Mercedes CLK Brabus parked across the street.

My daughter, Julie, was a couple yards away, checking her e-mail on her iPhone. She wasn't uncomfortable around crime scenes, but she wasn't eager to hang around dead bodies, either. Besides, she figured her job was getting Monk to the body, not examining it with him.

But she knew it was her responsibility to run interference for Monk, to make sure that he was free of distractions so he could concentrate on the task at hand, so when she glanced up and saw that he wasn't walking around the body, looking for clues, she sighed, stuck her phone in her back pocket, and walked over to him.

"What's the problem, Mr. Monk?"

"I'm revolted," he said.

"You can't see most of the body," she said. "It's under a tarp. Only his feet are sticking out. But his shoes are clean and his laces are tied."

"I'm not talking about the body," Monk said.

Julie followed his gaze to the Mercedes across the street.

If it were me, at that point I'd have tried to figure out what Monk found objectionable about the car, then attempted to make him see how petty and irrelevant the problem was compared to the dead body that was right in front of him.

It was an argument I would lose, which meant I'd have to find the owner of the car, then convince whoever it was to fix whatever was dirty, crooked, or imbalanced about the Mercedes, and then get Monk to calm down and focus on the investigation.

But my daughter took a different approach. She slipped her messenger bag off her shoulder, went over to the forensic unit van, foraged around inside it as if it were her own, and emerged with a folded blue tarp, which she carefully spread out evenly over the Mercedes so that it was completely covered.

Then she walked back over to Monk. "Is that better?"

"Thank you," he said. "But you need to make a note to have a police officer deal with that before we go."

"Will do," she said.

"You don't know what I am talking about, do you?"

She shrugged. "I'll just have them tow the car. That should solve the problem."

"But the back rests in the front seats will still be at different angles and the headrests at different heights."

"Yes, but the car won't be on the street anymore. Besides, having it towed will teach the owner an important lesson," Julie said. "Now he'll know not to leave his car without first making sure that all the seats and headrests are in the same position."

Monk thought about it for a moment, then nodded with approval. "You're right. Good thinking."

She smiled. "Just doing my job."

It was a job that was only supposed to last for a week or two, just until Monk found someone to replace me. But at the time the unemployment rate in California, a state teetering on bankruptcy, was at historic highs and she needed work, so she stuck with him.

It was a smooth transition for her. Julie didn't have to apply for a job, try to impress anybody, or learn new skills. Monk was like family. So unlike me, when she started working for him, she was already familiar with every bizarre facet of his obsessive-compulsive disorder. She wasn't startled by his behavior, confused by his arcane rules, or baffled by his phobias. It was life as usual for her.

And she certainly wasn't uncomfortable around cops.

Captain Stottlemeyer was like an uncle to her and she thought that his right-hand man, Lieutenant Amy Devlin, a former undercover detective with whom I had a rocky relationship, was probably the coolest woman she'd ever met.

It was a smooth transition for Monk, too. He'd known Julie since she was a little girl. And having her there almost made it feel like I hadn't really left him. It kept a big part of me in his life, even if I was thousands of miles away. Besides, he didn't like change. Sticking with her meant he didn't have to make any effort to find someone else or let a stranger into his life.

But their working relationship was definitely different from the one that he and I had. For one thing, Julie wasn't nearly as stressed out by him as I was. Nor was she as accommodating to his needs. Her attitude was that he was a grown man and that she was his assistant, not his babysitter. And this was her job, not her life.

Not only had she grown up around Monk, but more important, she'd grown up around me working for Monk, and she wasn't going to make the same mistakes that I had.

While Monk walked slowly around the BMW, his hands out in front of him, framing the scene like a director picking his shots, Julie stayed on the sidewalk and texted Devlin, who was with Captain Stottlemeyer in the victim's seventeenth-floor apartment, telling her what they were up to.

Devlin sent back a text telling her to come up to the apartment with Monk as soon as he was done surveying the scene.

Unlike my daughter, I wouldn't have been standing around texting. I would have been right beside Monk, evidence baggies and wipes at the ready, trying to see for myself what the clues were. I involved myself in the cases.

Not Julie.

She was more interested in getting home and salvaging what was left of her Saturday night. The call from Captain Stottlemeyer had interrupted her date with Ricky Capshaw, an aspiring singer, who was still in our living room watching movies on Netflix.

Monk took tweezers from his pocket and used them to pick up a pair of glasses from the street. Both of the lenses were cracked and one of the arms was broken. He held the glasses up in front of his eyes and squinted at them, then waved his hand at Julie. She knew what that meant.

She took an evidence baggie from her messenger bag and held it open for Monk. He dropped the glasses inside. "What's so special about the glasses?"

"Nothing," Monk said. "They are common reading glasses."

"So why are we bagging them?" She sealed the baggie and stowed it.

"He might have been wearing them when he fell."

"Is that significant?"

Monk shrugged, then tipped his head toward the corpse's feet, which were sticking out from under the tarp on top of the car. They reminded Julie of the Wicked Witch's feet peeking out from under Dorothy's house after it landed in Munchkinland. She half expected the feet to curl up and disappear underneath the tarp.

"He wears size eight shoes," Monk said. "They're New Balance 622s."

"What about them?"

"They are very clean," he said. "And a fine brand."

"So?"

"It shows he was a decent man," Monk said. "What else do we know about him?"

"All I was told was that his name was David Zuzelo and that he either fell, jumped, or was pushed from his apartment balcony," Julie said.

"Which apartment was his?"

Julie pointed up. "Seventeenth floor, second balcony on the left."

Monk staggered back and closed his eyes. Heights made him dizzy, even from the ground. "I'm going to need four bottles of Fiji water and fifty disinfectant wipes."

That's because he was afraid of elevators, which meant that he'd be taking the stairs to the seventeenth floor, counting each step and disinfecting the handrail with a wet wipe as he went along. The Fiji waters, the only water he drank (and brushed his teeth with), were to hydrate him during his climb.

If this had been Saturday afternoon, Julie would have wished him luck and told him she'd meet him at the apartment later. And while he was climbing, she'd have gone to a Starbucks, bought a coffee, and made a few calls before taking the elevator up to the apartment.

But it was Saturday night, her boyfriend was on our couch at home, and she didn't want to waste time.

"I have a better idea," she said. She tapped a key on her iPhone, then held the device up in front of the two of them. Julie's iPhone was connected to the apartment's wireless network and so was Devlin's. An instant later Devlin appeared live on screen and they could see each other thanks to Face-Time.

"Are you two ready to come up?" Devlin asked. Her hair looked like she'd cut it herself blindfolded and using hedge shears. She was not a woman who cared much about her appearance. Not that she needed to. She was in great shape and had perfect skin, except for a few little scars here and there from the fights she'd been in.

"Mr. Monk won't get in an elevator, so he'd have to take the stairs all the way up, which he'd be glad to do," Julie said. "But since the apartment is on the seventeenth floor, that adds an unnecessary risk."

Monk smiled at Julie with pride. She knew him so well.

Devlin looked bewildered. "What's the risk?"

As far as Devlin was concerned, risk in any situation was a plus. It's why she became a cop.

Monk leaned in so his face appeared on-camera. "This is Adrian Monk speaking."

"Yes, I know," Devlin said. "I can see you."

"The risk is that it's an odd-numbered floor," Monk said. "Very high up."

"So?"

"Look what happened to David Zuzelo," Monk said.

"It's not going to happen to you," Devlin said.

"It could," Monk said. "Or worse."

"What could be worse than dying?" Devlin asked.

"I have a list," Monk said. "It's indexed. You can borrow Captain Stottlemeyer's copy."

"No, she can't." Stottlemeyer leaned in close to Devlin so his face was on-camera, too. Devlin moved the iPhone at arm's length to include him. Even so, at the angle she was holding her phone, Stottlemeyer seemed to be peering over his own bushy mustache to look at us. "It's a family heirloom. You know it never leaves the locked display case in our living room."

The sarcasm was wasted on Monk, who didn't understand it and couldn't recognize it. But that didn't stop people from using it on him anyway, mostly as a way to alleviate the stress he caused them.

"So you understand why I can't come up," Monk said. "Naturally, it would be different if the apartment was on the sixteenth or eighteenth floor."

"Even you can't tell what happened to the guy without seeing where it happened," Stottlemeyer said.

"There's a simple solution. All the apartments are identical," Monk said. "Only the furnishings are different. There's a vacancy on the fourteenth floor. You can re-create his apartment there and call me when you're done."

"That's your simple solution," Stottlemeyer said.

"You can thank me later," Monk said.

"Get your ass up here, Monk, or I will have two officers handcuff you and bring you up in the elevator."

"That won't be necessary, Leland," Julie said. She was far less formal with Stottlemeyer than I was. He'd asked her to refer to him by his first name before she'd started working for Monk and she saw no reason to change now. Besides, the captain didn't seem to mind the informality. But I knew it bothered Monk. "You can show him the apartment with the iPhone camera. He can tell you what he wants to see."

"Sure, we can give it a try," Stottlemeyer said, then looked at Devlin. "You up for it?"

"Of course I am," she said. "If this works, maybe he'll never come to another crime scene again."

Julie looked at Monk. "Are you willing to try it?"

He rolled his shoulders. "I suppose it couldn't hurt."

"All right," Devlin said. "Where do we start?"

"Walk in the front door, just like I would," Monk said. "While you are on your way, what can you tell us about Mr. Zuzelo?"

"He's single, lives alone, and taught math at Northgate High School in Walnut Creek for thirty years until his retirement," Devlin said, keeping the camera on her face as she went to the door. "He inherited this apartment from his mother."

"What do you think happened to him?" Monk asked.

"A dumb accident," Devlin said. "He was standing on a chair, trying to change the lightbulb on his deck, lost his balance, and fell over the railing."

Devlin reached the front door, turned around to face the apartment, and clicked the flip icon, switching to the camera on the other side of the iPhone.

Now Monk and Julie could see what Devlin saw: a narrow hallway that led to an open kitchen on the left, a hallway to the right, and a big room straight ahead that served as both the dining room and living room.

The far wall was dominated by a sliding glass door that opened to the deck and a view of the office building across the street. Stottlemeyer sat on a barstool at the counter that separated the kitchen from the living room.

In the living room, against the wall to their left, was a couch with a coffee table in front of it.

"Proceed," Monk said. "Slowly."

Devlin did. And on Monk's instruction, she aimed her

iPhone into the kitchen, holding it at various angles. She was told to do the same on the floor, the ceiling, the artwork on the walls, and in the hall closet, where several coats were hung and shoes were stored. Monk's instructions were giving my daughter and Devlin a startling and dizzying peek into how he looked at the world.

It made Julie want to take a Dramamine.

After what seemed like an eternity, Monk finally asked Devlin to walk into the living room, where he spotted a Jonathan Franzen novel on the edge of the dining table.

Monk asked Stottlemeyer to pick the book up and show it to them. Stottlemeyer did and they could see that the corner of a page was folded down.

"Open the book to the marked page, please," Monk said.

"I've heard that reading Franzen has made some people want to kill themselves," Stottlemeyer said. "But I doubt that's what happened here."

"Me, too," Monk said.

Stottlemeyer opened the book and showed Monk the page. "So what difference does it make what the victim was reading before he died?"

"It makes no difference at all," Monk said.

"Then why are we looking at the page?"

"So we can unfold the corner and iron it."

Stottlemeyer closed the book and put it back on the table. "Moving on."

"Okay, we can come back and do that later," Monk said. "Could you push in the chair at the head of the table?"

"No," Stottlemeyer said.

"Okay, we can do that later, too. Let me see the couch."

Devlin walked over to the couch. There were two pillows on the left-hand side, one by the armrest and the other atop the back of the couch, suggesting that Zuzelo had rested his head against it while he was reading. There was a coffee cup on a coaster on the side table.

"Do you see those two pillows?" Monk asked.

"Yes," Stottlemeyer said.

"Take the one on the top and put it beside the armrest on the opposite end of the couch."

"We're showing you the apartment, Monk, not redecorating it," Stottlemeyer said.

"I understand," Monk said. "The bowl of seashells and the other items on the coffee table are in disarray."

The items appeared to be neatly arranged in the center of the table, but that wasn't what made Stottlemeyer grimace. "You said you understood what I just told you."

"I did, but this isn't redecorating," Monk said. "It's making things right."

Stottlemeyer turned to Devlin. "Let's take him to the deck."

"I am not done looking around inside," Monk said.

"Yes, you are," Stottlemeyer said and led them to the sliding glass door that opened onto an unlit narrow balcony with a wrought-iron railing, two wicker chairs, and a very small table with a lightbulb box on top. One of the chairs was tipped over and there was a big hole in the seat where it appeared Zuzelo's foot had fallen through the wicker webbing. There was a broken lightbulb on the floor.

"Show me the fallen chair," Monk said.

She did.

"Show me the light fixture," Monk said.

She aimed the camera up at the round, recessed light socket in what was basically the bottom of the balcony on the floor above.

"Show me the lightbulb that's on the tabletop," Monk said.

It was a hundred-watt bulb, still in its protective cardboard box.

"Show me the broken lightbulb," Monk said.

Devlin aimed the camera at the broken glass on the ground.

"Let me see the part that screws into the socket," he said.

Stottlemeyer bent down and carefully picked it up. The stems that held the filament were still intact and there were some jagged bits of broken glass around the rim.

"Okay," Monk said. "It's obvious what happened here."

"I told you so," Devlin said.

"No, you told me he was changing a lightbulb, lost his balance when his foot went through the seat, and he fell over the railing," Monk said.

Devlin hit the flip icon so the camera was now showing her angry face to Monk and Julie. "And that's what happened. You saw the evidence."

"I did," Monk said. "That's how I know it's murder."

# CHAPTER THREE

# Mr. Monk Sees the Light

"**N**o way," Devlin said.

She knew better than to question Monk's conclusion. He was never wrong about homicide. But that didn't stop her. He'd spotted something amiss that she had not, and it was a blow to her pride. What made it worse was that this was the second death in a week that she'd initially determined was an accident but that Monk immediately concluded was murder.

Captain Stottlemeyer knew how she felt, but he had long since stopped worrying about how his observational and deductive skills stacked up to Monk's and instead chose to appreciate the results. Besides, the captain knew the price Monk paid for his brilliance and, all things considered, felt he had the better end of the deal.

But Devlin had a long way to go before she could achieve Stottlemeyer's peace with Monk's genius and stop taking it as a personal insult every time he solved something before she did. The captain knew that questioning Monk's conclusions was a necessary step toward acceptance.

"There's no other possible explanation," Monk said.

"I just gave you one," Devlin said.

As much as Julie liked Devlin, she would have preferred it if the lieutenant simply accepted Monk's conclusions and moved on. It would be easier for everyone.

"Look around," Monk said. "The place has been trashed."

"Everything is clean and orderly," Devlin said. "There's no sign of forced entry or a struggle."

"I didn't say that anyone broke in or that there had been a fight," Monk said.

"But you said the place was trashed," she said.

"I did," Monk said.

"But it hasn't been," she said.

Stottlemeyer sighed. "How about we agree that you both have different definitions of what constitutes a mess, okay? Tell us what happened, Monk."

"Here's what happened," Monk said. "Zuzelo was sitting on his couch, reading a book, when someone rang the bell in the lobby. It was someone he knew, so he buzzed his friend up and set his book on the edge of the table on his way to answer the door. He greeted his friend and led him in. As they passed the dining room table, the friend picked up the book and, as Zuzelo turned, hit him across the face with it, knocking him out."

"That's pure speculation," Devlin said.

"That's how Zuzelo's glasses got broken," Monk said.

"What glasses?" Stottlemeyer asked.

"The reading glasses that he forgot to take off in his eagerness to greet his guest." Monk nudged Julie, who produced the evidence baggie containing the glasses and held it in front of her so Stottlemeyer and Devlin could see it. "I found them beside the body."

"Because he was wearing them when he fell," Devlin said.

"The killer had to throw the glasses over the railing with the body to cover up the fact that they were broken first by the book. You'll find some bits of the broken frame in the carpet by the table. But I'm getting ahead of myself."

"I never pointed the camera at the floor," Devlin said.

"You did when you aimed it at the book, which the captain picked up and held above the floor," Monk said.

"And in that brief moment, on a tiny iPhone screen, you could see a speck of plastic in the carpet that you can positively identify as coming from a pair of glasses."

"I could see the crumbs from the sourdough toast that he had for breakfast, too."

"Not even Superman could see that," Devlin said.

"That's why Clark Kent wears glasses," Monk said. "The killer got a fresh lightbulb from the closet, turned out the lights in the apartment, and went out on the deck. The killer wanted the apartment dark so he wouldn't be seen by anyone in the building across the way."

Monk went on to explain that the killer set the new bulb on the table and stood on the wicker chair to reach the light fixture above. But he was too heavy for the chair and his foot went through the worn wicker seat. So he went back into the apartment, banging his shin on the coffee table in the darkness, and carried out one of the dining room chairs, which he stood on to remove the bulb from the light fixture. He purposely dropped the old bulb on the ground, brought the chair back in, then picked up Zuzelo and threw him over the railing to the street below.

"That's quite an elaborate story, almost bordering on slapstick," Devlin said. She glanced around the apartment and then looked back into her iPhone camera. "But I don't see any evidence to back up a word of it."

"Then you need to see an optometrist right away," Monk said. "Because the evidence is everywhere."

"Like what?" Devlin said.

"There's the hole in the wicker chair," Monk said.

"Yes, I can see that. How do you know Zuzelo didn't put his foot through it standing on the chair himself to change the bulb?"

"There are four reasons. One, his shoe size. Whoever made that hole wears a size twelve shoe. Second, his height. Although I didn't see his body, I saw his jackets in the closet. He was five foot six. Even if he stood on that chair, he would not have been tall enough to reach the fixture. Third, the lightbulbs. The old bulb is a sixty-five watt and the fixture has a seventy-five-watt capacity, but the new bulb is one hundred watts, the kind used in the lamp beside the couch. The killer grabbed the wrong bulb. Fourth, everything on the coffee table is in disarray."

She looked at the table. "It looks fine to me."

"I'm surprised you're allowed to drive," Monk said. "The sunlight pours into the apartment and, over the years, has bleached the tabletop. When the killer banged the edge of the table with his shin, he shifted all the items that were on top of it, exposing the darker wood underneath them."

Devlin turned to look, pointing her camera at the table at the same time. Sure enough, Julie could see the outline of the bowl of seashells was burned onto the tabletop. It looked like a shadow.

Julie hadn't seen that the first time. Then again, she hadn't been paying any attention. It wasn't her job to look for clues. There were plenty of cops around for that. So she didn't feel dumb for missing it the way Devlin had and, to a lesser degree, Stottlemeyer had as well.

"You'll also find bits of wicker on the seat of the dining room chair," Monk added, "the one that is not pushed all the way under the table the way it should be."

Devlin turned the iPhone camera back on her and Stottlemeyer, who was shaking his head.

"I've got to hand it to you, Monk. You got all that without even coming up here. That's a first."

"I think he's making half this stuff up," Devlin said. "It's guesswork."

"Maybe so," Stottlemeyer said. "But I'll bet my pension that forensics will prove he's right about what's on the floor and on the chair. I'm pretty sure Monk can spot pollen with his naked eye."

"There's no reason to be pornographic," Monk said.

"I meant you could see it without glasses or a microscope," Stottlemeyer said.

"Then that's what you should have said instead of being unnecessarily crude."

"You're right," Stottlemeyer said. "I apologize."

"You do?" Devlin said.

Stottlemeyer shrugged. "It doesn't cost me anything."

"Only a measure of your pride."

"Pride is grossly overrated," Stottlemeyer said.

Julie turned the phone so it was just on her. "Are we done here, Leland?"

"Yes, you are," Stottlemeyer said. "But I'd appreciate it if you'd hang around for a minute. I need to come down and talk with Monk about something."

Julie clicked out of FaceTime, then sent a quick text to her boyfriend, Ricky, letting him know she'd be home in about an hour.

Monk kept his eye on the tarp-covered Mercedes, as if it might come alive and attack them both.

"The car hasn't been towed yet," Monk said.

"That's because I haven't had a chance to mention it to any officers," she said. "But rest assured, it's on the top of my to-do list."

"I don't see the list," he said.

She held up her iPhone. "I keep it on here. Asking the police to tow the car is item number one, right above getting you to your tuxedo fitting tomorrow at Ambrose's house. The wedding is only a week away."

Both Monk and his brother were buying tuxedos, even though they would probably never wear them again. Renting tuxedos was not an option because both of the Monk brothers were repulsed by the idea of wearing clothes that had been worn by others. (In fact, Monk felt that the whole business of renting formal wear should be outlawed. He was also vehemently opposed to the sale of vintage clothing, which Julie bought from stores in the Haight all the time and had to keep secret from him, but I digress.)

Since Ambrose wouldn't leave the house for a fitting, the tailor was coming to him. So it made sense for Monk to have his fitting done at the same time.

"I'm not looking forward to the wedding," Monk said with a shudder. "The noise, the confusion, and all those people, crowded together in one place."

"There's only going to be eight of us, and that's counting the bride, the groom, and the judge," Julie said. "It's just you, me, Mom, Ellen, and the mailman."

Monk's father had been invited, but hadn't responded to the invitation, so Ambrose invited the mailman to be sure that there would be an even number of guests. Before Yuki came along, the mailman was one of the most important people in Ambrose's life.

"Yes, but the mailman handles thousands of letters, some of them sealed with drool, and he doesn't wear gloves," Monk said. "His mailbag is a sack of plague."

"I don't think he's bringing it to the wedding," Julie said. "There are more people at this crime scene right now than will be at the wedding next week."

"You don't have to dress up, embrace people, or kiss anyone at a crime scene."

"Who are you planning on embracing and kissing?"

"Absolutely no one," Monk said. "And I am counting on you to prevent anyone from doing it to me."

"Does that include Ellen Morse?"

Before Monk could answer that question, Stottlemeyer emerged from the building and joined them.

Monk nudged Julie. "Tell him."

"Leland, that Mercedes over there, the one covered with a tarp, needs to be towed," Julie said.

He glanced at it. "What for?"

"The front seats and the headrests are not identically aligned," Julie said.

"How can you tell with a tarp over the car?" Stottlemeyer asked.

"I put the tarp over it," Julie said.

"Doesn't that solve the problem?"

Monk shook his head. "The seats and headrests are still not equally adjusted."

"But you're the only one who knows it," Stottlemeyer said.

"You can't see radioactivity, sarin gas, or bubonic plague, either," Monk said. "But they are still deadly."

Stottlemeyer gave him a long look, then sighed. "I'll have the car towed."

"Really?" Monk asked.

"No," Stottlemeyer said. "I'm humoring you."

Julie was startled by the remark, but not half as much as Monk was.

Now Monk gave him a long look. "Is that true?"

"You've come a long way in the last year, Monk. You only need an assistant part-time, you rarely see your shrink anymore, and you're dating a woman who sells actual crap. I think you can handle a little more honesty and a little less patronizing now."

Julie smiled. She liked that approach and had been toying with it herself, until she realized that Monk could fire her and then she'd have to join the hordes of unemployed scrambling for good jobs in the Bay Area.

Monk tipped his head from side to side, rolled his shoulders, and shifted his weight as if his body were out of alignment and needed to be set right. "So in the past you'd say you'd take care of a problem like this, but actually you'd do nothing about it."

"Pretty much," Stottlemeyer said.

"You've betrayed my trust."

"I watched your back," he said.

"You put a knife in it."

Stottlemeyer sighed. "The car isn't parked in a red zone or impeding traffic or presenting any kind of danger. I can't tow the car, or even ticket it, because no laws have been broken. So if I were to do what you asked, in this instance and all the times before, I'd actually be abusing my authority and jeopardizing my badge, and by extension my house and my pension. Then you'd be out of a job, too, because I created this consulting gig and I'm the guy who fights to keep you on the payroll despite massive budget cuts. So I've ignored some of your demands for your own good. That's the reality of the situation, Monk, whether you like it or not."

"Wow," Julie said. "That's some tough love you're dishing out tonight."

"I felt it was time I contributed to Monk's personal growth."

"Is that what you came down here to tell me?" Monk said. "Because if it is, I could have lived without it."

"No, I have something else to tell you," Stottlemeyer said.

"I was adopted."

"No," Stottlemeyer said.

"I have six months to live."

"No," Stottlemeyer said.

"I have gum under my shoe."

Stottlemeyer raised an eyebrow. "Tell me those questions weren't asked in order of importance to you."

"Please just tell me what it is and get it over with."

"Dale the Whale is getting out of prison tomorrow."

# CHAPTER FOUR

## Mr. Monk and the Fitting

**D**ale Biederback, aka Dale the Whale, was an outrageously obese and extremely wealthy businessman that Monk's late wife, Trudy, an investigative reporter, revealed to be a criminal through a series of scathing newspaper articles that aroused the interest of the FTC, the SEC, and the FBI.

In the wake of that humiliating scandal, Dale made it his personal mission to destroy her and her husband. From his bed, which he was too fat to ever leave, he filed one lawsuit after another against Trudy. The legal fees alone cost Monk his house, which Dale bought from the bank and used to store his massive collection of pornography.

Not long afterward, Trudy was killed by a car bomb and Monk suffered a devastating mental breakdown.

For years Monk suspected Dale of her murder. It turned out Dale had nothing to do with it, but Monk later proved him guilty of another murder, and got the fat lunatic sent to prison for life.

But even behind bars, Dale was able to continue harassing Monk. In fact, he almost succeeded in framing Monk for murder, but that's another story.

Suffice it to say that the news that Dale the Whale was getting out of prison was something Stottlemeyer knew Monk would not take lightly, so he was quick to qualify his remark.

"Don't worry, Monk. He's not being set free."

"I don't understand," Monk said.

"Because of Dale's enormous weight, he's been treated in prison by licensed caregivers, who keep him on a special diet, bathe him, and give him physical therapy to keep his muscles from atrophying. It's very expensive."

"He can afford it," Monk said. "He owns half the real estate this city is built on."

"All his holdings are tied up in lawsuits that could drag on for decades," Stottlemeyer said. "So in the meantime the state has had to pay the bills. And, befitting a guy who weighs more than five hundred pounds, they have been huge."

"He's lost weight," Monk said. "He was close to eight hundred pounds when he was arrested."

"Dale lost three hundred pounds?" Julie said. "That's amazing. I have a hard time losing three pounds. If word gets out about his weight loss, there will be women lining up outside San Quentin just to go on the prison diet. The Department of Corrections could make a fortune."

"They could use it," Stottlemeyer said. "You may have noticed California is in the midst of a crippling financial crisis."

"I'm a student at UC Berkeley," Julie said. "Tuition has skyrocketed. At the same time, they've cut classes, enrollment, professors, and services. Why do you think I'm still in this temporary job?"

"Is that the only reason?" Monk said.

"And I love it," Julie quickly added.

"The prisons are feeling the pinch, too," Stottlemeyer

said. "They are overcrowded, understaffed, and their funding has been slashed. They simply can't afford to pay what it costs to imprison Dale the Whale anymore. So the state has opted to take a radical approach to the problem, one that Dale has agreed to."

"Let me guess," Monk said. "He's graciously accepted house arrest in the comfort of his mansion."

"He's being transferred tomorrow afternoon to San Francisco General Hospital, where he will undergo massive liposuction, gastric bypass surgery, and the removal of all his excess flab," Stottlemeyer said. "And after his recovery, assuming he doesn't die on the table, he will go right back to prison, where he will be integrated into the general population and won't cost the state any more to support than any other lifer."

Monk shook his head. "It's a trick. He'll try to escape."

"He's too fat now to just slip away and he'll certainly be in no shape physically to try anything after being gutted, but even so, we both know how clever he is. That's why I insisted on handling security at the hospital," Stottlemeyer said. "And that's why I want you there with me tomorrow when he arrives."

"You can count on it," Monk said.

Julie had been to Ambrose's house in Tewksbury, a small town in Marin County, many times in her life. And whenever she visited, the house and its single occupant were always exactly the same, as if frozen in time.

Inside, the place was meticulously maintained, all the décor and furnishings treated as if they were on permanent display in a museum. The living room was filled with rows of file cabinets containing every piece of mail that had ever arrived at the house and neat piles of newspapers going back decades. Monk's childhood bedroom looked exactly as it was the day he went off to college.

And Ambrose Monk, who'd left the house only four times in decades, always greeted his occasional guests wearing a long-sleeve flannel shirt, a sweater vest, corduroy slacks, and Hush Puppies loafers, and stood a few steps back from the screen door, as if afraid he might get sucked out if he wasn't very careful.

So it came as a shock to Julie when Ambrose answered the door that Sunday morning wearing a tuxedo.

"Salutations," Ambrose said. "What a distinct pleasure it is to see you both."

Julie stepped in and gave him a hug. "You look very dashing, Ambrose. You were born to wear a tuxedo."

That's when she looked over his shoulder and noticed something extraordinary: The living room was empty.

Monk walked past them both into the living room, where outlines of everything that had been there before were burned by decades of sunlight into the hardwood floors as permanent shadows.

"You got rid of the file cabinets," Monk said.

Ambrose walked to the edge of the entry hall but not quite into the room. "Ever since Dad abandoned us when we were kids, I've been saving all the mail that came for him. But now that he's come back, and we know where he is, Yuki convinced me I should ship it all to him so he doesn't have to come here to go through it."

"He must have loved that," Julie said.

"I'm a good son," Ambrose said, proving that, like his brother, he had no ear for sarcasm.

"What about the newspapers?" Monk asked.

"I donated them to the library. You can find just about all of the articles online now anyway."

Monk rolled his shoulders. "Everything is changing so fast."

"I thought you'd be happy about this, Adrian. You've been complaining about my files and newspapers for thirty years."

"But I've never seen the room empty before," Monk said. "Not even when we were growing up."

"That's because no one ever got married in here before," Ambrose said.

"What have you done with the couch, the coffee table, and the two matching chairs?"

"I sold them," Ambrose said. "On Craigslist."

Monk staggered back as if he'd been struck. "How could you?"

"We're redecorating."

"Why?"

"Because Yuki lives here now," Ambrose said.

"So?"

"It has to be her house now, too."

"I still don't understand," Monk said.

"Our home should reflect her taste and mine, though almost all the existing furnishings were selected by Mom."

Monk shook his head. "Mom had an incredible eye for balance and symmetry. The couch, table, and chairs were part of a set. They were perfect. How could you possibly improve on that?"

"Aren't you being a bit hypocritical?" Julie said. "You moved out of here and into an apartment with Trudy that you two furnished yourselves."

"We bought the same living room furniture that was in this room," Monk said.

"Oh," Julie said. "I never noticed."

"That's because it was in the center of the hedge maze created by all those file cabinets and newspapers," Monk said. "You can see the outline of it over there." He pointed to the shapes burned into the floor. "That's all that's left of them."

"Except for the copies in your house," Julie said.

"It's not the same," Monk said.

"You just said that it was," Julie said.

"You're missing the point," Monk said.

"Yes, I am," Julie said, then turned to Ambrose. "So, where's Yuki?"

"She's out. She didn't want to see me in the tuxedo before the wedding," Ambrose said. "She presumed that I'd be irresistible in this attire, though I do have a flannel shirt that she finds particularly erotic."

"Don't be disgusting," Monk said.

"It's a natural part of life, Adrian."

"Disgust?" Monk said.

"Sexual attraction."

"Shh," Monk said, waving his hand. "What's the matter with you? Do you have Tourette's or something?"

Ambrose shook his head. "The tailor, Morris Abish, is waiting for you upstairs, Adrian."

Monk sighed and shuffled past Ambrose. "Now that you've gutted the place, what are you going to do next? Tear down the house?"

"Now that you mention it, we are talking about doing some remodeling—"

Monk held up his hand, interrupting his brother. "I don't want to hear any more. A man can only take so much."

He started up the stairs, but took only a few steps before a short, balding man in his sixties, wearing a three-piece suit and a length of yellow measuring tape draped around his neck like a doctor's stethoscope, appeared on the landing. His face was flushed with anger.

"What have you done?" Abish said, pointing at Ambrose with a piece of chalk.

"My sentiments exactly," Monk said.

Ambrose looked at himself from top to bottom. "What? Did I miss some chalk?"

"That's what I am talking about," Abish said. "You brushed off all my chalk marks!"

"Of course I did," Ambrose said. "I couldn't answer the door in filthy clothes."

Monk nodded. "It's a relief to know you still retain some shred of human decency."

"Now I have to do all the measurements again," Abish said, glowering at them both. "Get up here, you two, and make it snappy."

Monk and Ambrose did as they were told.

Julie headed to the kitchen to help herself to Ambrose's stash of Pop-Tarts, but before she could get to the pantry, she glanced out the window above the sink and saw Yuki stepping into the RV that was parked in the driveway.

Julie hadn't spent much time with Yuki, who was only a few years older than she was and had long black hair almost all the way down her back. But Julie was intrigued by Yuki because she'd spent some time in prison for killing a man (something Monk never tired of reminding Ambrose), had a snake tattoo coiled around the base of her spine, and rode a Harley-Davidson motorcycle.

To say that Yuki and Ambrose appeared to have very little in common was an understatement. But if you looked below the surface, you'd see that they were both very much alike. They were outsiders, quirky and troubled individuals who didn't fit into conventional society, so they cut themselves off from it, living in worlds of their own.

Now they had each other.

Julie stepped outside and knocked on the open door of the RV. "Permission to enter?"

Yuki leaned out. She was wearing a T-shirt and jeans and was holding a soapy sponge.

"Oh, hello," Yuki said. "I was so busy cleaning I didn't even notice that you'd arrived."

"It's a shame Mr. Monk wasn't able to hear that," Julie said. "You would have scored big points with him."

"I don't need Adrian's approval," she said.

"Why are you cleaning the motor home?"

"I'm getting ready for our honeymoon."

Julie nodded. "I can see how going from the house to the

driveway would seem like a big getaway for a guy who almost never leaves the house."

"We're driving across the country."

"You're kidding."

Yuki tossed the sponge in the sink and sat down on the steps of the motor home. "We might not ever leave the RV, which is sort of the point of a honeymoon anyway, but at least he'll see the country through the windows."

Ambrose and Yuki met during his first and only trip in the motor home, though Monk and Julie had to slip drugs into his food and abduct him to pull it off—but that's another story. The upshot is that the trip worked out fine for him. Ambrose fell in love with Yuki and ended up buying the motor home that we'd rented on the off chance he'd ever summon the courage to venture out again.

"How long will you be gone?" Julie asked.

Yuki shrugged. "Who knows? We're in no hurry. Ambrose can write his owner's manuals from anywhere."

"I can't believe he's going to do this."

"He hasn't done it yet," Yuki said.

"He will," Julie said. "He's in love. Maybe you can finally cure him of his agoraphobia."

"It doesn't matter to me. I'll take him as he is," Yuki said. "At least if he never leaves the house, I won't have to worry about losing him."

Julie laughed. "I hadn't thought of it that way."

"People adapt but they don't change," Yuki said. "They stay who they are. Anybody who expects anything else of a person is setting themselves up for disappointment."

"Ambrose is adapting a lot for you."

"I know," Yuki said.

"Mr. Monk would never do that. He doesn't adapt for any-body," Julie said. "He expects everyone else to adapt to him."

"He's with Ellen Morse even though she sells crap."

"I wouldn't say that he's *with* her. They hang out. But that's only because they don't talk about her work at all. He pretends that side of her life doesn't exist."

"So he's deluding himself," Yuki said. "That's an adaptation."

"Or a mental illness," Julie said.

"We're all a little crazy," Yuki said, getting up again. "That's what makes life fun."

"Or in the case of working for Mr. Monk," Julie said, "a living hell."

"You're beginning to sound just like your mother."

"Oh God, anything but that!" Julie said.

She said that in mock horror, of course.

At least I hope it was.

# CHAPTER FIVE

## Mr. Monk and the Whale

**M**onk would have preferred to go to a nuclear power plant, or slog through a sewer, or visit a trash dump, or even step into Ellen Morse's Poop shop, than to walk into a hospital.

That's because hospitals are full of sick people, and he spent every waking minute of his life trying to avoid getting an infection or catching some horrible disease.

Stottlemeyer refused to let him come in wearing a full-on hazmat suit with its own air supply, so Monk was forced to settle for scrubs, rubber gloves, a surgical mask, and protective goggles.

He looked like a surgeon preparing to go into the operating room. But in his mind, he might as well have been a naked man walking into a village stricken with Ebola.

The fact that he was there at all was a testament to the risk he felt Dale the Whale posed to society. Monk, Julie, and Stottlemeyer stood at the loading dock on the first floor, looking out at the street. They could hear the sirens of the approaching prison motorcade.

"I don't like this at all," Monk said.

"Really?" Stottlemeyer said. "I hadn't noticed. You hide it very well."

"Letting Dale out of prison for any reason is a big mistake," Monk said.

"No pun intended," Julie said.

"Of course not," Monk said. "I never pun. Why would I pun?"

"Never mind," Julie said. "Forget I said it."

"This is no time for puns," Monk said.

"You can relax. I've got officers stationed at every entrance and exit," Stottlemeyer said. "Nobody comes in or out of the building, much less into the OR and recovery room, without getting screened. Besides, Dale is far too big to be snuck past anyone. It's going to take a forklift just to get him into the building."

Stottlemeyer gestured to the forklift, which was on the other side of the loading dock, a cop at the controls.

"He won't need a forklift after all the fat has been removed," Monk said.

"He's having hundreds of pounds of fat ripped from his body. It's major surgery that could actually kill him," Stottlemeyer said. "So it's not like he can just leap off the table and run out of the building."

"Someone could help him out," Monk said.

"He'd have to get past us first," Stottlemeyer said. "And that's not going to happen."

The motorcade rolled into the parking lot. It was a moving truck escorted by two cop cars and four motorcycle cops. The moving truck backed up to the loading dock.

Two prison guards, one of them cradling a shotgun,

emerged from the cab of the truck and came around to the back. One of the guards stepped forward, unlocked the rear latch, and rolled up the back door to reveal Dale the Whale in all his corpulence, spread out and handcuffed to a queen-size bed that was bolted to a pallet. He wore a bright orange prison jumpsuit that made him look like a deflated hot-air balloon.

Julie let out a gasp and immediately covered her mouth in embarrassment.

"Ah, how I will miss that gasp of awe at my fleshy magnificence," Dale said with theatrical pomposity, even as he struggled for breath.

"It was a gasp of horror," Julie said, "you fat—"

Now it was Monk's turn to gasp.

I won't repeat the profanity that she used, but rather than offending Dale, it delighted him.

"I like you, Julie," he said.

"You know me?" she said.

"I know everything," Dale said. "I'm omniscient, omnipotent, and omnipresent. Just ask Adrian."

Monk took a step up to where the back of the truck met the loading dock. "Whatever scheme you have in mind, it's not going to happen. I'll foil it, as I always have."

"But as smart as you think you are, you weren't able to stop your wife from being blown to bits in her car. You didn't see that coming, did you?" Dale asked, smiling as Monk went rigid. "Oops, was that a sore point?"

Stottlemeyer marched into the truck, stopped beside the bed, and leaned close to Dale's ear, which was nearly lost in the fleshly folds of his cheek and neck.

"If you don't die on the operating table, I hope you try to escape," Stottlemeyer said. "It would be my pleasure to shoot you during the attempt."

"I'd tremble," Dale said. "But I'm too fat. You'll have to try to scare me again when I'm thin."

Stottlemeyer straightened up and gestured to the cop on the forklift.

"Get this blob out of here," he said.

The forklift scooted forward, turned, and moved into the truck, its long tines sliding under the pallet that held the bed. Then it backed up, turned again, and carried the bed into the hospital and down a long corridor to the first-floor suite of operating rooms.

Monk, Julie, and Stottlemeyer, as well as the two armed guards, followed behind the forklift.

The doors to the operating room had been temporarily removed to accommodate the forklift. Julie could see two maintenance workers standing against the wall, holding up the detached doors and staring wide-eyed at the arrival of the special patient.

A surgeon in his forties wearing blue scrubs was waiting at the entry to the OR. He held up his hand to signal the forklift operator to stop, then stepped up to meet his patient.

"Mr. Biederback, I'm Dr. Damian Wiss. I'll be your surgeon," he said, without offering his hand. He had an almost militaristic bearing, like a Navy SEAL about to parachute into Osama bin Laden's compound.

"Are you any good at this?" Dale asked.

"I've done hundreds of these operations," Dr. Wiss said. "You're my third patient today."

Monk smiled at Julie. "That's promising."

"I appreciate your confidence," Dr. Wiss said to him.

"That's not what Adrian meant, Doctor," Dale said. "He thinks that because three is an odd number that my chances of serious complications or death are vastly increased."

Dr. Wiss gave Monk a cold look, then shifted his gaze back to Dale. "There are significant risks involved in this operation, but the numerology surrounding it is not one of them. You do need to be fully aware of what you are facing."

"I've already been told about the risks by the prison doctor."

"But not by me, so you are going to hear them again. I'll be making a series of buttonhole incisions, inserting a metal tube between your skin and muscle, and sucking out the fat. I'll also perform a gastric bypass, decreasing the size of your stomach by dividing it into two pouches, the smaller of which will be directly attached to the middle of your small intestine. Afterward, I will make a series of elliptical cuts, remove the excess skin between them, and sew you back up."

"Sounds delightful," Dale said. "While you're at it, could you throw in a nose job? I've always wanted something more regal."

"During the course of those procedures," Dr. Wiss continued, ignoring Dale's comment, "I could puncture a major blood vessel or penetrate your abdomen, bladder, or bowel. You could die from dehydration, blood loss, or a heart attack. And if you survive the operation, the risk of infection is significant. There is also a chance of wound dehiscence."

"Dehiscence?" Stottlemeyer said. "What is that?"

"The wounds ripping open," Monk said. "Dale could burst like a piñata."

"Wishful thinking, Adrian," Dale said.

"You're this doctor's third operation on the seventh day of the week on the seventeenth day in the third month of an odd-numbered year," Monk said. "You're doomed, Fat Man."

"That's enough, Monk," Stottlemeyer said, then turned to the doctor. "What's Dale's post-op going to be like?"

Although the captain asked the question, Dr. Wiss addressed his answer to Dale. "You will be sewn up tight, covered in antibiotic ointment, and wrapped in bandages like a mummy to protect the wounds. You're looking at spending two days in the ICU so we can monitor fluids, then another five days under regular care. Do you still consent to the operation?"

"By all means," Dale said. "I am looking forward to the new me and a bright future as a model prisoner. Fashion model, that is."

Dr. Wiss stepped back and gestured to the cop driving the forklift that he should proceed to the center of the room, where an anesthesiologist and several nurses were waiting amid numerous pieces of equipment and trays of tools ready to be wheeled into position.

The forklift went into the operating room, lowered the pallet, and then backed out. As soon as the forklift was in the corridor, the nurses wheeled the surgical equipment into place and the workers brought up the doors and began to reinstall them.

Dr. Wiss turned to Stottlemeyer. "I'll check on Mr. Biederback tonight, but I'm going to Maui tomorrow with my family. My wife won a contest."

"Lucky you," Stottlemeyer said.

"My colleague, Dr. Auerbach, will handle Mr. Biederback's post-op care after that. It should be routine. I've handled larger patients than Mr. Biederback."

"But none as dangerous," Monk said.

"He'll be unconscious and quite helpless," Dr. Wiss said. "See you in about three hours."

The doctor turned and went inside, so he didn't see the big smile on Monk's face.

"Did you hear that?" Monk said to Julie. "Three hours. That's encouraging."

"You really want him to die on the table?" Julie asked.

"Hell yes," Monk said.

Stottlemeyer spoke up. "But on the assumption that he survives, and on the chance that he might have been planning an escape of some kind, two officers will be stationed outside this door."

"Where are you going to be?" Monk asked.

"In the operating room the whole time."

Julie grimaced just thinking about it. "It's going to be incredibly gross. Are you sure you want to see that?"

"I'm sure that I don't," Stottlemeyer said. "But I've been preparing myself by watching videos of Japanese fishermen stripping blubber from whales."

"What about us?" Monk asked.

"Stick around, keep your eye on things, make sure everything is in order," Stottlemeyer said. "After the operation, Dale will be taken to the ICU by elevator. It will be the first time he's ridden in one in decades. I'll call you when we're on the move."

Stottlemeyer went into the operating room, leaving Monk and Julie in the corridor.

"It sounds like the captain has everything under control," Julie said. "Don't worry."

"I was born worrying," Monk said.

# CHAPTER SIX

# Mr. Monk Plays Doctor

**F**rom where Monk and Julie were sitting in the hospital hallway, they could see the two officers standing guard between the operating room, which was to their left, and the ER, which was to their right.

The ER was a lot more interesting. Doctors and nurses rushed around and patients were wheeled to and fro, activity that generated a buzz of energy and urgency. Plus there was the instinctive rubbernecking attraction of seeing the injured, suffering, and emotionally distraught people that was hard for either Monk or Julie to resist. It was like watching an episode of that old series *ER*, only this was live and none of the doctors looked half as good as George Clooney, and the nurses were no Julianna Margulies.

Once patients got past the admitting desk and were buzzed through the security door, they were quickly assessed by a nurse or a physician, who determined how serious their medical situations were.

At that point, patients would be rushed into one of the trauma rooms, or into one of the exam rooms, or into a large treatment room where there were eight beds that could be curtained off for privacy, or parked in the hallway on a gurney or in a chair, until somebody could get to them.

Julie kept an eye on Monk for the next two hours, wondering when just sitting there and watching wouldn't be enough for him and he'd have to get up and straighten something out, literally or figuratively.

It finally happened when he saw a little girl in the treatment room getting a nasty gash on her right leg stitched up by a young doctor with two days of carefully curated stubble on his chin, the hair on his head meticulously askew.

The little girl, who was maybe ten years old, was brave through it all, biting her lower lip and fighting the urge to cry while her mother held her hand and looked away, apparently unable to handle the sight of blood.

When Dr. Stubble left them to attend to something else, Monk rolled his shoulders, tipped his head from side to side, and went over to the girl.

Julie sat very still in her chair, not sure what to do, and braced herself for an embarrassing incident.

Monk gave the little girl a smile, complimented her on her bravery, and applied a bandage that was identical to the one on her right leg to the same, uninjured spot on her left leg.

Neither the little girl nor her mother questioned the reasoning behind this. In fact, they thanked Monk. They probably assumed that he was another doctor and that he had a very good reason for what he was doing.

Monk patted the little girl on the head, gave her another smile, and then walked away, pulling off his gloves and dropping them in the hazardous waste bin.

He picked up a new pair from a box on a counter and put

them on as he returned to his seat beside Julie, who also didn't say anything about what he'd done.

Giving the girl matching bandages on both legs was harmless and made Monk happy, so Julie figured why make an issue out of it?

I wish I could say I would have handled the situation as reasonably as my daughter did. But I know better and I bet you do, too.

Although there was a lot of activity, the ER seemed to be humming along smoothly.

But then everything changed.

Julie overheard Dr. Stubble gather the nurses and inform them that a set of bleachers on a high school football field had collapsed during a practice game and that paramedics were bringing in a dozen injured people.

Within a few moments of that announcement, the injured started arriving.

Monk stood up and watched suspiciously as one ambulance after another rolled up to the ER. He wasn't the only one watching closely. There were four police officers stationed at the ambulance bay by Captain Stottlemeyer, and they immediately put their hands on their guns and scanned for trouble.

"What's wrong?" Julie asked, joining Monk.

He turned and looked past her to the two guards in front of the operating room doors. They were also on alert, braced for trouble.

"This could be a trick," Monk said. "An attempt to break Dale out of the hospital."

"But he's on an operating table getting his fat sucked out," Julie said. "It's not a great time for an escape."

"I wouldn't put anything past him."

One ambulance after another arrived and injured people were rolled in on gurneys. The police officers kept a close eye on everybody who came in, quickly searched each gurney and bag, and patted down each person just in case any of them was attempting to bring in a weapon.

Each victim was met by Dr. Stubble, a nurse, and some orderlies. The doctor did a quick exam, then took out a red, yellow, or green pen from his lab coat pocket and made a big *X* on the patient's wrist while giving out orders to the nurses.

The nurses and orderlies then took the victim to the proper room for the care they needed.

Anyone who left the ER, such as the paramedics and ambulance personnel, were closely scrutinized by the officers and Monk.

Once the ambulances and paramedic units had all left and things returned to the previous level of activity, Monk rolled his shoulders, tipped his head from side to side, and then went to a nurse's station, where he helped himself to several red, yellow, and green pens, which he clutched in one hand since he had no pockets on his surgical scrubs.

"What are those for?" Julie asked, gesturing to his fistful of pens.

"It's triage color coding," Monk said, heading for the treatment room, Julie in tow. "The doctor marked each patient with a color that represents the severity of medical need. Red is the most serious, and those people are already in the trauma rooms. Yellow is for major burns, multiple fractures, that sort of thing. Green is for minor fractures or simple cuts and abrasions."

He approached the first patient he saw, a man sitting on the edge of a bed, clutching what looked like a broken arm with his left hand, which had a green *X* on the wrist.

"Remain very still," Monk said, then drew a green *X* on the man's broken arm. "You're going to be fine now."

Monk tossed the green pen in the hazardous materials bin and headed for the next patient. Julie hurried after him.

"You're not a doctor," she said.

"I know that," Monk said.

"Then what are you doing?"

"What the captain asked me to do," Monk said. "Making sure everything is in order."

"I'm pretty sure that he was referring to hospital security," Julie said.

"That's exactly what I am doing."

Monk whipped back the curtain around the next bed, revealing a woman with a badly broken leg—a big shard of jagged bone jutting from her bloody flesh—and startling the nurse, who was injecting something into the IV.

"What are you doing?" the nurse asked.

"This won't take a moment," Monk said. He carefully applied a yellow *X* to the patient's other arm, then gave the nurse a nod. "Carry on."

Monk slipped out again, drawing the curtain behind him, and tossed the pen in the hazardous materials bin. He was about to go to the next curtained area when Dr. Stubble appeared and cut him off.

"I'm Dr. Frank Jessup, and this is my ER. Who the hell are you?"

"Adrian Monk. I'm a consultant to the San Francisco Police and this is Julie Teeger, my assistant. We're here as part of the security detail assigned to Dale the Whale, the morbidly obese homicidal maniac from San Quentin who is being operated on down the hall."

"That doesn't explain what you are doing here meddling with my patients."

"We were just leaving," Julie said and turned to go, tugging on Monk's sleeve. But Monk yanked his arm from her and held his ground.

"I admire your triage system, Doctor, but in your effort to quickly treat patients, you forgot to mark them on both arms."

"I didn't forget," Dr. Jessup said. "I only mark them on one."

"You need to mark them on both and dispose of the pen afterward," Monk said. "In fact, you should throw out the pens that you have in your pocket in the nearest hazardous waste receptacle right now and get new ones."

He stared at Monk. "Why should I?"

"Because it's unsanitary."

"No, it's not," Dr. Jessup said.

"You wouldn't use the same tongue depressor on two different patients, would you? So how can you use the same pen?"

"Because I am not sticking the pen in their mouths," Dr. Jessup said.

"I don't see the difference," Monk said.

"I don't care," Dr. Jessup said. "Get out of my ER right now or I will call security and have you dragged out."

"But I am a consultant to the San Francisco Police," Monk said. "And I'm right and you're wrong."

"We apologize and will stay out of your way," Julie said to

the doctor. She grabbed Monk firmly by the arm and led him away.

"We need to notify the Department of Public Health and the American Medical Association," Monk said.

"We need to focus on our job," Julie said.

"To protect and to serve—that's our job. Every time that doctor touches someone's flesh with his germ-soaked pen, he's spreading pestilence and death. I can't just turn a blind eye to that."

"And what if Dale the Whale knows that?"

"What are you talking about?"

"What if Dale knew that you'd become so distracted by Dr. Jessup's triage system that you'd forget all about keeping your eye on his security?"

"Oh my God, you're right," Monk said, and immediately looked down the hall, where the two officers still stood in front of the operating room doors.

Julie forced back a smile, pleased that Monk bought her argument, which she'd improvised on the spot.

I couldn't have done it better myself.

That's when the operating room doors opened and Dr. Wiss and Captain Stottlemeyer emerged.

Monk and Julie hurried down the hall to join them. Dr. Wiss removed his mask. His face was damp with sweat. Stottlemeyer looked pale.

"How did it go?" Julie asked.

"The operation went smoothly," Dr. Wiss said. "It's remarkable how much fat and skin we were able to remove."

"Horrific is more like it," Stottlemeyer said. "I may never eat again."

The orderlies wheeled the gurney out the door toward the elevator across the hall. As the gurney passed, Monk and Julie got a good look at Dale. All they could really see were his eyes. He was unconscious and wrapped up like a mummy, but what astonished them both was that his whole body fit well within the edges of the gurney, which would not have been possible before.

"My God," Julie said. "It's like you cut him in half."

"I freed the man that was trapped under all the flesh," Dr. Wiss said.

"I certainly hope not," Monk said. "The last thing anyone wants is Dale Biederback going free."

"I'm sorry, that was a poor choice of words," Dr. Wiss said, following the gurney into the elevator. "We're taking him to the ICU now."

"He'll be under armed guard 24/7," Stottlemeyer said, joining the doctor in the elevator. "I'm taking the first shift myself."

"We'll take the next one," Monk said.

"We will?" Julie said.

"No, you won't," Stottlemeyer said. "Now that the operation is over, I want you out there on the street, helping Lieutenant Devlin if any bodies drop. I've told her to call you in on everything."

"She must have been thrilled about that," Julie said.

"Go home, Monk. I've got it from here," Stottlemeyer said, and the elevator doors closed.

# CHAPTER SEVEN

# Mr. Monk Goes to the Police Station

**M**onk and Julie went from the hospital to police head-quarters. Although Devlin hadn't called them in, Monk was too keyed up to go home and there were two unsolved murders that he needed to investigate.

I know what you're thinking. *Two* murders? You probably remember only one, the murder of David Zuzelo, the high school math teacher who was thrown from the balcony of his seventeenth-floor apartment the previous night by someone he knew.

That's because I told you about Zuzelo in detail and only mentioned the other murder in passing. But I did say that Zuzelo's death was actually the second case that week that had appeared to be an accident at first but that Monk quickly proved to be a homicide.

The victim in the first case was Bruce Grossman, a big name in local business circles, a CEO-for-hire who took over troubled companies and got them back on their feet. In fact, to show you what a small world it is, Grossman ran the Burgerville restaurant chain after their CEO was murdered, a crime that Monk solved years ago.

He'd been jogging in shorts and a T-shirt through Land's

End, a rocky and heavily wooded park on the northeastern edge of San Francisco, a spot known for its spectacular views of the Golden Gate Bridge. But he'd decided to go off-trail into the fenced-off area, lost his footing, and fell over the edge of a cliff to the rocky shore far below. If Grossman had fallen a few yards farther out, the waves would have pounded him to pieces and carried what was left of him out to sea. Instead, Grossman's broken body was hauled up more or less intact, and Monk was able to see his muscular, tanned legs.

And that's how Monk knew that Devlin, who'd met him at the scene, was wrong about Grossman's death being an accident.

If Grossman had scaled the fence and run along the cliff's edge, he would have had to go through the same junipers and prickly brush that Monk had navigated, a terrifying experience that took him an hour and a half and that he likened to crossing a minefield.

And yet, Grossman's legs were unscratched.

This proved that Grossman didn't fall off the cliff. He was thrown, contrary to Devlin's initial conclusion.

That was why she'd been so irritated at Zuzelo's place when Monk proved that she'd been fooled again by a murder disguised as an accident.

So Devlin wasn't very happy when Monk and Julie walked into police headquarters on that Sunday and she had to tell him that the forensics report from the crime lab had confirmed his observations in Zuzelo's apartment.

"Zuzelo was, in fact, murdered," Devlin said, sitting at her cluttered desk outside of Stottlemeyer's office.

"You say that as if it's a surprise," Monk said. "I'm never wrong about homicide."

"One of these days, you will be. You quickly jump to some pretty big conclusions based on some very tiny details, so you'll have to forgive me if I'd like independent confirmation of your findings."

"It's your time to waste, though I think it would be better spent cleaning your desk."

"I like my desk the way it is," she said. "Are you here for a reason?"

"We have two open homicide investigations."

"I do," she said. "I'll be sure to call you if I need a consultation."

"You never call me," Monk said.

"And what can you deduce from that?"

"Whoever killed David Zuzelo had to be buzzed in to the lobby," Monk said, ignoring her question. "Do you have any security camera footage of him?"

"Gee, I would never have thought of that," Devlin said, hitting a few keys on her computer. An image came up on her screen of a man wearing a hoodie who was standing at an angle that blocked his face entirely from view. "But it's useless."

"The killer knew exactly where to stand to avoid being photographed," Monk said. "He'd cased the place."

"We have an even worse angle of him leaving," Devlin said and showed it to him.

Julie, you may have noticed, didn't contribute anything to the discussion. While Monk and Devlin were talking, Julie plopped herself down on the couch in Stottlemeyer's office and got busy playing Words with Friends, a Scrabble-type game app, on her iPhone with her boyfriend. He beat her about nine times out of ten. She won only when she had Monk play on her behalf.

"So where does that leave us?" Monk asked.

"Us?" Devlin said. "I don't know what you're doing, but I'm searching for any enemies Zuzelo might have had."

"Who opens his door and invites his enemy into his apartment?"

"You know what they say—keep your friends close and your enemies closer."

"That's idiotic," Monk said. "Who says that?"

"Sun Tzu in *The Art of War*."

"He should retitle it *The Art of Losing a War*."

"He's been dead for thousands of years."

"Killed, no doubt, by an enemy that he let get up close to him. Everybody knows you keep your enemies as far away as you possibly can. If you can't do that, the very least you should do is close your door. That's what doors were designed for—to keep your enemies out. And wild animals, of course."

"Of course," Devlin said. "In any case, I can't find anybody with a grudge against Zuzelo. He was a retired high school math teacher, for God's sake. He led a pretty quiet life."

"He's a lot quieter now," Monk said. "Have you had better luck on the Bruce Grossman case?"

"Now there's a guy with lots of enemies. One of the ways that he saved the companies that he took over was by closing stores or factories and slashing jobs. The challenge will be narrowing the list of people who wanted him dead down to just a few names."

"What company was he running at the time of his murder?"

"None. He hasn't been in a corporate suite in three years. He'd lost his mojo. On his last few gigs, he performed worse than the guys he replaced. He's the genius who pushed out Cleve Dobbs at Peach and then released the Pit."

Of course, Monk didn't know anything about the Personal Internet Telephone, derisively known as the Pit, the lame and disastrous follow-up to Dobbs' revolutionary and adorable Peach multimedia recording device. That's because Monk didn't participate in, or follow, American popular culture or the devices that shape it. He was unaware that the pocket-size Peach, and the company that Dobbs founded of the same name, had changed the way we record and share home movies and all but rendered the camcorder extinct overnight.

Monk was still only slightly familiar with a mouse, mostly because he refused to use any device named after a rodent.

"You don't know who Cleve Dobbs is, do you?" she asked.

"No idea," Monk said.

"His memoir is the number-one bestselling book in the country and he created Peach, a company rivaled only by Apple for technological innovation."

"I am familiar with peaches and apples," Monk said. "But not the electronic versions."

"How can you possibly expect to be an effective investigator if you don't keep up on modern technology?"

"Murder is as old as man. Look no further than Sun Tzu. It is also disorder. All I've got to do is look for the things that don't belong, are out of place, unbalanced, uneven, or missing, and if I try to restore the order, and clean up the mess, the truth will reveal itself."

"And what if that thing that is not where it's supposed to be has something to do with a Peach, or an iPad, or some other piece of technology that everybody, including toddlers who can't even talk yet, and perhaps even some domesticated animals, are familiar with and you are not?"

Devlin's phone rang before Monk could reply, which is a shame, because I would have been curious about his answer to that question.

While she was on the phone, Monk took the opportunity to start organizing her desk, an activity he abruptly halted when she grabbed a letter opener with her free hand and brutally stabbed the stack of files that he was about to straighten.

"I'll be right down," she said. She hung up and took her gun out of her drawer.

"That won't be necessary," Monk said, holding up his hands and taking a step back from her desk. "You made your point with the letter opener."

"It's not for you." Devlin put the gun in her shoulder holster as she stood, then took her leather jacket off the back of her chair. "I've got to roll. I've got a body."

"A murder?" Monk asked.

"Looks like a woman out in Noe Valley had too much to drink before diving into her lap pool—cracked her head on the bottom and drowned."

"Or it was a murder," Monk said.

"If it is, I'll be sure to give you a call," Devlin said, turning her back to Monk and heading for the door.

"If it is," Monk said, "you might not notice."

She stopped and turned around very slowly. "You know I'm armed and you still said that to me?"

Julie stepped out of Captain Stottlemeyer's office at that point because she'd heard enough to know that Monk had created a situation in need of defusing, and she considered that a key part of her job.

"Leland sent us here because he wanted Monk around if any bodies dropped," Julie said to Devlin. "I think those were pretty much his exact words."

Devlin gave Julie a look. "You know it was just to get Monk out of his hair and into mine."

Julie shrugged. "Doesn't really make a difference though, does it?"

"I was just starting to like you, kid," Devlin said and walked out the door.

Julie smiled at Monk. "But now she loves me because I stood up to her."

"Then why doesn't she love me?"

"Because you irritate her," Julie said. "Come on, let's go. We have to follow her and she has a siren."

She went out the door. Monk started to go but doubled back, quickly straightened the stack of files on Devlin's desk, and then hurried after Julie.

Noe Valley is an upscale neighborhood of renovated Victorians and well-off young families south of the Castro District, with its strong gay community, and west of the Mission District, once known for its vibrant multiethnic working-class mix and now home to the largest percentage of BMW owners in the city.

(Okay, I made that last fact up, but the Mission is where all the hip dot-com millionaires are buying their lofts and all those little mom-and-pop taco places that I loved are being replaced by coffeehouses and artisan bakeries. But I digress. . . .)

The usual cluster of official vehicles was parked outside the dead woman's home, which was already cordoned off with yellow crime scene tape. She had a tiny garden that was beautifully maintained, with a small patch of grass and two flower beds covered with tan bark and bordered with smooth rocks that looked as if she'd scavenged them from a beach.

Monk and Julie arrived right behind Devlin, though they had to break a few traffic laws to do so. Devlin got out of her car, marched across the front yard, and went through the open wooden gate on the side yard.

Julie hurried after her, but she quickly noticed Monk lagging behind, crouching to study the flower beds.

"The body is in the backyard," Julie said.

"And it's not going anywhere," Monk said.

He cocked his head from side to side, nodded to himself, then straightened up and followed Julie. She didn't ask why he stopped or what he was looking at because she was afraid he might tell her.

The last thing she wanted was a long lecture on how beach rocks belonged on the beach and not alongside shards of bark from trees that grow nowhere near the ocean, or some such nonsense.

The backyard was tiny, and the lap pool was more of a narrow, short pond surrounded by a patio of aged bricks. There were two chaise lounges, a bottle of Scotch and a glass on the tiny table between them. One of the chaise lounges had a folded towel and the latest issue of *The New Yorker* on top of it.

The dead woman was slim. She wore a one-piece bathing suit and was lying on her back on the wet bricks. Julie figured she was in her mid-fifties, but wore her age well. The woman's eyes were wide open and so was her mouth. That face, frozen in death, was more disturbing to Julie than any bloodied, mangled corpse.

Julie took a seat on the edge of a chaise lounge while Monk crouched beside the body, staring at the woman's face and the bloodless gash on her forehead, before something in the water distracted him.

Meanwhile, Devlin conferred with two uniformed cops, and several forensic technicians took photos of the crime scene.

Monk squeezed past them all and walked the perimeter of the yard, peering into the bushes and planters, his hands framing the scene in front of him, bobbing and weaving, almost as if he were shadowboxing with open palms.

After a few moments, Devlin left the officers and stood over the body, giving it a once-over herself. She glanced over her shoulder at Julie sitting on the chaise lounge behind her.

"Are you okay?"

Julie nodded. "The expression on her face bothers me."

"It's not an expression. It's death."

"I guess that's what bothers me," Julie said.

"You've seen death before."

"But not on somebody's face."

Devlin looked down at the body again, cocking her head

to study the woman's face. "I suppose it's the open mouth that's unsettling, like a frozen scream. It invites you to read all sorts of drama into it. Your mind can't resist creating whatever it is that made her so terrified, and that conjures up all your own fears and demons."

"Is that what you see?"

"What I see is the typical face of a drowning victim."

Monk joined them. "What do you know about what happened here?"

"Not much more than I did at the station," Devlin said. "Her name is Carin Branham and she's the married mother of two kids, both off at college. Her husband is a lawyer. He's away in D.C. this week. Her body was found by the pool man."

"So it's been a week since her pool was cleaned."

"Since her pool man comes once a week, yes, I think that's a safe guess."

"But her pool is clean except for a couple of leaves and a tiny bit of tan bark."

"So she cleaned it before she went swimming," Devlin said. "I'd think you'd admire her for that."

"I would if she'd been the one who cleaned it," Monk said. "But she wasn't."

"It was the murderer who did," Devlin said.

# CHAPTER EIGHT

# Mr. Monk Counts to Three

**M**onk looked surprised. "You figured out that this is a murder?"

"Hell no, I just got here. The only conclusion I've reached is that she's dead," Devlin said. "But I can tell that you think it's murder."

"How?" Julie asked.

"I'm not sure. I suppose it's the same way my dog used to know I was going to take her for a walk even before I went for my coat, the leash, or said anything. Maybe it's his body language."

"So you are comparing me to a dog," Monk said.

"Of course not," Devlin said. "I adored my dog. Tell me why you think that Carin Branham didn't just have too much to drink, take a lousy dive, and crack her head on the bottom of her pool."

"For one thing, she's still wearing her contact lenses. Most people would take their lenses off before going in the pool or at least wear a pair of goggles to protect their eyes."

"That's it?" Devlin said. "It means nothing. If she had a few drinks too many, she probably forgot she was wearing them."

"And her watch, too," Monk said, pointing to her wrist. "It's not waterproof."

Julie leaned forward and looked at the watch. There was water under the crystal.

"That's not unusual," Julie said. "I've gone in the shower once or twice with my watch on and I was sober."

"Maybe so, but then there's this," he said and pointed at the pool.

Julie and Devlin stepped up to the edge and peered into the water.

"I don't see anything," Devlin said.

"Neither do I," Julie said.

"You don't see that piece of bark?" Monk said.

They both leaned closer and saw a speck of red wood floating on the surface.

"It's a sliver," Devlin said.

"But it's more than enough to send someone to death row."

Devlin turned and looked at him. "How do you figure that?"

"Because there is tan bark in the flower beds in the front yard and none in the back. So how did it get in the pool?"

"Does it matter?" she asked.

"When I arrived, I noticed a depression in the bed of bark where one of the rocks had been removed," he said. "That rock is in the dirt beneath the bush on the other side of the pool, and it is wet."

Devlin walked around the pool to the bush, got down on her knees, and peered underneath it. She took a pair of plastic gloves from her pocket, put them on, and reached into the bush for the rock. It was one of the smooth beach rocks from out front and it was wet. She sniffed the rock.

"It smells of chlorine." She looked over her shoulder at Monk across the pool. "I'll be damned."

"Here's what happened," Monk said. "The killer arrived at her door, picked up the rock, and slipped it into his pocket before he rang the bell. She answered the door, invited him in, and they had a few drinks. At some point, he hit her on the forehead with the rock and then held her head under the water in the pool until she drowned. Then the killer cleaned the rock off in the pool, washing away the blood but also bits of mud and tan bark, then tossed it in the bushes. The killer undressed Carin, put her in a swimming suit, and threw her body in the pool."

By now Monk had everyone's attention, including the two uniformed officers and the four forensic techs, who had stopped what they were doing to listen to him.

Devlin dropped the rock into an evidence bag and directed the nearest forensic tech to photograph the sliver of bark in the water and then bag it as evidence.

"Good work, Monk," Devlin said.

Julie was stunned. She'd expected Devlin to be angry with him. But then Julie realized that this was different from any of the crime scenes they'd been at with her before. This time, Monk and Devlin arrived on the scene together. He hadn't shown up after her to contradict her conclusions and make her feel foolish in front of her colleagues. She had nothing to feel defensive about in this situation.

"Thank you," Monk said. And everything would have been fine if he'd just left it at that, but he had to add one more comment. "But it was nothing. It was blatantly obvious what happened here."

Devlin's face tightened. "In other words, any fool could have seen it."

"Well, not any fool," Monk said. "But any reasonably observant person."

Julie spoke up. "I do have one question."

She didn't really. She just wanted to stop Monk from irritating Devlin any further. Now they were both looking at her, waiting for her question. She searched her mind for one and, after a long moment, finally came up with something.

"What makes you think the killer had drinks with her?"

"He wouldn't have put out the bottle of booze and the glass to suggest she'd had too much to drink unless he knew we'd find alcohol in her system during the autopsy."

"She could already have been drinking when he got here," Julie said.

"The tabletop is dirty," Monk said, pointing to the tiny glass-topped table between the two chaise lounges. "The second glass, which the killer removed, washed, and probably put away, left a ring. That proves she had a guest and they were sitting out here together."

"So she was killed by someone she knew," Julie said.

"A friend," Monk said. "Just like David Zuzelo."

"That's a huge leap, even for you," Devlin said. "There's nothing at all linking these two cases."

"Three," Monk said. "There's also Grossman."

"We don't know that he was killed by a friend," Devlin said.

"But all three murders were staged to look like accidents."

"That doesn't mean they were committed by the same guy," Devlin said. "Or do you have a piece of lint or a dust particle or a bread crumb that proves otherwise?"

"Nothing but a feeling," Monk said.

"It's probably gas," Devlin said.

"Impossible!" Monk said.

"You never have gas?" Devlin asked.

"Of course not. I'd die first, if not immediately afterward."

"Gas isn't fatal," Devlin said.

"Tell that to the countless species that were driven to extinction in the Mesozoic era due to massive and uncontrolled dinosaur flatulence."

Devlin stared at him. "You are making that up."

"A comprehensive report published by the journal *Current Biology* calculated that plant-eating dinosaurs produced five hundred seventy-two million tons of methane per year, almost as much as all of today's natural and man-made producers of the greenhouse gases combined," Monk said. "Their deadly emissions created catastrophic global warming that wiped out scores of creatures. It was a flatulence Armageddon."

"Even if there was a doomsday fart, I don't think you have to worry about that now," Devlin said. "Passing gas isn't deadly."

"It is if you have any shame," Monk said. "And I have plenty."

He turned and went into Carin Branham's house.

Devlin looked at Julie. "How can you stand to be with him all day?"

"He pays me," she said.

"It can't possibly be enough," Devlin said, and then the two women followed Monk inside.

The house was clean and contemporary. It had obviously been extensively renovated. Several walls had been removed to open up the state-of-the-art kitchen to the family room, which had a huge flat-screen TV and floor-to-ceiling built-in bookcases with lighted niches to display awards, knickknacks, and antiques.

The shelves were full of hardcover and paperback books, a small law library, bound journals, and binder-style photo albums, though everything was distinctly organized by type of binding, which I'm sure was something that Monk appreciated.

Monk examined the books, but his attention was quickly drawn to the photo albums, which were on an upper shelf. He brought over a nearby stepladder and tentatively climbed up while gripping the shelf for dear life.

"He isn't two feet off the ground," Devlin said to Julie as she observed Monk's ascent.

"He's afraid of heights," Julie said.

"It's two feet," she said.

"A fall from any height has the potential to break your neck," Julie said. "I know a guy who broke both of his arms falling off a curb."

"Was this curb over a cliff?"

"The point is, heights of any kind can be dangerous."

"You're just arguing his side to mess with me."

"Yes," Julie said. "I am. I have to do something to entertain myself."

Monk spoke up. "This shelf is very dusty."

"You're not dusting the house," Devlin said. "So if that's what you're thinking, you can forget it."

"The only place where there isn't dust on this shelf is in front of this album," Monk said, "suggesting to me that it was removed and replaced today."

He pulled the album out, an action that threw him off balance and sent him toppling off the stepladder. Julie bolted forward, catching his back with her hands and preventing him from falling.

Monk regained his footing and took a deep breath.

Devlin remained where she was, shaking her head.

"Thank you, Julie. You saved my life," Monk said.

"I wouldn't go that far," Julie said.

"If I'd continued to fall, I would have cracked my head open on the edge of the coffee table and, at the very least, suffered severe brain damage."

"Or actual decapitation," Devlin said. "I hope that album was worth the enormous risk you took scaling the bookcase without rappelling gear and a safety net to get it."

"It was," Monk said, bringing the album to the coffee table, where Julie and Devlin joined him. "Do you recognize that scent?"

"What scent?" Devlin asked.

"The wonderful aroma of Windex," Monk said. "The cover and spine of the album have been sprayed and wiped with it to remove fingerprints."

"I have no doubt that you can recognize the smell of Windex, since you probably bathe in the stuff," Devlin said, "but how do you know that's what it was used for?"

"Because he's a careful killer who wanted to remove any prints he left behind." Monk opened the album, which contained family photos held in place by a thin layer of transparent plastic film that pressed them against the sticky surface of the underlying page. "And he also didn't want us to know which pages he looked at because it could reveal his identity."

"You mean there are photos of the killer in here?" Devlin asked.

"No, but there might as well be," Monk said.

"I don't understand," Devlin said.

"You'll notice that several of the pages are stuck together. That's because they were damp. He sprayed them with Windex and wiped them down before he put the book away. Those are the pages that Carin showed him, and that he touched."

With that buildup, Julie expected some dramatic photos. But the pictures weren't that remarkable, just various shots of Carin's kids at different ages, on trips and at sporting events. They were the kinds of photos that every parent has of their kids. I have boxes of them.

"So Carin was proud of her kids and was showing them off to the friend who came to kill her," Devlin said. "I don't see how that incriminates anyone."

"Carin was very careful about the pictures she chose, picking key pages throughout the book rather than just flipping through it from beginning to end," Monk said. "She only chose pictures that showed her kids alone or with her. She didn't show him any photos that included her husband."

"You think her killer was an old lover or boyfriend," Devlin said.

"I don't think so," Monk said. "I know so."

# CHAPTER NINE

# Mr. Monk and the Mistake

**M**onk gave Devlin plenty to go on in the investigation and he had no problem walking away and letting her work on the leads without him.

That's because he wasn't the kind of detective who detected, at least not in the traditional sense of doing research, interviewing scores of people, and going through the forensics.

He was the kind who made his discoveries through the observation of people, places, and things, noticing what wasn't quite right in what he saw, or what they said, or what they did, and putting it into order.

So he'd take whatever facts Devlin came up with and use them to interpret whatever he'd observed and, from that, make his brilliant deductions, seemingly from out of nowhere.

And it really pissed off Devlin, because she knew better than anyone that his startling "out of nowhere" deductions were often based on facts that she'd worked very hard to dig up, even if the conclusions that she'd reached from them were wrong.

But regardless, it was his deductions that got all the attention and that moved the investigations forward. Her work was usually forgotten or simply ignored. She rarely got any credit for any of the work she did that helped Monk make his stunning deductions.

I could understand her frustration and anger. But what she didn't understand was that it wasn't personal or intentional. Monk didn't care about getting credit or attention. For him, it was all about restoring balance, cleaning up a mess, and making things right. It never occurred to him to thank or acknowledge anyone for their contribution to his process. The way he saw it, we were all fulfilling our obligation to maintain the natural balance of things. It would be like thanking someone for breathing.

That's just my theory, of course, but it explains why he could walk away and leave Devlin on her own with three murders left to solve.

There was simply nothing for him to go on yet.

So, as if the day hadn't been long and exhausting enough, he had Julie drive him that evening to Union Street and the stretch of trendy boutiques, galleries, and restaurants between Steiner and Octavia streets.

The shops there catered to the wealthy residents of Pacific Heights and most of the goods for sale were priced way outside Monk's comfort zone. Then again, so is everything at the Ninety-Nine Cent Store. That's because his wallet is hermetically sealed, figuratively and literally.

But that didn't really matter because he wasn't going there to shop. He was going to visit Ellen Morse, who'd opened up the West Coast outpost of Poop on Union Street.

Crap is a surprisingly high-end product, and on Union

Street Ellen could find plenty of buyers who would spend twelve thousand dollars on a Swiss timepiece with a face made of fossilized dinosaur dung, or twenty-five thousand dollars on a sculpture of a swan carved from panda poop, or twenty-five dollars an ounce for a bag of Kopi Luwak, the gourmet coffee beans gathered from civet droppings.

There were less pricey things at Poop, of course. The discerning Pacific Heights shopper could also buy inexpensively priced dung-based stationery, salad dressings, and shampoos.

What made those buyers special wasn't only their money. They were also trend-makers. If the women of Pacific Heights washed their hair with crap, then the women of Noe Valley, the Marina, and North Beach were sure to follow.

Monk never set foot in Poop. Julie always called Ellen to alert her that Monk was on the way so she could meet him outside.

It wasn't enough for Monk that they meet outside of the store—they also had to be a safe distance away. This time, Monk suggested they meet at Lush, a handmade, natural soap store a few doors down from Poop.

Ordinarily, Julie would have simply dropped Monk off for his date and driven away as fast as she could for a date of her own, especially given an already packed and exhausting day that began with a tuxedo fitting in Marin County, hours at the hospital and a confrontation with Dale the Whale, and a visit to another crime scene. But she loved Lush almost as much as Monk did.

The soaps were displayed like piles of candies, cheese, and pastries and were described as if they were meant to be consumed, not used for cleaning, moisturizing, and rejuvenating.

While they waited for Ellen to arrive, Julie admired a vanilla-bean and cocoa-butter bath bar that promised not only to moisturize her skin but to release a jasmine, vanilla, and tonka-bean blend that would make her irresistible.

Monk examined some soaps that looked like assorted brownies and promised to brutalize dirt and grime while exfoliating and energizing with their decadent dark-chocolate and cocoa-butter blends.

Ellen came in and gave Monk a hug so intimate that a car could have parked between them. Monk immediately blushed.

"Isn't this a wonderful store?" Monk said.

"It is," she said. "I love the way it smells."

"An alley would smell good compared to where you've been all day," Monk said.

Ellen laughed at that, which is one of the reasons both Julie and I liked her so much. She was one of the few people—okay, actually the only person—who found Monk's complaints and little digs adorable rather than infuriating.

"I look at these soaps and I want to have them all," she said.

"Me, too," Monk said. "There is nothing more wholesome, more admirable, than a soap store."

"I sell soap," she said.

Monk did a full-body cringe. "Yours is made of cow dung."

"Which is every bit as natural as what they make these soaps from," she said. "And handmade, too, just like these."

That image provoked another full-body cringe from Monk. Ellen laughed again and gave his arm a squeeze.

"Don't worry, I don't make them myself," she said. "My hands are clean. And, as we agreed, I didn't wash them with any of the soap that I sell."

"Let me buy you some soap," Monk said. "Made with soap."

"That would be wonderful," she said, and went over to greet Julie. "How was your day today?"

"Murder," Julie said with a smile.

"So business as usual," Ellen said, then looked to see what was in my daughter's shopping basket. Julie had picked up the vanilla-bean bath bar and was now examining a pink ball of soap that appeared to have a red rose embedded in the center. "What is this?"

"The end to the perfect Saturday night," she said.

Ellen read the description of the soap, a bath bomb of jasmine, clary sage, soya milk, and something called ylang-ylang, all of which, when combined and dissolved in water, were supposedly among "nature's most potent and seductive ingredients," turning any bath into an aphrodisiac.

Ellen took one of the pink balls. "I'd like this one, Adrian."

She tossed it to him and he caught it.

"What kind of soap is it?" he asked. As he looked it over, Ellen removed the display card with the description and hid it behind her back.

"Extreme antibacterial scrubber," Ellen said. "They call it the Germ Nuker."

"It's pink," he said.

"So as not to alert the germs to the utter annihilation that's coming," she said.

"Now that's my kind of soap," Monk said. He walked over and took two for himself.

"I hope so," Ellen said.

Monk walked away from them and headed to the cash register.

Julie smiled at Ellen. "Do you think it will work?"

Ellen replaced the description card. "If anything is ever going to get Adrian in a romantic mood, it's probably going to have something to do with soap or cleaning supplies."

"That's more than I ever wanted to know," Julie said and went to the register herself.

Monk was in such a magnanimous mood that he bought Julie her soaps, too.

"I want to encourage you to lead a healthy lifestyle," Monk said.

"Thank you," Julie said.

"How did the tuxedo fitting go?" Ellen asked as they headed for the door.

"The tailor was a strange man. He supposedly respects fine garments but thinks nothing of drawing all over them with chalk to indicate where he needs to make his adjustments." Monk held the door open for them and they stepped outside. "I objected, of course."

"Of course," Ellen said.

Julie looked at her and was surprised to see that Ellen was serious. Although Ellen sold Poop products, she and Monk shared an obsession with order, symmetry, and cleanliness.

But Ellen was more in control of her OCD tendencies and was also much more socially well-adjusted than Monk.

"So he then suggested that he use pins," Monk said as they continued on to Julie's car. "He wanted to deliberately put permanent holes in the clothing."

"Unbelievable," Ellen said.

"That's how rips and tears start. He might as well have taken out a pair of scissors and cut the clothes to shreds."

"Insane," she said.

Julie gave her another look, trying again to discern any sarcasm in her statement and realized, to her dismay, that Ellen was completely serious.

"So I introduced the man to the concept of writing down the necessary adjustments and measurements on a piece of paper instead of the garment."

"Did he thank you?" Ellen asked.

"Strangely, no," Monk said. "He actually seemed irritated. Perhaps he's illiterate and was trying to hide his disability. That would explain why he was using chalk marks."

"That's a very clever deduction," Ellen said.

"So I didn't press the issue and risk embarrassing him," Monk said. "Instead, I wrote the measurements down for him."

"You're so sensitive, Adrian," Ellen said.

They were just about at Julie's car when Monk stopped suddenly, cocking his head at an angle to look at something.

Julie turned to see what had attracted his attention. It was a poster-size blowup of the cover of Cleve Dobbs' memoir, *Just Peachy*, in the window of a small bookstore.

The cover featured a picture of a defiant Dobbs, his white

shirtsleeves rolled up, holding a Peach device in his hand, thrusting it out at the reader. The picture wasn't recent. It was taken several years earlier during his heyday, prior to his firing from Peach and after he got a trainer and lost his gut, but before his trademark bushy goatee became streaked with gray. He looked uncomfortable in the businessman's white shirt but clearly proud of his newly muscled arms.

Monk pointed to the tattoo—"CaringForever"—scrawled on his arm.

"What does that mean?" he asked.

"I think it's a statement of his personal commitment to charitable causes," Julie said.

"He's donated tens of millions of dollars to good causes," Ellen said. "Like sewage treatment plants in third-world countries that turn human waste into electrical energy."

Monk cringed. "That's just wrong."

"It's restoring balance," Ellen said, "turning waste into energy."

"I'm not talking about that," he said and pointed to the tattoo again. "There is no space between 'Caring' and 'Forever.' It's two words. He needs to add a space."

"They aren't words on a computer screen," Julie said. "It's a tattoo on skin. It's permanent. You can't do it over."

"That's why you shouldn't put anything on your skin that can't be immediately washed off," Monk said. "Because if you make a mistake, you have to live with it."

"I'm not defending tattoos, but the truth is, we have to live with most of our mistakes anyway," Ellen said. "It's better to own them than pretend they can be undone."

Monk faced the window again, rolled his shoulders,

tipped his head from one side to the other, and smiled, as if he were looking at the real Cleve Dobbs instead of his picture.

Julie sighed and looked at Ellen. "There goes my night and probably yours, too."

"What do you mean?" Ellen asked.

"Mr. Monk just solved a murder," she said.

"No, I didn't," he said. "I solved three."

# CHAPTER TEN

# Mr. Monk Is Peachy

**E**llen Morse was not at all pleased when Monk abruptly canceled their date and decided he had to go back to the police station right away.

Julie wasn't too thrilled about it, either, nor was her boyfriend, whom she feared wouldn't stick around with her for much longer the way things were going.

But both Ellen and Julie knew that Monk would not wait, and that it was possible someone else could be killed if the murderer wasn't caught quickly.

So Ellen went back to her store and Julie and Monk stuck their soap in the trunk of her car and headed back downtown.

Captain Stottlemeyer was in his office with Devlin, both of them eating McDonald's takeout at his desk, when Monk and Julie came in. Julie immediately took a seat on the couch and began texting her boyfriend.

"This is shocking," Monk said.

"Hello, Monk, it's nice to see you, too," Stottlemeyer said. "Please, come in and complain about something. It will help my digestion."

"It most certainly will," Monk said.

"How do you figure that?" Stottlemeyer asked.

"Because I won't stand by and let you continue to eat your meal on your desk," Monk said. "You might as well be eating your food off of a toilet seat."

"Contrary to popular belief, I don't urinate in my office," Stottlemeyer said, then glanced across the desk at Devlin. "Do you?"

"Only when you're not around," Devlin said. "And I really, really have to go."

"There is no need to be crude," Monk said. "Especially when impressionable youngsters are present."

He tipped his head toward Julie, who was busy texting and making a show of ignoring what was going on, though everyone knew that wasn't the case.

"The fact is," Monk continued, "that your desk is covered with files that have been all over the city, touched by hundreds of disease-caked hands, and coated with a layer of dust. As if that wasn't filthy enough, you walk all over San Francisco, on dirty sidewalks and streets, and through bloody crime scenes, and then come back here and put your feet up on the desk. And now you are eating off of that same disgusting surface."

"I've got a paper bag under my burger and fries, which is protecting them from my desk and vice versa," Stottlemeyer said, holding the Quarter Pounder in his hand.

"And where has that bag been?" Monk said. "Let's set aside for the moment where it was before it was in your custody. Think about where it has been since you drove through McDonald's on your way here from the hospital. The bag was on your car seat or on the floor. Now think about what has been on your seat and on the floor and how long it has been since your car has been washed."

Stottlemeyer did. He made a face and set his hamburger down on the bag. "Okay, you may have a point."

"If you're not going to eat that hamburger," Devlin said. "I will."

"Really? After all that?" Stottlemeyer said.

"Especially after all that," Devlin said. Defiance was her default mode.

Stottlemeyer lifted up the bag and set it in front of Devlin, then took a sip of his Coke and regarded Monk again. "I'm sure you didn't come all the way down here because you got a tip that I was eating at my desk. Was it to hear about Dale?"

Monk shook his head. "I assume he's conscious, in pain, handcuffed to his bed, and under constant guard."

"He is," Stottlemeyer said.

Monk nodded his approval. "I'm here because there's been a major break in the investigation into the serial killings."

"I wasn't aware we had any serial killings," Stottlemeyer said.

"Monk thinks the murders of Bruce Grossman, David Zuzelo, and Carin Branham are connected," Devlin said, speaking with her mouth half full.

"They are," Monk said. "They were all murders made to look like accidents by someone the victims knew."

"That may be true," Stottlemeyer said. "But we don't know the killer is the same person."

"I do," Monk said. "And now I can prove it."

Devlin swallowed what she was eating. "You couldn't at

the crime scene. What's changed since you left the crime scene two hours ago?"

"I bought soap," Monk said.

Stottlemeyer sighed. "I can see how that would change things."

"There's a bookstore that is selling Cleve Dobbs' memoir on the same block as the soap store," Monk said. "Are you familiar with him?"

"I am," Stottlemeyer said. "But I am surprised that you are."

"He wasn't until this afternoon," Devlin said.

"Dobbs has a tattoo on his arm, the kind that doesn't wash off," Monk said.

"Most are," Devlin said. "I've got a few myself."

Monk ignored her comment. "If you make a mistake on the tattoo, or change your mind, it's too bad, you are stuck with it."

"I am aware of that, too," Stottlemeyer said.

"This is what his looks like." Monk picked up a pen from Stottlemeyer's desk and wrote "CaringForever" on a yellow legal pad.

The captain glanced at it. "I don't see what this has to do with the murders of those three people."

Monk turned to Devlin. "How does the woman who was killed today spell her first name? Is it K-A-R-E-N?"

"No," Devlin said. "It's C-A-R-I-N. Why?"

Now Julie, suddenly interested, looked up from her phone, which indicated to Stottlemeyer that Monk might actually be on to something.

"What difference does it make how she spells her name?" Stottlemeyer asked.

"Because it was clear from the evidence at the scene that she was killed by an old lover or boyfriend," Monk said.

"To you," Devlin said. "I'm not convinced."

Monk ignored her and pointed to the drawing. "If you look at the tattoo, you'll see that the two words run together, and that the *F* in *forever* is capitalized. There should be a space between the two words. It's the *g* at the end of *Caring* that ruins everything."

"You think the tattoo used to say 'Carin Forever' and that when they split, Dobbs added the *g* to the tattoo," Stottlemeyer said. "That's why the two words run together."

"Exactly," Monk said.

"So, just to be clear, you believe that Cleve Dobbs, one of the most well-known men on this planet, and also one of the richest, killed Carin Branham," Stottlemeyer said. "And you are basing this theory on the fact that there's no space between the two words *Caring* and *Forever*."

"There's more," Monk said.

"There always is," Devlin said.

"Bruce Grossman, our first victim, replaced Dobbs on the board of Peach," Monk said.

"Do you know how many thousands of people in the Bay Area have worked for Peach?" Devlin said.

"How many of them have fired Cleve Dobbs or broken his heart?" Monk asked. "I am certain if you look into David Zuzelo you'll find a connection to Dobbs, too."

Stottlemeyer ran his hands through what was left of his

hair. "Let's assume that there is. You're saying that Cleve Dobbs suddenly decided, weeks after the release of his best-selling book, to stroll down memory lane and kill people. Not hire someone to do it, but murder them himself."

"Yes," Monk said.

"Why?" Stottlemeyer said.

"I don't know," Monk said.

"Is there anything else, perhaps something that would actually qualify as admissible evidence, that connects the three murders to Dobbs?"

"What more do you need?" Monk asked.

"Has it occurred to you that someone with a grudge against Dobbs, or Peach, could be killing these people?" Stottlemeyer asked. "Or that Dobbs, rather than being the killer, could be a potential victim?"

"No," Monk said.

"But that doesn't mean it isn't so," Devlin said.

"Usually it does," Monk said.

"Egomaniac," Devlin said.

Stottlemeyer glanced at Julie. "What do you think?"

"I'm not a detective," she said.

"I'm trying to include you in the discussions," Stottle-meyer said.

"Honestly, Leland, I'd prefer if you tried to end the discussion instead so I could go home. But I will say that what Mr. Monk is suggesting about the tattoo makes some sense. Johnny Depp had Winona Ryder's first name tattooed on his arm when they dated and he had it changed to 'Wino' when they split up."

"Who is Johnny Depp?" Monk asked.

"He's a pirate," Devlin said.

Stottlemeyer sighed. "Look, I've had a long day, one that included watching as a fat murderer got cut open and had all his blubber sucked out. So here's what I'm going to do. I'm heading home and so are you. In the meantime, Lieutenant Devlin will look into the pasts of both Carin Branham and David Zuzelo for any links to Dobbs or Peach."

"I will?" Devlin said. "Just because Monk saw a tattoo on Dobbs' arm?"

"It won't cost us anything to explore the possibility that he's right. You will have to admit, he usually is. And if Dobbs is a potential victim, I'd like to get to him before the killer does."

"He is the killer," Monk said.

Stottlemeyer looked at Monk. "If Devlin finds a Peach connection between the victims, then I'll give you a call and we'll go talk with Dobbs. But that won't happen until tomorrow morning at the earliest, so go home. I'm sure some dust has accumulated that needs your urgent attention."

Monk couldn't argue with that, nor could he possibly ignore the notion of dust piling up at his home once the idea had been planted in his head, which, of course, was exactly why Stottlemeyer mentioned it.

"You have to promise me one thing," Monk said.

"What's that?"

"You will clean all of the crumbs, ketchup drops, bits of lettuce, french fries, and grains of salt off of your desk before you go."

Stottlemeyer sighed. "I won't leave until every grain of salt is removed."

"Do you mean that in the same way that you said you'd tow that Mercedes at Zuzelo's building but then you really wouldn't?"

"No, Monk, this time I will do it," Stottlemeyer said. "You can sleep soundly tonight."

Monk stared at the desk, then back at the captain. "I will check the desk next time I am here."

"You check my desk every time you are here," Stottlemeyer said.

Monk nodded. "I'm glad we understand each other."

And with that, Monk walked out, Julie right behind him.

# CHAPTER ELEVEN

# Mr. Monk and the Broken Heart

**A**t that moment, I was in New Jersey, three hours ahead of everyone in San Francisco, and back in my hotel room after ending my shift.

During my day maintaining law and order in Summit, I ticketed a dozen drivers for speeding violations, figured out who'd been stealing Mr. Abernathy's morning paper for the last month (it was a dog across the street), and filled out a report for a woman who had an iPad stolen from the front seat of her unlocked Porsche.

It was not the most exciting day in the annals of law enforcement, and I found myself guiltily longing for a major crime wave to challenge my little gray cells, as Hercule Poirot would say.

I gave Julie a call on the pretext of giving her my travel information for the wedding, but I really wanted to find out what complex mysteries she and Monk were involved in so I could live vicariously through them.

I caught her at home, shortly after she'd dropped off Monk at his place and been dumped via text message by her boyfriend.

"You're better off without him," I said.

"How do you know?"

"Because he broke up with you by text," I said. "It proves he's a gutless, classless jerk."

"I deserved it," she said. "I would have dumped me, too. I was never around and totally undependable."

"You're dependable," I said.

"To Mr. Monk—not to anybody else. I blew off a date tonight at the last minute because Mr. Monk had one of his sudden inspirations."

"Did he catch the murderer?"

"No, but he's certain that he knows who it is, even though he doesn't have any concrete evidence. But his epiphany meant that I stood up my boyfriend for the one hundredth time. I never did that before I started working for Mr. Monk. This job makes it impossible to have a relationship."

"Believe me, I know," I said. "Now imagine doing the job while being a single mother and raising a child."

"You're fishing for appreciation," she said.

"I'm just making a point," I said.

"No, you're trying to score some off of my misery. Shame on you. This call is supposed to be about me."

"Who says?"

"I do," she said. "I was just dumped."

"By a jerk. He did you a favor. Suck it up."

"Thanks for the sympathy and understanding, Mom."

"That's not what you need now. Don't be hurt, be angry," I said. "It feels better. How's work going?"

"The usual. People have been murdered. Mr. Monk makes huge deductive leaps on the basis of tiny details nobody else notices. Amy is pissed off and defensive, though she had it a bit more under control today. And Leland just accepts it all and wants to go home."

"Sounds wonderful to me," I said, hoping I didn't sound too homesick and envious.

"Oh, and Dale the Whale is having lipo and a gastric bypass."

That made me sit up in my chair. "In prison?"

"In a hospital."

"It's a trick," I said. "He's plotting an escape."

"That's what Monk thinks, too, but Leland has it under control. Dale is in the ICU and under around-the-clock guard."

Murders to solve and Dale the Whale out of prison, perhaps plotting a grand escape. It sounded so much more interesting than catching a dog who liked to collect rolled-up morning newspapers and bury them in his yard.

For a moment, I wished I was there to help out. But I wasn't Monk's underappreciated, underpaid, overworked assistant anymore. Julie was.

I was a police officer now, recognized for my skills and decently compensated for my work. I carried a badge and a gun instead of a purse full of disinfectant wipes, bottled water, evidence baggies, and hand sanitizer.

I was independent and self-reliant in a way that I'd never been before.

I was respected for the first time in my life.

I actually had a profession.

So why was I so glum?

"Tell me about the murders," I said.

She did. "And you won't believe who Mr. Monk thinks the killer of all three of them is."

"You say that like it's someone I know."

"It's someone everyone knows—except Monk, of course. Cleve Dobbs."

I was stunned. "Founder of Peach? *That* Cleve Dobbs?"

"How many others do you know?"

"Why would he go around killing people? He has the money to hire an army to do it for him."

"I don't know, but Mr. Monk is usually right about his deductions, so I'm pretty sure we'll be over at Dobbs' place tomorrow. Leland will try to be polite and circumspect, but he will be totally undermined by Mr. Monk, who will probably come right out and accuse Dobbs of being a murderer. Maybe I'll record it all for you on my Peach."

I almost took her up on the offer, which made no sense. That's because the situation she described was one I'd been in a thousand times before with Monk and always found extremely irritating, frustrating, and uncomfortable. It was exactly the kind of stress I'd looked forward to eliminating from my life when I'd taken the Summit job.

And yet, at that moment, I found the prospect of being part of that potentially awkward and infuriating encounter with Dobbs so much more interesting, fun, and amusing than anything that was likely to happen in my life.

"If Monk says Dobbs is a killer, then he is," I said. "But proving it isn't going to be easy. Monk will become obsessed with solving the crime."

"So I won't have much time to wallow in my heartbreak," she said.

"Are you really heartbroken?"

"It wasn't love, if that's what you're asking. But I really liked him and, who knows, in time it might have turned into something."

"Not if he's the kind of guy who breaks up with you with a text message."

"Well, in his defense, it's probably the best way to reach me these days, so how he dumped me kind of underscores why the relationship wasn't working. I probably would have stood him up if he'd made a date to dump me face-to-face."

"You're not making it very easy to be angry at the guy," I said.

"I don't want to be angry at him," she said. "It just sucks, that's all. I guess I'm going to have to be single until the summer is over and Mr. Monk can find a new assistant. I need a job with regular hours once school starts again. I can't blow off my classes every time a dead body is found in San Francisco, or I'll never graduate. And I'd like to have a love life."

"Join the club," I said.

"What's stopping you?"

That was a good question. "I'm focusing on my career right now."

"And you're still living in a hotel?"

"I haven't had a chance to find a place yet," I said.

"Sounds to me like you're stalling."

"Stalling what?"

"Starting your new life."

"I'm hard at work," I said.

"But you're living out of a hotel room and not starting any new relationships," she said. "You're hesitating about putting down roots. Something is holding you back."

"Have you changed your major to psychology?"

"No," she said.

"Maybe you should," I said.

Okay, that's enough about me. The last thing you want to hear about is my emotional and psychological angst. You want to know about the three murders and Dale the Whale. I just wanted to remind you that I was around and that I'd soon be arriving in San Francisco, where I'd become part of the story rather than just your lovable, all-knowing if slightly neurotic narrator.

But I am getting ahead of myself.

Julie followed Teeger family tradition and drowned her sorrow in Oreo cookie ice cream, which is lousy for the waistline but a remarkable cure for whatever ails you. Unless it's worries about your weight, of course.

The next morning, she got a call bright and early from Captain Stottlemeyer summoning Monk to the police headquarters.

"Can I assume this means Amy found the connections between Dobbs and the three murder victims?" she asked.

"A brilliant deduction," Stottlemeyer said, but he declined to tell her any more details.

So Julie dutifully picked up Monk at his place, but it took them nearly an hour to get to the headquarters. The brakes failed on a moving truck on Powell Street, sending it barreling down the steep hill toward Union Square, where it plowed into a cable car and a bus, injuring scores of people and snarling traffic throughout the city.

Monk and Julie didn't have to make any excuses for their tardiness to Stottlemeyer, who was at the coffee machine when they came and was well aware of the accident. Besides, Julie got the impression that the captain was in no hurry to question Dobbs anyway.

He picked up his coffee cup and led them over to Devlin, who sat at her desk, which was covered with fast-food containers and empty soft-drink cans.

"I thought you said you weren't going to eat at your desk anymore," Monk said.

"The captain did, not me," Devlin said. "If I stopped eating at my desk, it would be the same as going on a hunger strike."

"You are wearing the same clothes you wore yesterday," Monk said.

"Wow, you really are observant," she said. "I haven't showered, either, thanks to you."

Monk took a big step back from her desk, which seemed to delight her.

"She's been here all night digging into the backgrounds of the victims and Dobbs," Stottlemeyer said. "You were right, they are connected."

"I wasn't aware there was any doubt," Monk said.

"We already know Grossman's connection to Peach. He was on the board that booted Dobbs from the company and took his spot as CEO," Devlin said. "And you were right about Carin Branham. She was Dobbs' girlfriend for two years before he developed the Peach. Supposedly, he was so depressed from the breakup that he went into virtual seclusion after that, which was when he created the Peach."

"So the breakup was the best thing that ever happened to him," Julie said. "Just because someone dumps you, it's not the end of something, but maybe the beginning. An opportunity. A blessing in disguise. Instead of wallowing in misery and feeling sorry for yourself, you should celebrate your heartbreak as the glorious gift that it might actually be."

Monk, Stottlemeyer, and Devlin stared at her.

"Did your boyfriend dump you last night?" Devlin asked.

"How did you know?" Julie asked.

"It's obvious from the drops of Oreo cookie ice cream on your shoe," Monk said. "And the fact that you ordinarily send or receive text messages from him once or twice an hour and yet you haven't today."

"I didn't notice any of those things," Devlin said. "I got it because Julie just told us she was dumped."

"She did?" Monk said.

"Your understanding of human nature is astounding," Stottlemeyer said.

"That's why I am sure I would have heard Julie say it if she'd said it," Monk said.

"Yes, I was dumped," Julie said. "But I am totally okay with it."

"We can tell," Devlin said.

"Can we move on, please?" Julie said. "How is David Zuzelo connected to Dobbs?"

"Zuzelo was Dobbs' high school math teacher who flunked

him," Devlin said. "Apparently, Zuzelo told him to pursue a career that didn't require any mathematics."

Monk nodded and turned to Stottlemeyer. "Shall we go arrest him?"

"We don't have any evidence," Stottlemeyer said.

"If you aren't going to listen when I tell you what happened, you should have Devlin take notes."

"His tattoo doesn't prove he's a serial killer," Stottlemeyer said. "We also don't have any motive."

"Zuzelo offended him, Grossman took his job, and Branham broke his heart."

"Decades ago, Monk," Stottlemeyer said. "Why kill them now?"

"We can ask him after you read him his rights," Monk said.

"We will go and talk with him," Stottlemeyer said. "But you aren't coming along unless you can promise me you'll behave yourself."

"I always do."

"Okay," Stottlemeyer said. "With all the traffic today, it's probably better if the three of us can go in my car."

"Your car?" Monk asked.

"I've got a siren," Stottlemeyer said. "And I've had it cleaned."

"You said three of us would be going."

"I'm sending Devlin home," Stottlemeyer said. "She's pulled an all-nighter on this."

"Then we'll need another officer," Monk said.

"I think we can handle Dobbs on our own," Stottlemeyer said.

"Three people in a car isn't safe," Monk said. "It's a deadly imbalance, particularly at high speed."

Devlin sighed and got up. "I'll come along. I don't get to meet many billionaires."

"Are you going to shower first?" Monk asked. "With a strong disinfectant soap and a scrub brush?"

"For you, no," Devlin said. "But for a billionaire, yes."

# CHAPTER TWELVE

# Mr. Monk and the Billionaire

**B**eing rich is certainly better than being poor, but it doesn't mean you're less likely to become a murderer, or get yourself killed, than anybody else. I can think of more than a dozen times that murder investigations led Monk to a mansion in Pacific Heights, where the city's elite live, supposedly above all the troubles that afflict us mere mortals.

The ruthless robber barons who built the city picked this spot in the 1800s as their Mount Olympus, using their gold and railroad riches to erect their castles high above everyone else, granting spectacular views of their domain.

Back then, and even more so today, to attain the kind of wealth required to live in Pacific Heights, and to keep it once you have it, you must be a strong-willed, aggressive, and fiercely protective person capable of going to extraordinary lengths to get what you want. Those are certainly great attributes for a murderer to have, and also the kind of personality traits that would make someone want to slit your throat.

Cleve Dobbs didn't rise to the top of the tech world, and make Peach a household name (except in Monk's household), without being tenacious and vicious and without plowing through any obstacles, human or otherwise, in his path.

I could see him as a murderer. Then again, after working so long for Monk, I could see anyone as a killer.

Even with the siren, it took Stottlemeyer nearly forty-five minutes to make his way to Dobbs' house, which was just a few doors down from the Victorian mansion that once belonged to Veronica Lorber, widow of Burgerville founder Brandon Lorber, whose murder Monk had solved a few years back.

Like I said, we'd been to the Heights a lot.

Veronica ended up marrying a twenty-four-year-old male model, who was easily thirty years younger than her, and moved to Marbella, where she died a mysterious death—but that's another story and not one we were involved with.

Dobbs' house took its design cues from Vaux-le-Vicomte castle in France. It didn't have the moat, but it did have a stone bridge over a large pond full of exotic and colorful fish.

Stottlemeyer rang the bell and held his badge up to the security camera. Monk, Julie, and Devlin stood behind him.

"May I help you?" a woman's voice asked over the speaker.

"Captain Leland Stottlemeyer, SFPD. We'd like to see Cleve Dobbs. It's urgent."

"Come right in," she said.

There was a buzz and the gate unlocked. They walked over the bridge to the front door, which was elaborately carved out of wood and probably thick enough to withstand an assault with a battering ram. The iron knocker was a lion with a ring in its teeth, which was no surprise. I saw them on the doors of rich people's homes all the time. I'm not sure why people think the knocker, or a statue of a lion with his paw on a stone ball, is so classy.

A woman opened the door. Her long, prematurely gray hair was in sharp contrast with her youthful features, perfect skin, and radiant blue eyes.

"I'm Jenna Dobbs, Cleve's wife. Can you tell me what this is regarding?"

"We really need to speak with him," Stottlemeyer said.

"Very well." She ushered them inside.

The entry hall had two vast, curving staircases that looked as if they'd been carved from two huge slabs of marble and a gigantic chandelier that resembled the mother ship in *Close Encounters of the Third Kind*. It probably was.

Julie had to suppress an urge to take a picture of it with her iPhone.

Jenna led them through the entry hall to the great room, which was two stories tall with a breathtaking view of the garden. The meticulously landscaped yard, also modeled after the gardens at Vaux-le-Vicomte, sloped downward in such a way that it created the illusion that their property stretched clear out to the Golden Gate beyond, as if the bridge and the bay belonged to them, too. A vast second-story balcony, supported by vine-wrapped Romanesque pillars, gave a commanding view of the bay from the upper floors.

My daughter had never been in a house that big, ostentatious, and opulent before, and it was all she could do not to gasp.

Devlin didn't seem impressed. If anything, the wealth seemed to irritate her. Julie couldn't read Stottlemeyer, but based on what she knew about him, she figured he wouldn't let himself be intimidated by the trappings of money and power and would treat Dobbs like anybody else.

Monk, of course, was interested only in how clean, orderly, and symmetrical everything was and, on that score, he had to be impressed.

Jenna led them outside, where they found Cleve Dobbs on his knees, planting roses. He stood up as they approached. He was deeply tanned and was dressed in a sunhat, polo shirt, and cargo shorts. He wore thick leather garden gloves and he had rubber pads strapped to his knees with Velcro.

"Cleve, this is Captain Stottlemeyer with the San Francisco Police," Jenna said. "He says it's urgent."

"Is this about my parking tickets?" Dobbs asked, limping slightly as he approached them.

"I'm not in parking enforcement," Stottlemeyer said. "I'm in homicide. This is Lieutenant Devlin, our consultant Adrian Monk, and his assistant, Julie Teeger."

Dobbs pulled off his gloves and stuck them in the pockets of his shorts. "What can I do for you?"

"You could confess," Monk said.

Stottlemeyer gave Monk a sharp look of warning, then shifted his gaze back to Dobbs. "We're investigating the deaths of Bruce Grossman and David Zuzelo."

"I heard on the news that Bruce fell off a cliff or something a few days ago," Dobbs said. "What happened to Mr. Zuzelo?"

It's funny how we think about the teachers we had as kids. No matter how many years have passed since we were in their classes, or how old we get, they will always be Mr. or Mrs. Whoever to us.

"He fell from the deck of his seventeenth-floor apartment here in the city," Stottlemeyer said.

"That's terrible," Dobbs said.

"Who was he?" Jenna asked.

"My high school math teacher," Dobbs said.

"The one who said you would never amount to anything?" Jenna said.

"Yeah," Dobbs said. "In fact, those were his exact words, pun intended."

"What pun?" Monk asked.

"Amount to anything," Dobbs said.

"I don't get it," Monk said.

"He was a math teacher," Dobbs said. "And he was referring to what he considered my lack of mathematical comprehension."

"I still don't get it," Monk said.

"It doesn't matter, Monk," Stottlemeyer said, then turned back to Dobbs. "The point is, Mr. Dobbs, that they weren't accidents. Both men were murdered."

"By someone they knew," Devlin added.

"I'm sure they knew lots of people besides me," Dobbs said. "So why are you here?"

"Because yesterday Carin Branham drowned in her swimming pool," Stottlemeyer said. "And that wasn't an accident, either, though someone tried to make it look like one."

Dobbs sighed and rubbed his arm, the one with the "CaringForever" tattoo. "I see."

"I don't," Jenna said.

"Three people were murdered in what initially appeared to be accidental deaths," Devlin said. "And the one thing they had in common was that they all knew your husband."

"And he hated them," Monk said, then gestured to Dobbs' feet. "You wear a size twelve shoe."

"Yes, I do," Dobbs said. "But I don't see what that has to do with anything. And I certainly didn't hate any of those people. Quite the contrary. I owe them the success that I have today."

"How do you figure that?" Devlin asked.

"I wanted to prove Mr. Zuzelo wrong. That's what motivated me to get past my fear of math and to embrace it. I would never have been able to write the code for the Peach software without that," Dobbs said. "If it wasn't for Carin dumping me, and the heartbreak that drove me into seclusion, I probably never would have created the Peach. And if Bruce hadn't fired me, and taken over my company, I would never have realized and acknowledged the serious management mistakes that I'd been making that would have doomed the company if I'd stayed on. Thanks to him, I was able to come back to Peach and make it a bigger success than it was before."

That was pretty much the rationale that Devlin predicted he'd use, so she must have been pleased with herself.

"You have scratches on your ankle," Monk said.

"That's what you get when you work in a rose garden," Dobbs said. "Roses have thorns. What's your point?"

"I think you got those scratches when you stood on the wicker chair on Zuzelo's deck and your foot went right through the seat," Monk said. "The limp, too."

"You're kidding me," Dobbs said. "You think I threw my high school math teacher off a roof?"

"His deck," Monk said.

"We aren't saying that," Stottlemeyer said firmly.

"I am," Monk said.

"This is going well," Devlin whispered to Julie.

"I find your insinuations highly offensive," Jenna said. "My husband has been limping for a while now. In fact, he went to the doctor about it last week."

"Sprained my ankle playing racquetball and it won't go away," Dobbs said, but he kept his eye on Monk. "You think I pushed Bruce off a cliff and drowned Carin, too?"

"No, we don't," Stottlemeyer said.

"I do," Monk said.

"Why would I do that?" Dobbs said.

"I don't know," Monk said.

"Isn't that something you should know before accusing someone of multiple murders?" Dobbs asked.

"We aren't accusing you of anything," Stottlemeyer said.

"He is," Jenna said, pointing her finger at Monk. "And I've had enough. When did these murders happen?"

Devlin told her the approximate times of death and the days when the murders occurred.

"Well, that settles it," Jenna said. "He was here with me all of those times. On the morning Bruce was murdered, we were having breakfast on our deck. When that math teacher was killed, we were in bed together, watching Jimmy Kimmel."

"I love that guy," Dobbs said.

"And when Carin was killed," she continued, "I was inside but I saw Cleve out here puttering away in the garden."

"That's good to know," Stottlemeyer said. "But an alibi isn't really necessary. The reason we're here is because you seem to be the only connection between these three victims. We're hoping you can offer us some insight into who might be doing this."

"Isn't it obvious?" Dobbs said.

"It is to me," Monk said.

"My book just came out and is a huge best seller. Clearly some twisted individual, someone who resents me for some reason, is killing people who played a significant role in shaping the man that I have become," Dobbs said. "What you should do is read my book, identify other possible targets, and warn them that they could be in danger."

"Or you could just give us your list," Monk said.

"I don't know how a killer thinks," Dobbs said.

"Oh, sure you do," Monk said.

"That's enough, Monk," Stottlemeyer said, then looked at Devlin. "Take him back to the car, Lieutenant. He's done here. If he won't go, put him in handcuffs and drag him out."

"With pleasure," Devlin said, then grabbed Monk by the arm and led him away.

This put Julie in an awkward position. Her reflex was to leave with Monk. On the other hand, she was tempted to stay, just in case anything was said that might prove useful later on in Monk's investigation. Then again, she was afraid of what Stottlemeyer might do if he saw her lingering.

So she split the difference. She walked away, but didn't leave. She stayed within earshot, admiring the house and the big balcony with its well-tended potted trees and flower boxes. She imagined what it would be like to live in such a place.

"I apologize for my colleague," Stottlemeyer said.

"Adrian Monk," Dobbs said. "I've heard of him. He's supposed to be brilliant."

Monk would have liked hearing that.

"He is," Stottlemeyer said. "He's also a difficult personality."

"People have described me the same way," Dobbs said. "So how can I help?"

"Your theory about the murders makes a lot of sense," Stottlemeyer said. "Except for one thing."

"What's that?"

"Whoever killed these people wasn't some wacko off the street," Stottlemeyer said. "At least two of the victims invited the killer into their homes."

"That's scary," Jenna said.

"I don't know, but I'd be cautious if I were you," Stottlemeyer said. "I'd also warn your friends to keep their eyes open and be extra careful, but that's not going to be easy."

"What do you mean?" she asked.

"The killer could be someone close to you," Stottlemeyer said. "Someone you trust. The person you warn could actually be the one you should be afraid of."

"If he's been close to us for that long," Dobbs said, "why start killing now?"

"That's a good question," Stottlemeyer said. "Something you did, or something you said in your book, must have ticked him off and sparked these killings."

"I've got no idea who that could be," Dobbs said.

"Unfortunately, neither do we."

"This guy Monk," Dobbs said. "They say he's solved every case he's ever investigated."

"He has," Stottlemeyer said. "He'll solve this one, too."

"So what do you do?" Dobbs said.

"I get to make the arrest and go home early," Stottlemeyer said.

"But right now Monk suspects my husband is the killer, which is absolutely absurd," Jenna said. "If any of that man's insane accusations get picked up by the media, you'll be hearing from our lawyers. It will sound a lot like a firing squad."

"Message received," Stottlemeyer said. He walked away toward the house and Julie joined him, leaving Dobbs and his wife behind in the garden.

"What do you think?" Julie asked him.

"He's the guy," the captain said.

# CHAPTER THIRTEEN

# Mr. Monk and the Perfect Storm

"That was you behaving yourself?" Stottlemeyer asked Monk when they got to the car.

"Yes," Monk said.

"The first thing you did was ask him to confess."

"He asked what he could do for me," Monk said. "I answered honestly. Did you expect me to lie?"

"No, I expected you to be you, and you certainly were," Stottlemeyer said. "Which allowed me to be clever and crafty."

"I don't understand," Monk said.

Julie sighed. "Leland is saying that you did exactly what he expected you to do."

"And, as a result of throwing you out, I got into his good graces," Stottlemeyer said. "He thinks I'm on his side."

"His wife wasn't with him when the murders happened," Monk said. "She's lying."

"Of course she is," Devlin said.

Monk turned to her. "You agree with me?"

"As much as I hate to admit it, yes, I do."

"So do I," Stottlemeyer said. "She's the second-worst liar I've ever seen."

"Who's the first?" Monk asked.

"That would be you," Stottlemeyer said.

"So you know that Cleve Dobbs is a murderer," Monk said. "A serial killer, in fact."

"I do," Stottlemeyer said.

"Then why aren't you arresting him?"

"Because we have absolutely no evidence and no motive," Stottlemeyer said.

"But what if he kills someone else?" Julie asked.

"He might like to, but he won't," Stottlemeyer said. "He knows we're on to him now. If he's got other people on his kill list, he's going to wait until the pressure is off him before he strikes again."

"It won't be," Monk said. "I am going to be on him like disinfectant on a countertop until he's behind bars."

"I'll dismantle his alibis for starters," Devlin said.

"Even if we can prove that his wife lied for him," Stottlemeyer said, "that still doesn't put Dobbs at the crime scenes."

"So how are you going to do it?" Julie asked. "You've already collected all the evidence and there's nothing directly linking Dobbs to the murders."

"There is," Monk said. "There has to be. We just haven't seen it yet."

"How can you be so sure?" Julie said.

"Because he killed those people," Monk said. "Everybody leaves a mess wherever they go. It's inevitable. But most people aren't as good at cleaning them up as I am."

"And that, in a nutshell, is how Monk always gets his man," Stottlemeyer said.

"You ought to be president of his fan club," Devlin said.

"I am," Stottlemeyer said. "I am also its only member."

Monk nudged Julie.

"I'm a member, too," she said.

Stottlemeyer smiled. "We're growing by leaps and bounds."

The traffic was terrible in San Francisco. Drivers who were trying to avoid the street closures caused by the truck accident north of Union Square were creating near-gridlock everywhere else. Even with the siren, Stottlemeyer was forced to take a circuitous route that avoided major north–south streets like Divisadero and Van Ness.

Devlin was up front with Stottlemeyer, and Monk and Julie sat in the back. Julie craned her neck to see the swarm of news and police choppers hovering over Union Square. Every so often a medevac chopper would rise up and then streak south toward the Mission District and San Francisco General.

Monk followed Julie's gaze and rolled his shoulders. "What do you know about this accident, Captain?"

"Just what I heard on the news. The brakes failed on a truck this morning on Powell Street, and it rolled down the hill and slammed into a cable car and a bus," Stottlemeyer said. "Couldn't have happened in a worse place or at a worse time."

"Can you find out more?" Monk asked.

"That shouldn't be too hard." Stottlemeyer turned on the radio to KCBS, the all-news AM station, and got an immediate update.

The newscaster basically repeated what Stottlemeyer had already told Monk, but far more colorfully, describing the "perfect storm" of a large moving truck roaring out of control down one of San Francisco's steepest streets, becoming a "runaway freight train of bloody carnage" at the exact moment that both a bus and a crowded cable car overflowing with tourists were crossing in front of it on Powell Street.

The speeding truck first T-boned the bus, turning it on its side and creating "a massive battering ram of twisted metal and showering sparks" that smashed into the cable car, "obliterating one of San Francisco's historic icons like a piñata."

Rescue personnel arriving on the scene likened the devastation to the aftermath of an earthquake or a bombing.

Four people were killed, and the number of those hurt, many critically, was in the dozens and climbing, overwhelming the emergency rooms of San Francisco General and other local hospitals. Medevac units were already taking some of the injured across the bay to hospitals in Berkeley.

It was shaping up to be one of the worst traffic accidents in San Francisco's history. The driver of the truck had not been found or identified.

"Oh my God," Monk said.

Stottlemeyer sighed. "With the steep hills we've got in this city, an accident like that was bound to happen one of these days."

"But it didn't happen on any day," Monk said. "It happened the day after Dale the Whale checked into San Francisco General for surgery."

Stottlemeyer glanced up at the rearview mirror to get a look at Monk. "You think he got someone to rent a truck and let it loose on Powell Street?"

"I think the only hope Dale has of escape is creating so

much chaos in the hospital that it would be impossible for the security team to stay on top of everyone who is coming and going."

"Damn it," Stottlemeyer said, slamming his palm against the steering wheel. "Get hold of the security teams, Amy. I want confirmation that Dale is secure. And tell them we are on our way."

The security teams admitted that keeping the hospital buttoned down wasn't easy with all the ambulances and medevac choppers arriving, but they said no patients had left the hospital that the officers hadn't seen coming in.

That report, received by Stottlemeyer in the car on the way to the hospital, didn't do much to alleviate his concern or Monk's. They still hadn't heard from the officers stationed outside the ICU and in the adjacent recovery rooms since no cell phones were allowed in those areas.

As soon as they arrived at the hospital, they rushed into the ER, which was overflowing with patients, paramedics, orderlies, and medical personnel.

Dr. Jessup was running around marking everybody up with his colored pens and, much to Monk's chagrin, not bothering to use new ones with each patient.

"He's making a deadly situation far worse," Monk said to Julie, who had never seen anything like the carnage she now saw. It seemed like everybody was covered with blood and wailing in agony.

"I think germy marking pens are the least of the problems these people have right now," she said.

"Now perhaps," Monk said. "But not later, when they are

virulent with horrific diseases far worse than the injuries they've sustained."

Monk and Julie hurried to keep up with Stottlemeyer and Devlin as they weaved their way through the crowds.

Monk shoved his hands in his pockets and drew himself in as much as he could to avoid contact with any of the injured people, concerned relatives, and beleaguered hospital staff that he passed, but that just wasn't possible in such tight quarters. He was bumped and jostled the whole way.

"My clothes are going to have to be incinerated when this is over," Monk said. "And this is my favorite coat."

"It's identical to all your other coats," Julie said, doing her best to literally run interference for Monk without actually pushing anyone aside.

"But this was the first one I bought," Monk said. "It held a special place."

"The first in the row hanging in your closet," Julie said.

"Now you understand," Monk said. "It also means another coat will have to be sacrificed."

"So you have an even number again."

"It's a tragedy all around," Monk said.

"It could be worse," she said. "You could be one of the people injured in the accident."

"I am collateral damage," he said.

They followed Stottlemeyer and Devlin up the stairs and down the corridor toward the ICU and the two officers stationed outside the door, who were checking patients as they came in and out.

"Where's Dale?" Stottlemeyer asked one of the officers.

"They moved him and the other lipo patients out of ICU

and into another ward to make way for all the incoming wounded," the officer said. Obviously, this was a man who'd previously served in the military or at least had watched a lot of episodes of *M\*A\*S\*H*.

"Where's the ward?"

"Down the hall and around the corner, into to the next wing," the officer said.

Stottlemeyer rushed off in that direction. Devlin, Monk, and Julie almost had to run to keep up with him.

They rounded the corner and at the end of the long, crowded hall, they could see a doctor in blue scrubs and a lab coat talking heatedly to two more uniformed officers. One of the officers, a woman built like a wrestler, kept pointing to the door behind them as she spoke, her face flushed with anger.

Julie didn't take this as a good sign.

The doctor was a big-boned man with a square jaw, deep-set eyes, and a strong nose. He was all edges and no smoothed corners.

"I'm a doctor, not a cop," he said. "My job is to take care of patients."

"Then the least you should know is where the hell your patients are," the cop said, and that's when she noticed Stottlemeyer approaching with Devlin, Monk, and Julie. She grimaced. "We just found out, Captain."

"Found out what, Claire?" he asked.

"We've lost Dale the Whale," she said.

# CHAPTER FOURTEEN

## Mr. Monk Goes Whaling

**S**tottlemeyer took a deep breath to calm himself and turned to Claire's partner. "Okay, you get on the radio to every cop and security guard in the building. I want this hospital locked down."

"Yes, sir," the cop said and went off to follow the captain's order.

Stottlemeyer looked at the doctor. "Who are you?"

"I am Dr. Donald Auerbach," he said. "I share the plastic surgery practice with Dr. Wiss. As he may have told you, he's on vacation and I've taken over his rounds and the care of his three patients from yesterday."

"How did you lose Dale?" Stottlemeyer asked.

"I didn't," Dr. Auerbach said firmly. "All three of our patients—Jason McCabe, Frank Cannon, and Dale Biederback—were here when I checked on them this morning."

"I can explain," Claire said, adjusting her utility belt. "The accident at Union Square brought a lot of critically injured people into the ICU, more than they could handle. They had to move Dale and the two other patients out to accommodate the emergency cases."

"Jason McCabe and Frank Cannon," Dr. Auerbach added.

"You stayed with Dale, didn't you?" Devlin asked Claire.

"Of course we did, but there was only the two of us up here and it was like a fast game of musical chairs. People on gurneys everywhere, getting in our way. On top of that, all three of the guys who were lipo'd were wrapped up like mummies on identical gurneys. We couldn't tell them apart."

"Of course not," Monk said. His arms were crossed and he was shifting his weight from side to side. "That was the whole idea from the start."

"I just came back a few minutes ago to check on them, to see if they were all right after the move," Dr. Auerbach said. "Cannon and McCabe were here, but Biederback was gone."

"Is this the only door into the ward?" Stottlemeyer asked.

Claire shook her head. "This all just happened. We didn't get a chance to scope out the room or cover the door."

"Could Dale have walked out of here on his own?" Monk asked.

"Absolutely not," Dr. Auerbach said.

"So he had to have had help," Devlin said. "He couldn't have left here unless it was on a gurney, and somebody had to be pushing it."

Stottlemeyer shook his head. "But none of our officers have seen anybody rolled out of here. Maybe he hasn't left the building yet."

The captain got on his cell and ordered more officers to the hospital for a room-by-room search.

"You're wasting your time," Monk said. "Whatever Dale's plan was, he's already pulled it off."

"We don't know that, Monk," Stottlemeyer said.

"I do," Monk said.

"If he's escaped, he's put his life in jeopardy," Dr. Auerbach said. "With all the fluids and blood that he's lost, he could die without close observation, the proper care, and the right medications. Even if he survives, there's a high risk of wound dehiscence and infection."

"He would know all that," Devlin said.

"He's had months to plan this," Monk said. "He also has the financial resources to build his own personal ICU somewhere in the city."

"Setting that ICU up, getting the equipment and the meds will have left a trail," Devlin said. "And he'd still have to staff it. So we're looking for at least one accomplice, maybe two. Possibly three or four if you count whoever sent the truck rolling down Powell Street and a dirty doctor to watch over him."

"Or one person with medical training who created the accident, got him out of here, and is caring for him now," Monk said.

"Anybody but me find it convenient that Dr. Wiss went on vacation today?" Devlin asked.

"Dr. Wiss has the utmost integrity," Dr. Auerbach said. "What you are suggesting is unthinkable."

"Check it out," Stottlemeyer said to Devlin, ignoring Auerbach's protest. "But I am not ready to accept that Dale is gone yet. He and his accomplices, no matter how many he's got, might still be in the process of sneaking him out. We're going to search every inch of this building and every vehicle coming or going from here."

Monk shook his head. "You're wasting your time, Leland. He's outsmarted us. He's gone."

Julie remembered the way Dale had looked at her and hoped that Monk was wrong.

Dozens of cops descended on the hospital, covering every exit and searching the building floor by floor, room by room, the entire effort coordinated by Stottlemeyer and Devlin.

Monk remained strangely detached from the whole thing as it was unfolding. Instead of walking the hospital, doing his Monk-Zen thing, looking for whatever might be out of place, he planted himself on a waiting room chair and just stared at the wall across from him.

He was sulking like a child.

Julie sat beside him, frustrated, helpless, and a little scared. So she texted me, told me about Dale's escape, and asked for my advice.

I wasn't surprised to hear that Dale had escaped and I can't imagine that Monk was, either.

All I could do was tell her what I'd say to Monk if I were sitting there with him. She took my talking points to heart and gave it a shot.

"It's not your fault," she told him after a long, silent hour had passed.

"I should never have left the hospital. I knew he'd try to escape."

"You thought the captain had it under control."

"I should have known that he was deluding himself," Monk said. "Instead, I deluded myself, too."

"Dale was gutted and under guard," she said. "It was hard to imagine how he could possibly escape under those circumstances."

"And that's exactly how he fooled us," Monk said.

"You'll catch him," she said.

"I'm not so sure," Monk said.

"You've caught every killer you've gone after."

"Solving murders is one thing, Julie. Catching wanted fugitives in something else entirely. I'm not a tracker. Dale has had a long time to plot his escape. I'm sure he's anticipated every move we're going to make."

"You're giving him too much credit," she said. "You've foiled his plots every time, even when he tried to frame you for murder and arrange the assassination of the governor, just so the lieutenant governor, who was in his pocket, could take office and pardon him. This can't be any more intricately planned than that bizarre scheme was."

Monk shook his head. "He's undoubtedly learned from his mistakes and studied the ways I caught him before. He is not going to repeat the past."

"Don't forget, he's at a disadvantage. He's been gutted on a surgical table and needs to recuperate. All you have to do is figure out where he is now and what he's going to do next."

"He will try to destroy me, the captain, and everybody that's close to the two of us," Monk said.

Julie knew that included her and me, and that made her stomach cramp. "By destroy, do you mean kill?"

Monk shook his head. "Dale only kills as a means to an end, to achieve a larger, more satisfying goal. Take today, for instance. He had an accomplice create that deadly accident, not to kill people, but as a diversion for his escape. He's a megalomaniac. It's all about control. He delights in crafting exquisitely complex ways to make his enemies suffer. Killing them would take all the fun out of it."

"How can you be so sure?"

"Because he's never tried to kill me and I'm his archenemy," Monk said. "His goal is to crush my spirit."

Julie stood up and faced him. "Well, it looks to me like he's already succeeded."

Monk shook his head. "This is only the beginning."

"Not if you suck it up and go after his ass."

He looked up at her. "There's no need for profanity."

"If this isn't a situation that calls for it, I don't know what the hell is."

"Your mom would be shocked if she heard you now."

"My mom wouldn't let you wallow in pathetic self-pity," Julie said and kicked his chair. "She'd make you man up."

"Have you met me?" Monk asked.

Stottlemeyer and Devlin approached them. Their faces were drawn with weariness and anger.

"I think we've discovered how Dale left the building," Devlin said. "He died."

"Excuse me?" Monk said.

"He left here in a body bag," Stottlemeyer said. "A dead patient named Walter Groh was picked up by Buffman Brothers. It turns out that the real Walter Groh's body is still in the hospital morgue and the Buffman Brothers reported their hearse stolen yesterday. We didn't have anybody checking to see that the body bags leaving the hospital actually contained corpses."

"Give yourself a break, Captain," Devlin said. "Our officers thought Dale was in his bed. There was no reason to check body bags."

"I left a door open," Stottlemeyer said. "This escape is on me."

"He had inside help," Monk said.

"We ran background checks on everybody on his surgical and post-op team," Stottlemeyer said. "They all came out clean, and they are all here and accounted for."

"And it wasn't Dr. Wiss," Devlin said. "I called the cops in Hawaii. They found him at his hotel and sent me a picture of him so we could confirm the ID."

"It could have been one of the paramedics who brought in a victim from the accident," Monk said. "There was no way you could have anticipated this particular scenario and checked out every first responder in the city."

Stottlemeyer's cell phone rang. He looked at the caller ID.

"Tell that to the chief of police."

He walked away and took the call out of earshot of Devlin and the others. But from his body language, it was clear that the captain was getting his head handed to him.

The three of them watched, feeling his pain. Devlin spoke up, drawing their attention away from the captain.

"Dale must have had contact with one or more of his accomplices while he was in prison," Devlin said. "I'll contact the warden and get his visitor logs and whatever mail he's received."

Monk sighed. "Don't you think Dale is aware that's the first thing we'd do?"

"I'll also contact drug companies and medical equipment suppliers, find out if they've had any unusual purchases or thefts."

"Another obvious move," Monk said.

"Do you have a better idea?" Devlin asked.

Monk stayed silent, which was all the answer Devlin needed. Stottlemeyer ended his call and dragged himself over, a beaten man.

"The chief wasn't very happy to hear that a convicted killer is loose in the city," Stottlemeyer said. "I told him that Dale is unlikely to be running around committing any mayhem, at least not for now, but that didn't make the news go over any better."

"What's the chief going to do?" Devlin asked.

"Hold a press conference as soon as possible. As embarrassing as this is for the department, he thinks it's imperative that we notify the public and get Dale's face out there so everybody in San Francisco is on the lookout for him."

"Dale isn't going to be out in public for weeks," Monk said. "And even if he is, what are you going to use for a picture?"

"Well, we'll use his—" Stottlemeyer stopped himself and grimaced. "The bastard looks completely different now, doesn't he? Damn. We'll get Dr. Auerbach to sit down with a police artist, work up a rendering of what a thin Dale would look like without his bandages."

"It's pointless," Monk said.

"What would you like us to do, Monk?" Stottlemeyer said.

"Turn back time," Monk said.

# CHAPTER FIFTEEN

## Mr. Monk Has a Blast

**W**hile all the detectives at the station tried to shake down some leads, there really wasn't much for Monk to do but clean Devlin's desk.

And since Devlin was off at San Quentin, searching Dale's jail cell and getting the visitor logs, she wasn't around to complain about it.

Stottlemeyer stayed in his office, fielding one call after another, sometimes juggling two at once, one on his desk phone and another on his cell.

Julie sat in a chair and played games on her iPhone.

The captain rushed out of his office. "Monk, we've got something. I got a call from Amy. Dale had love letters from a girlfriend. Her name is Stella Chaze."

"What could any woman possibly see in him?" Monk asked, directing the question to Julie.

"Why are you asking me?" Julie said. "I think he's repulsive."

"Some women find revulsion and fear incredibly exciting," Stottlemeyer said. "Haven't you noticed that convicted serial killers always have women lining up to marry them? In this case, it probably doesn't hurt that he's also obscenely rich."

"He's obscene all the way around," Julie said.

"Though there's not so much around his around any-more," Monk said. "He's not Dale the Whale anymore."

"Dale the Frail," Stottlemeyer said. "Stella visited him doz-ens of times, even appealed to the warden for conjugal visits."

"I think I may be sick," Julie said.

"She's a graphic designer who works out of her home in Potrero Hill," Stottlemeyer said, heading for the door. "It's real close to the hospital."

Monk and Julie hurried after him.

"This is too easy," Monk said.

"I'm not expecting Dale to be staying in her guest room," Stottlemeyer said. "But I'm sure she knows something."

"Whatever she knows is what Dale knows she knows and wants us to know," Monk said. "You know that, right?"

Stottlemeyer stopped and turned to face him. "You're right. So let's not bother."

"Really?" Monk asked.

"Hell no," Stottlemeyer said. "Are you coming or not?"

Monk nodded and the captain continued on his way.

Stella Chaze lived on a quiet, upscale residential street in a small one-story house with a new Lexus parked in the drive-way. It was an older home but so well kept that it looked as if it had been built yesterday. The yard was nicely landscaped and maintained.

This was not at all what Julie had expected. She'd pic-tured a rotting dump with peeling paint, a tarp over a hole in the roof, and a yard filled with trash, junked cars, and overgrown weeds.

Stottlemeyer pulled up in his car, followed by two black-and-white patrol cars. He directed the two officers in the first car to go around back and stationed the other two out front. Then he, Monk, and Julie went to the door.

The captain rang the bell. A woman in her thirties opened the door. She was tall and slim and wearing nothing but a pair of stylish glasses and a small Band-Aid on her left arm.

Julie was expecting a crazy, overweight, stringy-haired woman with bad skin donned in a flowered blouse and smoking a cigarette.

But at least Julie got the crazy part right, or so it appeared.

Monk immediately turned his head and shielded his eyes from the harsh glare of her nakedness with his hand, which prompted a delighted laugh from her.

"Adrian Monk, you are such a prude," Stella said. "Surely you've seen a naked woman before."

"Do you always answer the door in the nude?" Stottlemeyer said.

"You caught me as I was showering," she said.

"We'll wait while you put on some clothes," the captain said. He glanced back at Monk, who was looking away, and at his two officers, who were unabashedly staring at Stella with goofy smiles on their faces. Those smiles evaporated when they saw Stottlemeyer glaring at them.

"I wasn't planning on dressing today," she said.

"I insist," Stottlemeyer said.

"You can stomp your feet and cry if you like, Captain. But this is my house. I make the laws under this roof. I will wear, or not wear, whatever I please. Are you going to come in, or would you prefer I stand here? Either way is fine with me."

"We'll come in," the captain said.

Stella stepped aside and beckoned the captain in with a sweep of her arm. He frowned at her and walked in.

Stella looked at Monk. "How about you, Adrian?"

Julie turned to Monk, who hesitated, taking a step forward and then immediately one back.

"You know she's doing this just to mess with your head, Mr. Monk," Julie said. "Don't give her the satisfaction."

"Aren't you adorable," Stella said to her. "You go, girl."

Monk took a deep breath, focused his gaze past Stella, and plunged into the house. Julie followed, Stella closing the door behind them.

The place was clean and smelled of incense. It burned on several tables and shelves around the house, which was decorated straight out of the IKEA catalog. Monk sniffed the air as they came in.

"How did you know who we are?" Stottlemeyer asked Stella.

"I Googled you both ages ago. I had to put faces to the names. Dale has spoken about you many times," she said, taking a seat in one of the two armchairs facing the couch.

"Warmly, I'm sure," Stottlemeyer said, taking a seat on the couch across from her.

Stella turned to Julie. "But I don't know you."

"How nice," Julie said. "Let's keep it that way."

Stella laughed. "I like you."

Monk took a seat in the armchair that was beside Stella's so that he was facing Stottlemeyer instead of her. Julie took a seat on the couch next to the captain so she could watch Monk and Stella.

"So," Stella said. "What can I do for you?"

"You can put your clothes on now," Monk said, sniffing some more and staring straight ahead at Stottlemeyer and Julie.

"I could," she said, "but I won't. I am much more comfortable in the nude. Besides, this way you can see I am not carrying any concealed weapons and won't be tempted to shoot me."

"Where's Dale?" Stottlemeyer asked.

"At San Francisco General having his tummy tucked," she said. "Though I must say, I'll miss those love handles, not that I've had much opportunity to handle them."

Monk squirmed and sniffed some more. The burning incense put off a strong odor.

"He's escaped," Stottlemeyer said.

"Good for him," she said.

"You don't seem surprised," he said.

She shrugged. "Dale is brilliant and you're not."

"You have been writing him love letters and visiting him in prison," Stottlemeyer said. "And now you're putting on this little show in a pathetic and degrading attempt to distract us. Do you really expect us to believe you don't know anything about his escape and that you didn't help him pull it off?"

"You're welcome to search the house for him if you like. Look in the closets and under the bed. Who knows where he could be hiding. But if you think I'm going to help you in any way, you're dumber than even Dale thought."

Monk sniffed in her general direction. "You smell like nail polish."

"I was doing my nails when you arrived."

"In the nude?" Julie asked.

"I'd just stepped out of the shower," she said.

"But there's no polish on your fingernails," Monk said.

"That's because I removed it, hence the smell of nail polish *remover*," she said. "I would have thought a supposedly brilliant detective such as yourself would have made that deduction. You really aren't very bright, are you?"

"Bright enough to put that fat lunatic Dale in prison," Julie said.

"But not to keep him there, sweetie," Stella said.

Stottlemeyer spoke up. "If you helped Dale escape, or had anything to do with that runaway truck in Union Square, you could be the one going to prison, and it won't be to visit Dale."

"I had nothing to do with his escape," she said.

"Do you smell gas?" Monk asked.

"It's incense," Stella said. "I bought it at Poop. Perhaps you're familiar with the place."

"I've never been inside," Monk said.

"You don't know what you are missing," Stella said. "The proprietress is lovely, don't you think?"

"It seems you've taken a very active interest in Monk," Stottlemeyer said.

"He means a lot to Dale and Dale means a lot to me." She got up, making a point of standing directly in front of Monk, who immediately turned his head and curled up in a fetal position to avoid the possibility of her naked body brushing his feet or legs. "I'm getting a cigarette. Would anyone else like one?"

"No," Monk said. "And you don't want one, either."

"Of course I do," she said and walked through the open kitchen door and out of their sight.

"You have to stop her, Captain," Monk said.

"It's not illegal to smoke in your own home," Stottlemeyer said.

"It's no different than if she pulled a gun on us," Monk said. "She's putting our lives at risk."

"She's only doing it to needle you," Stottlemeyer said. "That's what this whole little show is about, to throw you off your game. It's a diversion, just like the runaway truck in Union Square. You have to see past it to whatever she's trying to hide."

"She isn't hiding a thing. She's buck naked and Dale obviously isn't here," Julie said to the captain. "Can we go now? She's creeping me out."

"Because she's nude?" Stottlemeyer said. "I'm pretty sure it's nothing you haven't seen before."

"It's because she's scary-crazy," Julie said.

"Of course she is," Stottlemeyer said. "She's hot for Dale, a convicted killer. You're welcome to leave, but I'm not going until we get some information from her."

"She won't talk," Julie said.

"She doesn't have to," Monk said. "She's the accomplice that we're looking for."

Stottlemeyer looked at him. "How do you know?"

That's when Stella returned with a pack of Marlboros and a silver lighter. She walked past Monk and sat down in her chair. He turned away from her and that amused her.

"I bet you won't even look at yourself naked," she said.

She was probably right about that.

"You were in the hospital today," Monk said.

"No, I wasn't."

"You came in pretending to be a victim of the terrible accident that you instigated," Monk said. "Your only hope of being spared the death penalty is to cut a deal and help us find Dale."

She lit her cigarette with her lighter. "What am I supposed to do now, confess?"

"That would be appreciated," Monk said, then sniffed. "I still smell gas."

She blew smoke at Monk, who nearly gagged. "Isn't it customary before making an accusation to actually confront me with some kind of evidence?"

"I thought it was obvious," Monk said, his hand over his nose and mouth. "It's all over you."

"I am not wearing anything," she said.

"You're wearing a Band-Aid," he said.

"That's all you noticed about me?" she said. "What about my birthmark?"

"It's on your inner elbow, the area known as the antecubital fossa."

"Wrong. It's a lip-shaped mark above my left nipple. It looks like someone with lipstick kissed my breast. Just ask the captain—he's been sneaking glances at it since you got here."

Stottlemeyer wasn't embarrassed or thrown by the remark, but Monk was. *Nipple* and *breast* were two words he didn't like to hear, much less think about. He did a full-body cringe, much to Stella's delight.

"I'm talking about your Band-Aid," he said. "It's on the spot on your arm that is the preferred location for starting an IV. Medical professionals choose that spot because the antecubital vein is very easy to raise with a tourniquet."

"That's a wonderful little factoid. You must have been an avid viewer of *Diagnosis Murder*. But what does any of that have to do with me, or Dale, or the price of yams in Bermuda?"

"Here's what happened: You sent that truck rolling down Powell Street. You purposely timed it so the truck would hit the cable car and bus, causing the most damage, injury, and confusion possible. You then insinuated yourself among the injured. You probably covered yourself in their blood to appear more injured yourself, which is why you had to shower as soon as you got home and why you are naked now. You fooled the paramedics in Union Square into believing you were, at the very least, in shock, so they started an IV of saline and administered a bolus where you have the Band-Aid now," Monk said, then cocked his head. "Do you hear a hiss?"

"What I hear is a lot of babble," she said. "A Band-Aid on my arm proves nothing except that I have an owie. Is that all you've got? My expectations of you were so much higher. You're disappointing me, Adrian."

"The ER doctor at San Francisco General uses a pen to put triage marks on the arms of all his patients," Monk said. "There's still a fleck of green on your wrist, despite your efforts to remove the indelible ink with nail polish remover. Green indicates that you arrived in the ER complaining of soft-tissue injuries and the doctor determined you were not a priority case. But all you really wanted was to get into the hospital, and you succeeded. You then stole an orderly's gown and, in all the confusion in the ICU, wheeled Dale down to the morgue to make your escape."

"The puncture in your arm for the IV and the mark prove you were in the hospital," Stottlemeyer said.

"I definitely hear a hiss." Monk stood up and began walking around the room, cocking his head, trying to pinpoint the sound.

"They prove nothing," she said, answering the captain's comment but looking over her shoulder at Monk.

"We also found your fingerprint on the runaway truck that you stole," Stottlemeyer said. "And the attendant in the hospital morgue ID'd you from a photo as the woman from the nonexistent mortuary who came to pick up a body."

That was an outright lie, of course.

Stella kept her eye on Monk. "If you had all of that, you would have arrested me when you walked through the door."

"To be honest, I'm just waiting for the green light from the ADA to arrest you, but I thought we'd have a friendly chat in the meantime," Stottlemeyer said. "What you ought to be asking yourself is this: Do you really want to be rotting away in prison while the thin, new Dale is sunning himself on some tropical island with a new girlfriend?"

That's when three things occurred, almost all at once.

The first thing that happened was that Monk looked into the kitchen. What he saw was a lit candle on the counter, two open gasoline cans on the floor, and the dials on the gas stove turned to full blast, but no flames were flickering on the burners.

The second thing that happened was that Stella bolted up

from her chair with a scream of fury, flicked on her lighter, and threw it into the kitchen.

The third thing that happened was that Monk yelled *"Run!"* with sufficient horror and authority that Stottlemeyer and Julie didn't second-guess his command and ran with him to the front door.

Monk and Julie got outside but Stottlemeyer was still passing through the doorway when the kitchen full of flammable gas ignited and the explosion blew the house apart, the fireball blasting out the windows and splitting the roof.

The concussive force of the blast blew Monk and Julie off their feet, while the flaming edge of the fireball kicked Stottlemeyer through the air and set the back of his jacket ablaze.

The captain hit the lawn hard and cried out with pain. Monk looked up, saw the fire on Stottlemeyer's back, and quickly sprang to his feet, taking off his coat and smothering the flames with it.

Julie joined Monk and together they pulled off Stottlemeyer's jacket, rolled him over, and then gently sat him up.

"Are you all right?" Julie asked. Her ears were ringing and she was trembling all over.

The captain was dazed. The hair on the back of his head was singed, his nose was bleeding, and he clutched his right arm close to his chest. But he nodded affirmatively, gazing past them to the burning house.

"Holy crap," Stottlemeyer said.

# CHAPTER SIXTEEN

# Mr. Monk and the Surprising Accusation

**S**tottlemeyer sat on the back bumper of the ambulance and watched as the fire department crew extinguished the last of the hot spots in Stella's charred but still standing house while a paramedic splinted his arm.

Another paramedic tended to Julie, who'd wrapped herself in the blanket that the firefighters gave her and leaned against Stottlemeyer's car.

Julie hadn't sustained any injuries beyond some minor cuts and bruises, but she couldn't stop trembling, even after she'd eaten all the cookies and drank all the Gatorade that the paramedic gave her to deal with the shock.

Monk, meanwhile, gave a detailed report to the arson investigator about what he'd seen and smelled before the explosion. It was the most detailed witness report that the arson investigator had ever taken. By the time Monk was done, there wasn't a whole lot left for the investigator to investigate. Monk finished up his story just as the team from the medical examiner's office wheeled out Stella Chaze's corpse in a body bag and a crime scene unit arrived to process the scene for evidence.

The four police officers who'd accompanied Stottlemeyer, Monk, and Julie to Chaze's house, but who had remained outside during the interview, came through the blast with minor injuries. Only one of the officers was cut badly enough by flying glass to require some stitches.

Although the hair on the back of Stottlemeyer's head had been singed, he hadn't suffered any serious burns. But the paramedic wanted to take the captain in to the hospital right away to have his arm x-rayed, since it was likely that it was broken. The captain refused to go just yet, though, promising the paramedic that he'd see a doctor later that day, after he was certain that the crime scene was secure.

So the paramedic put the captain's splinted arm in a sling, gave him an ice pack to put on it, and went back to his unit to wait for his partner.

Stottlemeyer joined Julie and sent the other paramedic away with a nod of his head. He leaned against the car beside her and winced. His arm really hurt, despite the ice.

"How are you doing?" he asked.

She looked at him. "I almost got killed."

"I know," he said.

"I can't do this job anymore, Leland."

"This doesn't happen every day," he said.

"Once is enough, and thankfully I survived. I only took this job because it was an easy way to make some money and pay my bills. It's not something I care enough about to die for."

"You're scared and in shock," Stottlemeyer said. "It will pass."

She shook her head. "When I was flying through the air on a fireball, time slowed down for me. And do you know what I was thinking in that long split second? A crazy naked woman just tried to blow me up in her house. What the hell was I doing in there? I knew she was nuts, but I sat there anyway. What does that make me? Maybe as crazy as she was, only better dressed. I don't want this insanity and risk in my life."

"Fair enough," he said. "So what are you going to do?"

"Get a job selling yogurt or something," she said. "You don't hear about many yogurt servers getting blown up by the naked girlfriends of imprisoned murderers."

"I meant about Monk."

"I'll stick around for a little while," she said, "but not for long."

Stottlemeyer nodded and gestured to Monk, who was now heading their way. "When are you going to tell him?"

"Tonight, tomorrow, I don't know yet."

Monk joined them.

"I realized as I was giving my report to the arson investigator that Stella was burning that poop incense not just to unsettle me and hide the smell of gas but also to create additional ignition points," Monk said. "She was insane, but deviously so."

"Now you know what she had in common with Dale," Stottlemeyer said.

"You saved our lives, Mr. Monk," Julie said. "Thank you."

Monk shook his head. "I don't deserve any gratitude. I shouldn't have let you go into that house in the first place. And I should have thrown you out the instant Stella started smoking her cancer sticks and disclosed that she was burning excrement. At that point, the lethal danger she posed was obvious. I was just too distracted to see it. You're my assistant, but that's secondary to the fact that you're Natalie's daughter. She entrusted me to look after you and I failed miserably."

"I'm alive, Mr. Monk," she said. "I'd say that you succeeded."

"Accept the gratitude, Monk, and here's some more," Stottlemeyer said. "Thanks for putting out the fire on me. I'm sorry it cost you your coat."

"No worries. I was planning on incinerating it anyway."

"You were?" Stottlemeyer said.

"We're in deep trouble now," Monk said as he glanced back at the morgue wagon. "There's no question Stella was Dale's key accomplice, responsible for the accident and spiriting him out of the hospital, but now that she's gone, we may have lost the one person we know who could lead us to him."

"Which is exactly why she sacrificed herself," Stottlemeyer said.

"Maybe she really did love him," Julie said.

An officer drove Monk and Julie back to the station and another officer took Stottlemeyer to the hospital to get his arm treated.

Although she was still shaky, Julie felt well enough to drive Monk home and then head back to our house.

Once she was in the empty house, she immediately broke into tears, and after a good, long cry on the couch, she gave me a call and told me what happened, which scared me to death, even though she'd come through it all unharmed.

I won't lie to you, I was relieved when she told me she

intended to quit working for Monk. This is going to sound stupid, but it hadn't occurred to me, despite my own years of personal experience, that working with him would put her life in danger. I'd simply forgotten how dangerous the job was because I'd become so used to it.

But after Julie told me about her near-death experience, I remembered something that had happened years earlier. I'd been in a life-threatening situation with Monk and a killer, and through an unusual turn of events my cell phone was on and the whole deadly encounter was recorded on my home answering machine. Julie listened to the message and heard it all. And when I came home, she'd confronted me about it. This is how our conversation went back then:

*"What were you thinking, going into an abandoned warehouse in the middle of the night?"*

*"I was doing my job,"* I said.

*"Going after murderers."*

*"I think maybe it's what I'm good at,"* I said.

*"You are,"* Julie said.

*"You think so?"*

*"This job makes you happy, happier than I have ever seen you doing anything else. But you have to promise me that you will be more careful."*

*"Hey, I'm the one who is supposed to do the worrying in this relationship."*

*"That changed when people started pointing guns at you."*

I loved the job, and the jolt I got from the potential danger that comes with dealing with killers was probably a part of that. I developed a genuine passion for the detective work (and, immodestly, some skill at it) and I didn't mind the risks. It was how I'd ended up as a cop in Summit, New Jersey, and yet was also probably among the reasons I was so bored by what I was doing.

But my daughter didn't love the job. She had no affinity for or interest in it. Working for Monk was just a way to earn money. And while I was willing to risk my life doing it, I was glad that she wouldn't gamble with her own.

"Tell Monk tomorrow that it's your last day," I said without the slightest hesitation.

"I want to, but how can I leave him in the lurch with Dale on the loose and the possibility of Cleve Dobbs getting away with murder? He'll fall apart."

"I'll be on the first flight back to San Francisco that I can get," I said. "I was going to come back for the wedding this week anyway, so I'll just move my flight up a couple of days. I'm sure Randy will understand. In the meantime, call Ellen Morse, let her know what you're doing. She'll keep him together and Leland will be there for him, too."

"Thank you, Mom," she said. "I wish you were here now."

It was the first time in years that I'd heard Julie say something like that and it made my heart melt.

"Me, too," I said.

Julie picked up Monk at eight the next morning to drive him down to the station. Monk hadn't heard about any new developments in the search for Dale, nor did he have any new insights himself, but he didn't have the patience to sit around his place waiting for news. He wanted to be at the station to help interpret any information that might come in. Monk knew that a fact that might seem insignificant to the police could end up being the key to solving the mystery of Dale's whereabouts for him.

He didn't have to tell Julie this, though. She knew it because she knew Monk.

And it was this unspoken interaction that made her delay telling Monk that she was quitting. She realized just how important she was to him, and how long it would take to not only find a replacement but for that new assistant to get in sync with his thinking and his moods.

She figured it would soften the blow if she waited until I was in town to tell Monk that she was leaving.

My daughter is a smart cookie.

They found Stottlemeyer and Devlin at a big dry-erase board that had been wheeled into the squad room. It was covered with a timeline of events, photographs, blueprints, and papers containing facts related to Dale's arrival at the hospital, the crash in Union Square, and the explosion at Stella Chaze's house.

Stottlemeyer's right arm was in a dark blue cast and a matching sling and he looked like he hadn't slept. Devlin didn't look much better.

"Morning," Stottlemeyer said to them without shifting his gaze from the board. He was hoping that if he stared at the damn thing long enough, the answer would emerge.

"How are you feeling?" Monk asked.

"Eternally grateful to whoever invented Vicodin," Stottlemeyer said.

"You're on drugs?" Monk asked.

"Hell yes," Stottlemeyer said and tipped his head to Devlin. "You want to fill them in on what we don't know?"

Devlin sighed, pointing first at an artist's sketch taped to the board. "This is a rendering of how Dale might look now, derived from Dr. Auerbach's description and some photographs we dug up of him in his teen years, when he was plump but not yet morbidly obese."

Julie squinted at the picture. "It doesn't look much like Dale. It looks like two entirely different people Photoshopped together."

"You would, too, if you had a couple of hundred pounds of fat sucked out of you and the excess skin cut away," Stottlemeyer said. "But I don't think that sketch is of much use to us anyway. For all we know, Dale is undergoing additional plastic surgery as we speak, or he will once he's recovered from the lipo and gastric bypass that he just had."

Devlin tapped a photograph of a black Chrysler Town & Country hearse.

"This is the hearse stolen from the Buffman Brothers mortuary. It was found on the docks at Mission Bay," she said, referring to the long-abandoned, decaying Bethlehem Steel warehouses, foundries, and machine shops on the piers. "We discovered tire tracks at the scene that match Chaze's Lexus and dirt in her treads that match the docks."

"That means that she drove Dale from the hospital to the pier, where her car was already parked. She left the hearse and drove back home in the car, where she cleaned herself up," Stottlemeyer said. "We'll never know what she planned to do after that because she ran into us first."

"So Dale could be hiding out in one of those empty warehouses in a makeshift ICU," Monk said.

"We're searching every inch of those piers," Stottlemeyer said.

"Or she could have delivered him to a waiting boat," Monk said. "From there, he could have gone across the bay or out to sea."

Devlin nodded. "We've alerted the Coast Guard, and they're spot-checking sailboats, tankers, anything that floats, but they can't possibly search every boat off the California coast."

"Then again," Monk said, "we don't know that Dale's nude girlfriend didn't drive him somewhere in the city in her Lexus and drop him off before she got home."

"That's true," Stottlemeyer said. "So he could be anywhere in the city or not in the city at all."

"That narrows it down," Julie said.

"We know he's got to have another accomplice, someone who can take care of his medical needs," Monk said. "What do we know about Dr. Auerbach? He was the last person to see Dale. He could have helped with the escape and bought the drugs and equipment necessary to care for Dale without raising suspicion."

"He's been Dr. Wiss' partner for fifteen years," Devlin said. "He's a stable family man, married with kids, with no arrest record and no significant debts. We've also had him under surveillance since he left the hospital and he's gone from there to their clinic and back to his house."

"We checked his clinic," Stottlemeyer said. "Dale isn't there and we doubt he's in Auerbach's house, though we are keeping our eye on it."

"And what about Dr. Wiss?" Monk asked.

"He's still in Hawaii with his wife," Devlin said. "The cops there have been keeping an eye on him for us, too."

"You're being very thorough," Monk said.

"Thank you," Devlin said.

"But we have nothing to go on," Monk said.

"We were hoping that you'd spot something that we missed," Stottlemeyer said.

Before Monk could answer, Deputy Chief Harlan Fellows marched in wearing a doubled-breasted suit and black shoes so shiny they put Dorothy's ruby slippers to shame. Fellows was accompanied by two grim-faced uniformed police officers.

Monk couldn't look at Fellows. It wasn't the glare off those shoes or any personal animosity that made Monk turn away, but rather Fellows' front teeth, which were crooked and overlapping. Monk found them repulsive.

"Captain, I need to talk with you," Fellows said and gestured to Stottlemeyer's office. "Now."

"If it's about the investigation into Dale Biederback's escape, we can talk right here," Stottlemeyer said. "You know Lieutenant Amy Devlin and Adrian Monk. I'm not sure if you've met his assistant, Julie Teeger."

Fellows nodded and glanced at the two uniformed officers, who lingered behind him, before continuing. "The moment we heard that Biederback was going to be released from prison for this surgery, you rallied hard to be the one to handle security at the hospital. You assured us you had it covered and that building was locked down tighter than the secret formula for Coca-Cola."

"I thought it was," Stottlemeyer said. "Clearly I was wrong, and I take full responsibility for that."

"As you should," Fellows said. "We don't think Biederback could have escaped without help."

"That much is obvious," Stottlemeyer said. "We know at least one of his accomplices was Stella Chaze, who—"

"Blew herself up when you went to question her," Fellows said, interrupting him. "Taking what she knew with her to hell. From what I understand, you made her think we had more evidence against her than we actually had."

"I might have exaggerated the strength of our case," Stottlemeyer said.

"Exaggerated her right into suicide," Fellows said. "Thus losing the best lead we appear to have."

Monk spoke up, but he wouldn't look directly at Fellows. "That isn't an accurate chronology of events. Besides, she'd already set up the mechanism for the blast before we arrived."

"But it was your questions that encouraged her to go into the kitchen, under the guise of getting cigarettes, and set her plan in motion," Fellows said.

"We don't know that," Monk said.

"Here is what we do know," Fellows said, turning his gaze back to Stottlemeyer. "You are upside down on your mortgage and have been desperately trying to renegotiate your loan without success. You are behind on your alimony and child support payments and your credit cards are maxed out."

Monk looked at Stottlemeyer. "I didn't know that."

"And I wish you didn't know, because it's none of your

business." Stottlemeyer's face reddened with anger and he turned to Fellows. "Are you insinuating that Dale paid me off?"

"I'm not insinuating a thing, Captain," Fellows said. "I am stating a fact. One hundred thousand dollars was wired into your account from the Cayman Islands within hours of Biederback's escape. We know that you are the inside man."

# CHAPTER SEVENTEEN

# Mr. Monk and the Call

"**H**ow dumb do you think I am?" Stottlemeyer asked.

"I suppose we're about to find out," Fellows said.

"This is so obviously a setup that it's laughable," Stottlemeyer said, shaking his head. "If I was on the take, do you really think I'd have Biederback put money in my account hours after his escape?"

Fellows shrugged. "Maybe you didn't. Maybe you had some very clever plan to make sure we never discovered the payoff. Maybe this is Dale double-crossing you for putting him in prison in the first place."

"Yes, I did. I put him there," Stottlemeyer said. "So think about it. Why would I help Dale, a killer I put away and who once framed my friend Monk for murder, escape from prison?"

"For an end to your financial problems and a chance to give some misery to your so-called friend," Fellows said, tipping his head toward Monk, "who has decisively proved, day after day, year after year, how brilliant a detective he is and how mediocre you are."

Stottlemeyer took a step toward Fellows and immediately

the two uniformed cops moved protectively to the deputy chief's side.

"If my right arm weren't in a cast," Stottlemeyer said, "you'd be on the floor right now looking for your teeth."

"And you would have thanked him later," Monk said to Fellows. "Because then you could have had your teeth replaced. You still can, by the way. You don't have to wait for someone to hit you."

Fellows ignored Monk's comment and addressed Stottlemeyer. "You're suspended, pending the outcome of an internal affairs investigation. Leave your badge and your gun on the desk, take your personal items, and go. These officers will escort you out of the building and to your car."

"You can't do this," Monk said, talking to Fellows but looking at some indefinite point over the man's shoulder. "Don't you see? This is exactly what Dale wants. It's another diversion, a blatant attempt to distract us from focusing our full attention on the hunt for him."

"We aren't distracted at all," Fellows said. "I'm placing Lieutenant Devlin in charge as acting captain and putting all of the department's resources on this, including you."

"I work with Captain Stottlemeyer," Monk said, "or I don't work at all."

"Your contract is with the San Francisco Police Department, so you work for me," Fellows said. "Secondly, we both know you will obsess over this investigation until you find him, so you might as well get paid while you're doing it."

"He's right, Monk," Stottlemeyer said. "You walk, and Dale wins. Work with Devlin and bring the bastard in."

"You can't just give up, Leland," Monk said.

"Who said anything about giving up?" Stottlemeyer said, then looked at Fellows. "You'll catch Dale and I'll sue the department."

"Good luck with that," Fellows said. "You'll be doing it from prison."

Stottlemeyer shook his head and went into his office, followed closely by the two officers.

Devlin watched as Stottlemeyer put his gun and badge on the desk, grabbed his jacket, and walked out, accompanied by the officers. Monk shook his head.

"You're making a big mistake, sir," Devlin said to Fellows. "Captain Stottlemeyer is right. It's an obvious frame."

"You let me worry about that. You find Dale Biederback," Fellows said and then looked at Monk, who wouldn't look back at him. "What is your problem? Why won't you look at me?"

"He can't because your teeth are crooked and you are a pompous idiot," Julie said. "What I want to know is how someone as dumb as you ever became a deputy chief."

"I'll have you know I have degrees in accounting and criminology," Fellows said. He turned to Devlin. "Who is this kid?"

Julie snapped her fingers. "Over here, Chief. This kid is your boss, a taxpaying citizen of the city of San Francisco. Adrian Monk is going to find Dale Biederback and when he does, he's going to hold a press conference telling the public how he did it and how you not only had nothing to do with it but aided and abetted Dale with your toxic stupidity. So if I were you, I'd start thinking about what your new career is going to be."

Devlin bit her lower lip, holding back a laugh, but Monk was ashen, staring at Julie as if her head had spun completely around on her neck and she'd projectile vomited in the chief's face.

Fellows glared at Julie and pursed his lips as he tried to think of something to say. Instead he looked back at Devlin, told her to keep him informed on her progress, and then walked out.

Monk faced Julie. "That was disrespectful and rude."

"It was wonderful," Devlin said. "You're my new hero."

I wasn't there to hear it myself, but I wish I had been. Because at that moment, she became my hero, too. I like to think I would have had the guts to say the same thing to Fellows if I'd been there, but I'm glad that my daughter did.

"I'm mortified," Monk said. "The man has hideous teeth, and that deserves our pity, but he's deputy chief of the San Francisco Police Department, and that demands our respect."

"Respect is something that's earned, and he hasn't earned mine," Julie said. "I don't have to tolerate his ignorance."

"Sadly, I do," Devlin said.

"How could he have a degree in criminology and still think Leland is on the take?"

"I don't know, but the best way to help the captain is to find Dale. I'm open to any ideas. What have you got, Monk? What have you deduced from a wrinkled shirt, a bread crumb, or a fleck of dandruff? I don't care how wild, unsupportable, or outrageous your theory is. I'm ready to run with it."

Monk lowered his head and slumped his shoulders. "I've got nothing."

"Then I need you to pick up the slack on our open murder investigations while I concentrate on finding Dale," she said. "What have you got on Cleve Dobbs and our three unsolved cases?"

In all the excitement, Julie had forgotten all about the murders and Dobbs and, from the look on Monk's face, so had he. Then again, it had been only a day since their confrontation with Dobbs and a lot had happened since.

"I've got nothing," Monk said.

"That is not the Adrian Monk that I know," Devlin said.

"I feel the same way," Monk said.

Monk was determined to make a discovery that would move the search forward, so while Devlin and the other detectives pursued all previously mentioned avenues of investigation, he rearranged all the things on the dry-erase board by subject, type of item (photo, diagram, blueprint, sketch, witness statement, et cetera), color, and size.

Devlin allowed him to do this for two reasons. One, she knew it might help him spot some obscure detail he'd missed before, and two, it kept him occupied while she not only tried to run the search for Dale but also absorb all of Stottlemeyer's responsibilities as well.

Julie went out in the hall and tried to call me to bring me up to speed on the latest developments, but I was already en route to San Francisco, so she called Ellen Morse at her store and filled her in.

When Julie was finished, Ellen was quiet for a long moment before speaking. "Can I talk you out of quitting for a couple of weeks, at least until Dale Biederback and Cleve Dobbs are behind bars?"

"No, you can't. I think quitting when Mom arrives for the wedding is perfect timing," Julie said. "Having his old assistant back, even temporarily, will soften the blow."

"And what happens when Natalie leaves again next week?"

"Monk will have to adapt."

"To your leaving, his brother's leaving, and Natalie's leaving. He'll be all alone."

"You'll be here."

"But I represent a change, a big one, and he's going to have to deal with plenty of that as it is."

"He has a good shrink."

"That's cold," Ellen said.

"My mom always put his needs first, before her own, sometimes even before mine. I love her, but I am not going to be like that. I am not his wife, his daughter, or his caregiver. I love Mr. Monk, but I have to look out for myself, too."

"I know and I'm sorry for what I said. It's just that I'm worried about him."

"There's a good side to what happened today."

"I don't see it," she said.

"Leland is free now, so I'll talk to him and see if he's willing to fill in as Mr. Monk's temporary associate. It will do them both some good."

"That's a great idea."

"Yeah, to you and me," Julie said. "I don't know how Leland and Mr. Monk will feel about it."

That's when Julie's phone beeped, indicating another incoming call. She took the phone away from her ear to look at the caller ID on the screen.

It was Cleve Dobbs.

That was a call she'd never have dreamed she'd get.

She put the phone back to her ear. "I have a call I have to take. Can you pick up Mr. Monk for me at his shrink's office this afternoon? I have to pick up my mom."

"No problem," she said. "I look forward to seeing you both tonight."

Julie hung up on Ellen, took a deep breath, and answered the call from Dobbs.

"Hello, Mr. Dobbs. I take it you're not calling to see if I'm a satisfied Peach customer."

She knew she was being a smart-ass, an unenviable trait that she got from me, but it was the best way she knew not to sound nervous. He was, after all, superrich, internationally famous, and quite possibly a serial killer.

"Are you?" he asked.

"I am. It's terrific. How did you get this number?"

"It wasn't hard," he said. "You can find anything on the Web these days. I ought to know. Where do you think Google and Facebook got a big chunk of their start-up money?"

"I didn't know that," she said.

"I need to see Mr. Monk on a personal matter," he said. "Do you think that's possible?"

She opened the door to the squad room and saw Monk emptying the garbage cans at each desk into a large black Hefty bag. It was sad and it was a waste, no pun intended. Another encounter with Dobbs, and the chance to confront a man he was convinced was a killer, might kick him out of his funk and reenergize him.

Or get them both killed.

"Yes, I think it is," she said. "Where would you like to meet?"

"My house," he said.

"We'll be there, but we're at police headquarters now, so we'll have to get out of what we're doing and tell them where we're going in case they need to reach us."

In other words, she was telling him that the police would know where they were going and who they were going to see, just in case he was planning to kill Monk.

Then again, if his plan was to strip naked and blow up his house with them in it, this warning wouldn't make much of a difference.

"That's fine," he said. "I'll be here all day. But please hurry."

Julie was right. Just the idea of seeing Dobbs allowed Monk to focus in a way that he hadn't been able to since, well, his last encounter with Dobbs.

But in the car ride over, they didn't talk about Peach's founder. They discussed what had happened that morning at the station.

"I had no idea Leland was in such financial trouble," Monk said.

"I'm not surprised. The bottom fell out of the housing market and hasn't recovered. He's been complaining about his mortgage for years."

"He has?" Monk said. "Not to me."

Actually, Stottlemeyer had, several times, starting three years back when he brought Monk in to figure out how Mike Clasker, CEO of Big Country Mortgage, was strangled while driving alone to court in a locked car in broad daylight on a public street under police escort. But that's a story I've already told.

"On top of that," Julie said, "cops aren't paid a lot and he's not only supporting himself but he's sending money to an ex-wife and two kids who are going to college."

"I hadn't thought about that."

Of course he hadn't. Julie couldn't think of a polite way to say that Monk rarely thought about other people's troubles, so she didn't say anything.

"Whatever his financial problems may be," Monk said, "he would never, ever accept a bribe, and the department should know that. He's an honorable man and has proved it again and again."

"I am not an expert on politics, or anything really, but I'm guessing the brass are extremely embarrassed about Dale's escape and are desperately looking for someone to blame."

"I understand that, and he was ready to fully accept that blame, though it's rightfully mine. What I can't comprehend is how they can believe that he was on the take."

"Because it's easy and convenient," Julie said.

"But it's wrong," Monk said.

"Doesn't matter when something is easy and convenient. They don't have to think too hard."

"They aren't thinking at all."

"It's panic and embarrassment and ass-saving," she said. "Their own, not Leland's."

"I don't feel comfortable talking about rear ends," he said. "Or even thinking about rear ends. Especially not the rear ends of people I know."

"Sorry," she said.

"I knew this would happen. I told you it would, back at the

hospital, as soon as Dale escaped. He enjoys playing games and destroying lives."

"What you said was that it was just the beginning. Do you think he'll come after me? Or Mom?"

Monk looked over at Julie and tried to offer her a reassuring smile. Instead, he came off looking queasy. It wasn't very reassuring. But to reassure him, she pretended that it was.

"I'll catch him before that can happen," he said. "Just like I am going to catch Cleve Dobbs."

He said that just as they pulled up in front of Dobbs' mansion and parked. Julie looked up at his house.

"I have a feeling that Dobbs likes to play games, too," Julie said. "And his might be starting right now."

Monk rolled his shoulders and tipped his head from side to side, like a boxer loosening his muscles before a fight.

"I hope he's not a sore loser," Monk said.

# CHAPTER EIGHTEEN

# Mr. Monk and the Game

**M**onk pressed the doorbell at the gate and Dobbs buzzed them in, instructing them over the intercom that he was in the backyard and that they should meet him there.

They went over the bridge and followed the path around the large house to the garden, where Dobbs was shoveling rich, dark potting soil out of large yellow bags and spreading the mixture over a path of tilled dirt.

"That's not a pot," Monk said, gesturing to the ground.

"I know, but the soil mixture helps the plants thrive," he said.

"You shouldn't use potting soil unless it's in a pot."

"Why not?" Dobbs asked, plunging his shovel into the ground like a post and resting one of his gloved hands on the upright handle.

"It's for pots," Monk said. "It says so on the bag."

"Dirt is dirt," Dobbs said.

"But this is pot dirt," Monk said. "Not ground dirt."

Dobbs rubbed his brow, getting dirt on his sweat-dappled forehead. "I didn't ask you here to talk about dirt. I have something more important to discuss with you."

"Do you want to confess?" Monk asked.

"I know that you think that I killed those people, but I didn't, and I am afraid that whoever did might not be finished," Dobbs said. "That he won't stop until he gets to me."

"Not unless you're planning to kill yourself," Monk said. "Are you?"

"Of course not," said Dobbs. "I want to hire you to find the killer."

"I already have," Monk said. "It's you."

"I want you to open your mind to other possibilities," Dobbs said.

"Are you trying to buy him off?" Julie asked.

"I want Monk to do his very best and follow the clues wherever they lead. But I am asking that he also consider the possibility that it's a misdirection, one designed by someone out to destroy me."

Even one day ago, the suggestion that the evidence pointing to Dobbs was a deliberate misdirection would have been absurd. But now, considering the events of that morning, it struck a nerve with Monk. Julie could see it in the way Monk adjusted his balance between his two feet as if he'd been hit by a sudden, and totally unexpected, gust of wind.

"I'll think about it," Monk said.

"I appreciate it," Dobbs said and offered his gloved hand to Monk to shake.

Monk ignored the outstretched hand and walked away. Julie looked back at Dobbs, meeting his gaze for a moment, and then left, too.

When they got back to the car, she stopped to talk with Monk.

"What do you make of that?" she asked, looking back at the big house.

"He's rich and cunning and a killer," Monk said. "He's a lot like Dale, only thinner."

"Not anymore," Julie said. "But if you feel that way about him, why did you tell him that you'd think about his offer?"

"To have an excuse to come back and talk with him again," Monk said. "Remember what Sun Tzu said in *The Art of War*: 'Keep your friends close and your enemies closer.'"

"You told Amy that was stupid," Julie said, "that it's what got Sun Tzu killed."

"Perhaps Sun Tzu was investigating a murder," Monk said. "I'll try not to let Dobbs kill me."

"That sounds like a wise strategy," Julie said.

Julie drove Monk to Dr. Neven Bell's office for his regularly scheduled appointment and told him that Ellen would be picking him up to take him home.

"Where are you going?" Monk asked.

"I'm picking up Mom at the airport," Julie said. "And three people in the car wouldn't be even or safe."

"I'm glad you're a conscientious driver," Monk said. "But why is Natalie arriving today? She's not supposed to be here until tomorrow."

Julie thought of a lot of ways she could answer the question, but then she considered where they were, and that Monk would soon be sitting with his shrink, and decided this was as good a time as any for the truth.

"She came early because of what happened yesterday," Julie said.

"The explosion. But you're fine."

"Physically, yes. But I'm not fine with doing this job anymore," she said. "I'm quitting, Mr. Monk."

Monk nodded. "Because I failed you and you're disappointed in me. And that's why Natalie is coming back early, to admonish me for not taking care of you."

"That's not it at all," Julie said. "I'm quitting because I don't want to die. I care about you, but there are other jobs I can do that won't put my life at risk, that don't involve my having to look at corpses with their faces frozen in terror or meet convicted killers and their crazy naked girlfriends."

"I understand," Monk said.

"Do you?"

"I've been trying to work up the courage all day to fire you," he said.

"Really?"

"After the explosion, I knew I couldn't live with the guilt if you got hurt. I just couldn't figure out how to fire you and spare your feelings at the same time."

Julie leaned across the seat and gave him a hug. "Thank you, Mr. Monk. You don't know how much better that makes me feel."

He got out of the car, but before he closed the door, he hesitated, rolled his shoulders, and turned back to face her. "That's a lie. I wasn't going to fire you."

"I know," she said. "But the fact that you tried to lie to me makes me feel good. It's the thought that counts."

Monk looked at Dr. Bell's building. "I think this is going to be a long session."

He took a deep breath, closed the car door, and walked into Dr. Bell's office.

Julie was waiting for me in baggage claim.

I grabbed her in a tight bear hug and had to hold back tears. When I finally let her go, I took a step back and looked her over from top to bottom for cuts and bruises and any other injuries she didn't tell me about in our call. She stared at me like I was mentally ill.

"What is wrong with you?" she asked, glancing around to see if anyone else noticed my behavior.

"I love you so much," I said, filled with relief that she appeared to be healthy and whole and just as embarrassed by me as ever.

"You didn't before?" she said.

"Of course I did. But you nearly got killed," I said. "I guess it didn't really sink in until I saw you."

"Well, I am okay now. It's over. You can relax and start acting like a normal person."

"Because I am replacing you, effective immediately," I said. "While I'm here, I am going to be Mr. Monk's assistant and you are going to take a backseat, far away from naked psychopaths who blow up their own homes, and start looking for a new job."

"Then I guess I better fill you in on all that's happened since we talked," she said.

"There's more?"

"No one else has tried to kill me since we last spoke, if that's what you are worried about."

It was, but I didn't admit to it.

She told me about the accusations against Stottlemeyer and about Cleve Dobbs trying to hire Monk to find whoever had killed Bruce Grossman, David Zuzelo, and Carin Branham.

I'd met Deputy Chief Fellows once before and thought he was an ass. The fact that Fellows, with his cherished degree in criminology, couldn't see through Dale's inane attempt to frame Stottlemeyer only confirmed that impression.

"You'd think the department would know better than to accuse Stottlemeyer of a crime after they did it once before and were proved wrong," I said. "Are they looking for more embarrassment?"

"That was the one thing I didn't think to say when I unloaded on Fellows," Julie said.

"What you did say was great. Now it's up to me, Amy, and Mr. Monk to catch Dale and prove Stottlemeyer is innocent." I don't want to sound like I was benefiting from the misfortune of my friends, but these were challenges that I looked forward to taking on. They would be a nice change from what passed for law enforcement in Summit. "How is Mr. Monk taking all of this?"

"Well, before I quit, he was taking it glumly, or I should say, glummier than usual for Monk. Is *glummier* a word?"

"It is for Mr. Monk," I said.

"But I will say that the offer from Dobbs seemed to brighten him up considerably."

"It simply shifted Mr. Monk's attention from Dale and Stottlemeyer for a while and offered him a case he feels more equipped to solve."

"You've been watching *Dr. Phil* again," Julie said.

"Beats going to college for a psych degree," I said.

"I don't see how the Dobbs case is an improvement," Julie said. "Mr. Monk is at a dead end on that one, too. He's got no evidence at all."

I waved off the concern. Literally, I waved. "He's been in that position many, many times before. Like when he was convinced the killer in a case was someone whose alibi was that he was in a coma at the time of the murder."

"Or when Mr. Monk was certain that an astronaut killed his wife even though his alibi was that he was in outer space at the time," Julie said. "Those are the examples you always use."

"Mr. Monk overcame those impossible situations, and many others like them, because solving murders is what he does," I said. "But catching escaped felons is not his specialty."

We collected my bags and found the car in the parking structure. Julie had used her police vehicle pass to park in the red zone. I beamed with pride at her abusing her privileges. She was a fast study.

I put my bags in the trunk, unzipped one of the suitcases, and removed my gun and holster, which I put on my belt.

Julie looked at me oddly as I did this. "Is that really necessary?"

"I'm a cop now," I said.

"In New Jersey," she said.

"There's a killer and his acolytes who might be targeting my family and friends, so yes, I think it's necessary."

"Plus it's cool and you like wearing it," she said.

"Not especially," I said. "It's a real drag on my pants, so I have to cinch my belt pretty tight, and that cuts down on my consumption of donuts in a big way. Also makes me want to use the bathroom a lot more often."

"More information than I needed to know," Julie said.

"Are you going to keep looking at me like that?"

"Like what?"

"Like I've grown a tail."

"It just feels odd to see my mom packing heat," she said.

"Armed and dangerous, that's me," I said. "So I hope your room is clean and you've done your chores."

I closed the trunk and got in the car. Natalie Teeger was back in Frisco and ready to kick some bad-guy butt.

Monk was setting the dining room table and Ellen Morse was making dinner in the kitchen when we walked into Monk's apartment without knocking, as if it was our home (which I suppose it was, in many ways).

Nothing had changed, and I mean that literally. Everything was exactly as it had been when I left, and as it had been for years. And at that moment, I found a lot of comfort in that stability, just as Monk did every single day.

Monk's face lit up when he saw me. He approached me, his arms outstretched like a robot, his way of preparing himself for a hug.

He put his hands lightly on my sides and leaned toward me at the waist.

I had no patience for this and pulled him into a tight hug. Much to my surprise, he didn't resist much.

"I am so glad to see you," he said, his head on my shoulder and mine on his.

"Me, too," I said.

He stepped back and looked at me. "You've become a cop."

"You knew that," I said.

"No, I mean it's on your face and in your stature," he said. "You aren't easygoing, sweet Natalie anymore. You've got authority."

"Not with me she doesn't," Julie said. "So don't get any ideas, Mom. I'm an adult now."

Ellen emerged from the kitchen. Of all the people in the room, she was the one who'd actually seen me a few times since I'd left, so this wasn't a reunion for her.

"It's good to see you back home," she said. "You must be starving after your long trip. Sit down. Dinner is ready."

We all took our seats at the table, Julie and I on one side, Monk and Ellen facing us on the other.

Ellen served us meat loaf (sliced into perfect squares) with rice (which she served using an ice cream scoop so we all got perfect, round balls), twelve peas, and two spears of asparagus to start with.

Ellen and I had wine, Julie and Monk had Fiji water. I know Julie would have preferred a Coke, but the balance of beverages had to be maintained.

The meal was tasty, symmetrical, and balanced, and each entrée item was kept in its own segment of our plates. I felt like I was eating a TV dinner.

The dinner conversation had nothing at all to do with the investigations or the troubles that Monk faced. Instead, I told them what Disher and Sharona were up to and shared stories about some of my adventures in Summit, including the Tide detergent caper, which I knew Monk would enjoy.

"That was exceptional police work," Monk said. "And for a noble cause."

"Isn't all police work for a noble cause?" Ellen asked.

"Some causes are nobler than others," he said.

I noticed the easy rapport that Monk and Ellen had and it made me feel good. They were relaxed and comfortable with each other, which is no small feat where Adrian Monk is concerned. She fit right in. And that, especially, was meaningful to Monk. He liked things that fit. It meant they were where they should be, that balance and symmetry had been achieved.

Perhaps Monk had, at long last, found a companion. Besides me, that is. Although my role in Monk's life had been entirely different, and didn't really apply anymore. I was just a visitor now.

Julie's cell phone rang. She answered the call. She listened for a moment, then replied.

"I'll pass along the message, but in the future, and until further notice, call Mr. Monk directly at home. I've resigned as his assistant." She listened for a moment. "No, it was completely amicable and my own choice. I'll tell you about it some other time. Hold on a moment." She put the phone down. "It's Amy."

"Have they caught Dale?" Monk asked.

She shook her head. "It's about Cleve Dobbs."

"He's killed someone else," Monk said.

"No," she said, hesitating. "Someone has killed him."

## Mr. Monk Is Wrong

**M**onk leaned back in his chair, the color draining from his face. Ellen put her hand on Monk's arm. He let her.

First Dale had escaped, then Stottlemeyer's badge was taken away, and now the unthinkable had happened: Monk had been proven wrong.

Cleve Dobbs wasn't a killer. He was a murder victim, and he'd become one mere hours after he'd asked for Monk's help. But Monk hadn't believed Dobbs was in any danger. Quite the opposite, in fact. He'd believed Dobbs was a threat to others.

Julie spoke very softly. "Amy wants to know if you'd like her to send a patrol car to bring you to the scene."

I answered for him. "That won't be necessary, Julie. We'll drop you off at home and I'll take him."

Monk looked at me. "You will?"

"Until I go back to New Jersey on Monday, I'm your new assistant. Would you like to see my résumé and references?"

"You'll do," he said and went to get his coat. Was that sarcasm? From Adrian Monk?

I made a note to analyze the remark later to be sure, because if it was sarcasm, it was a big step for Monk under pretty dark circumstances.

I hate to admit it, but I was actually thrilled at the prospect of going to the scene of a homicide, of helping Monk solve a string of murders.

I tried my best to hide it and to look grim instead, because let's face it, that was what things were. If Monk was truly wrong, and if the man he'd identified as the killer was innocent, then this was a cataclysmic event for him.

And, a cause for celebration for Amy Devlin. But as much as she'd want to rub Monk's nose in this, I was betting that she wouldn't, because this victory had come at the price of a man's life. Besides, with Stottlemeyer gone and Dale on the loose, she needed Monk now, imperfect or not.

I rose from my seat and turned to Ellen. "It was a lovely dinner. I'm sorry this had to happen in the middle of it."

"It comes with Adrian's job," she said.

"It might not be my job any longer," Monk said, rejoining us. "Not after word gets around about this."

"You don't know anything about the murder yet," Ellen said.

"I know that I thought Cleve Dobbs was the killer and now he's been killed," Monk said. "That's enough."

Monk trudged to the door as if going to his own execution.

Julie handed me the keys to the car. "Welcome home."

I flashed my badge to the officer who secured the scene at the end of the block, and then we drove the car right up to Dobbs' gate. When we pulled up to the curb Monk gave me a look. Despite the pain and insecurity that he was undoubtedly feeling, I saw warmth in his eyes. And I'm sure he saw the same thing in mine.

It was great to be together again at a crime scene, even if it was the case that could be the unmaking of his perfect record. We might never be able to say again that Monk was always right when it came to homicide, no matter how perfect the suspect's alibi might be or how outlandish Monk's reasoning might seem.

We got out of the car and, as we approached the house, I folded my badge wallet in such a way that it allowed me to put it in the front pocket of my jacket and display my shield.

Some of the officers on the scene knew me casually from before and seemed startled to see the badge and, I presume, the gun. I walked a little bit straighter, trying to exude that authority Monk thought I had.

We followed the path to the backyard, which was lit up by all the available outdoor lights already on the property and augmented by more brought in by the police.

Amy Devlin was wearing gloves and stood over Dobbs' corpse, which was splayed faceup on the patio. His body was twisted in such a way—his arms and legs and neck and back bending in places where there were no joints—that it was obvious that most of his bones had to be broken. His white shirt was slashed and torn and soaked with blood, indicating that he'd been stabbed multiple times.

It was a horrific sight, made even more troubling since it was someone I knew, not personally, but as the ubiquitous face of Peach. Dobbs was seemingly everywhere, on the cover of his bestselling book, on billboards, and in commercials and other advertisements.

Devlin looked up at us as we approached, her eyes drifting to my badge. I tensed a bit, preparing myself for a snide remark about wearing a badge she didn't think I'd earned.

"It's good to see you, Natalie. We could use your experience on this one." She shifted her gaze to Monk. "We need you at your best, Monk. Can I count on you?"

It wasn't the reaction he'd been expecting, either. I admired her for saying the right thing to both of us. I decided that she might have the makings of a captain after all.

"Of course," he said.

"Here's what we know. Dobbs' wife, Jenna, was out shopping when she got a call from him at six thirty, asking her when she'd be home and what she wanted to do for dinner, to eat in or go out."

"What did she choose?" Monk said.

"I don't know. She didn't say and I didn't ask."

"You might want to follow up," he said.

"I'll put that at the top of my list. When she got home a half hour or so after the call, she found him like this," Devlin said, gesturing to the body. "Someone attacked him with a knife in his office upstairs. The fight spilled out onto the deck and Dobbs toppled over the railing to the patio. The fall killed him on impact, but the medical examiner says he would have died regardless. He was mortally wounded already."

"So he was killed after he called his wife and before she came through the door," I said. "That's a tight window."

Monk tipped his head and made a circle around the body,

doubled back, and circled again. I studied the body, too. There were slash and stab wounds all over his chest and stomach, defensive cuts across his arms and palms, but no wounds on his back.

The attacker had faced Dobbs head-on. He wanted Dobbs to see who was betraying him.

But the wounds indicated that Dobbs hadn't turned to run, that he'd faced his attacker and took him on.

A gutsy and ultimately fatal move motivated by anger and ego rather than self-preservation.

It must have been a savage, bloody, and horrifically one-sided fight: an unarmed man, still reeling from the shock of betrayal and that first stab wound, up against an enraged killer wielding a large knife.

"Have you found the murder weapon?" I asked.

Devlin shook her head. "But there's a big knife missing from the set on the counter in the kitchen. We're checking the street to see if it might have been ditched in a drain or a trash can."

"How did the killer get past the locked gate and the alarm system?"

"Dobbs must have buzzed in whoever it was, which means that the killer was someone he knew, just like the other three victims. Did Monk tell you about them?"

"Julie did," I said.

Monk looked over at the flower bed that Dobbs had been working on that afternoon. It was finished now, the perennials planted in neat rows, the shovel propped against a bench, the gloves laid out on the seat.

"This isn't anything like the other killings," Monk said.

"Those were staged to look as if they were accidents. This was a brutal, angry attack."

"All the killings were about rage," Devlin said. "But the rage was always directed at Dobbs, not the people that were murdered. That rage came out when the killer finally got to Dobbs himself."

Monk rolled his shoulders and shifted his weight. "Why now? Why not continue killing the people who'd helped, in their own way, to make him the success that he was?"

"Maybe the point of the first three killings was to scare Dobbs and implicate him at the same time," Devlin said. "But we got onto Dobbs too quickly. He knew that if Dobbs was being watched, any new murders would clear him rather than dig the hole deeper. It took the fun out of murdering anyone but Dobbs himself."

"Did Dobbs mention having a guest when he spoke to his wife on the phone?" I asked.

"Nope," Devlin said. "He didn't give any indication that he wasn't alone."

"I'd like to see the office," Monk said.

Devlin led us into the house and up the grand staircase to a second-floor landing that was large enough to be the banquet hall at the Hyatt.

There were three large sets of double doors leading to the three upstairs suites. One set led to the master bedroom, another to the guest room, and the third to Dobbs' office. That set of doors was open.

I could smell the copper scent of blood even before we stepped through the open doors of the office, which was like stepping into one of his white, airy Peach stores.

The blood was everywhere, as if someone had taken a bucket of it and splashed it on the walls and floor. It was hard to believe one man's body could contain so much blood. Several forensic techs were taking pictures and measurements and collecting samples.

Monk held his hands up in front of him, framing his view so he took in the room in sections, rather than all at once. He moved methodically around the office, tracking the blood like it was a map to the solution of the murder.

The office was an open and uncluttered space, with bleached hardwood floors, a glass-topped desk with just a Peach computer, a Peach device, a notepad, and a phone on top. The desk chair was wing-backed, all chrome and black leather, something from the Dr. Evil / SPECTRE collection.

The walls were adorned with silver-framed photos of Dobbs with politicians and actors, but also of a young Dobbs slaving over early prototypes of the Peach and other products his company produced.

I was struck by how cold and impersonal the office was and wondered which came first, his office or the identically designed Peach stores that were now in every upscale shopping mall in America.

Monk followed the blood trail out to the deck, his hands out in front of him. The potted plant was spattered with blood and so was the side and top of the plexiglass railing.

"From the blood spatter and stains, it looks like Dobbs was initially attacked in front of the desk, and then fell on the floor, where he was stabbed again," Monk said. "He scrambled to his feet, was stabbed twice more, then backed up against that wall, where he took some brutal hits before sliding to the floor, then staggering to the deck."

"Why did he come out here?" I asked, joining Monk.

Devlin spoke up. "Perhaps the killer was blocking his path to the door. Or maybe he was disoriented, or maybe he was hoping to call for help. But it looks like his last stand was in front of this pot, and then he went over the side."

"Or was pushed," Monk said.

"Doesn't really matter," Devlin said. "Murder is murder."

Monk peered over the railing at the body below. Dobbs' dead eyes stared back up at him.

"Where's Jenna Dobbs?" he asked.

"In her bedroom," Devlin said, "being treated by paramedics for shock."

"I'd like to talk with her," Monk said.

"I don't think it's a good time," she said.

"But I have questions for her."

"Like what she was planning to do for dinner?"

"Like why she lied for her husband and gave him an alibi for the murders," Monk said.

"It hardly matters now," Devlin said.

"Everything matters," Monk said.

"It's obvious, isn't it?" Devlin said. "She was being a good wife, protecting her husband."

"So why not let the truth speak for itself?"

"The truth can be twisted and people don't always think things through when they hear their spouse being falsely accused of murder. Her natural reflex, right or wrong, was to defend him."

The "falsely accused" bit she stuck in there had to sting. I wondered if she'd done it on purpose to needle Monk just a little for his "everything matters" rebuke. If so, I couldn't blame her. He deserved it.

"Did you check out her alibi?" Monk asked.

"Of course I did," Devlin said.

"And she lied," Monk said.

"Badly. On the morning Grossman was killed, her credit card activity shows she parked her car with the valet at the Belmont Hotel in Union Square, probably to go shopping. We don't know where she was when Zuzelo was thrown off his balcony, but her Golden Gate Bridge FasTrak pass indicates that she was in Marin County somewhere when Carin Branham was killed."

"Didn't she think we'd check up on her?" Monk asked.

"I don't think she thought at all," Devlin said. "Like I said before, defending her husband was a reflex. But that's all moot now that he's been murdered, probably by whoever killed Grossman, Zuzelo, and Branham."

"I wonder why he didn't try to run," Monk said, "and why he never turned his back on his killer."

"Would you turn your back on a man with a knife?" Devlin asked.

"I might look over my shoulder at him as I ran," Monk said. "But yes, I would. But Dobbs didn't."

"Maybe he was facing his killer and pleading for his life," I said. "Maybe that first wound injured him too badly to run."

Monk frowned. "So the killer was someone Dobbs knew and trusted. He invited the killer in. The killer snatched a knife from the kitchen at some point, came upstairs with Dobbs to the office, then attacked him."

"Looks like it," Devlin said.

"Why didn't he bring a weapon of his own?" Monk asked.

"To make it less likely we could track the weapon back to him if it's ever found," Devlin said.

"Why didn't he attack Dobbs in the kitchen rather than hide the knife and wait to make his move until they came up here?"

"Maybe the office had some meaning to him," I said. "Maybe the killings all spring from something that occurred between the two men in this room."

"There are things about this murder that just don't fit," Monk said.

"Fit what?" Devlin said.

"Fit together in a way that's coherent and clear," Monk said.

"To you," she said.

"Which is the same as everybody."

"Not really," she said. "But I'm sure it will all fit for you after we find the killer and discover his motive."

"Usually it's what doesn't fit that leads me to the killer," Monk said.

"It didn't this time. It led you to Dobbs," Devlin said. "So let's try it my way and see what happens."

# CHAPTER TWENTY

# Mr. Monk Has Changed

"**T**his is why I hate change," Monk said as I drove him back to his place from Dobbs' house. It was nice to be driving in the city again, so I took the long way.

"What does the murder of Cleve Dobbs have to do with change?"

"The fact that I didn't see it coming," Monk said.

"You were never psychic," I said. "Though I hear there's a PI down in Santa Barbara who is supposed to be a pretty good one. I met his assistant here once at a gathering for assistants of detectives."

"You had gatherings?"

"It was more like a support group," I said. "Me, Jasper, Arnie, Sparrow, and a few others."

"They had nothing in common with you."

"They assist detectives."

"Chow is certifiably insane, Wyatt has severe anger-management issues, and Porter is senile," Monk said. "They aren't assisting detectives—they are caring for people with debilitating psychological issues who can't function in normal society. They weren't like you at all."

"Yes, I see your point," I said. "I was definitely the odd man out."

"You were their voice of reason," Monk said.

"Probably so," I said. "But let's get back to what you were saying about change. There was no way you could have foreseen the murder of Cleve Dobbs."

"The old Monk would have known how and when Dale was going to escape," Monk said. "The old Monk would have known there was another killer out there besides Dobbs."

"Besides Dobbs?"

"I still think Dobbs murdered those three people," Monk said. "But now I won't ever be able to prove it, thanks to whoever killed him."

I couldn't decide whether he was simply unwilling to accept that he was wrong about Dobbs, or if there was justifiable grounds for him to suspect there were two murderers at work. But I wouldn't know until I had more facts and, at the moment, it was actually the least interesting aspect of the discussion to me.

"What do you mean when you say the old Monk?"

"The Monk I was before all of this change made me the Monk I am now."

"You mean the Monk you've become after you solved your wife's murder, after Disher moved to New Jersey to be with Sharona, and after you began to feel your life had become balanced in a way it hadn't in a very long time?"

"Not quite then," he said.

"You mean the Monk you became after you took your brother on a cross-country road trip in a motor home so he'd experience the balance you had in your own life?" I said. "And he fell in love with a woman who was a tattooed ex-con?"

"Not quite then, either."

"You mean after I solved a case on my own, and after Ambrose got engaged to Yuki, and after you got into a relationship with a woman who sells poop, and after I left you to become a cop in Summit?"

"Sometime after all of that."

"You mean after all of us went through big changes in our lives that you had to adapt to, and after you discovered not only that you could adapt, but that you were actually happy after you did?"

"Yes, that's it," Monk said. "Now you see my crushing problem."

"You think happiness has thrown you off your game."

"Denying my misery has distracted me from reality," Monk said. "I am not seeing the world as it really is or the details that really matter."

"Or maybe you're just seeing some things now that you never saw or appreciated before."

"I see what's important," he said.

"We see what's important to us," I said and pulled the car to the curb in front of his apartment. "Maybe what is important to you has changed."

"That's what I am getting at," he said. "Change is bad."

"Really?" I gestured to the light in his window. "Ellen Morse stuck around for you. Isn't it nice for a change to come home to a house that isn't empty, to someone who cares about you?"

He glanced at his window and rolled his shoulders. "I don't know if it's a good thing having her in my life."

"You like her, don't you?"

"But maybe that's where my problems started," Monk said.

"I'm not following you," I said.

"She sells poop products. It's repulsive. I pretend that part of her life doesn't exist so I can be in the same room with her. But when I put those blinders on, what else do I blind myself to? Is that why Dale was able to escape, Leland lost his job, and Cleve Dobbs is dead?"

"No, it absolutely isn't."

"How can you know that?"

"Because you're allowed to be happy."

"Am I?" Monk said. "Look what happened the last time I was. Look what has happened now."

He opened the car door and got out.

It was so nice to sleep in my own bed in my own house. Granted, a lot of my stuff was packed up, and Julie had pretty much made the place her own, but my room was more or less as I'd left it. And the house itself, which I'd bought with my late husband, Mitch, would always be filled with wonderful memories, even if someone else lived there someday. But for now, being in the house was like being wrapped in a big warm blanket.

I used to feel like that every day, before things changed.

It was also great to stroll into the kitchen in my nightgown early the next morning to find my daughter, in her T-shirt, sweats, and slippers, sitting at our scuffed-up table and drinking from a big mug of coffee and browsing on her iPad.

It was almost like it used to be, before she grew up and went off to college. Before things changed.

"How did it go last night?" she asked.

"This is going to sound terrible," I said, "but it was like the good old days."

Before things changed.

Good God, I was as bad as Monk.

"You didn't think things were so good at the time," Julie said. "You were constantly complaining about Monk's quirks, about the long hours, and the lousy pay."

"I have some perspective now that I didn't have before."

"Or everything looks better from your rearview mirror when you're leaving," Julie said.

"When did you get so cynical?"

"When I became an assistant to a guy who investigates murders," she said. "I thought you enjoy being a cop, that it validates you in a way no other job ever has. That you feel you've finally found yourself outside of being a mother to yours truly."

I put a bagel in the toaster, poured myself a cup of coffee, and sat down next to her at the table.

"Yes, I like being a cop, and I feel all those things that you mentioned," I said. "But it's not as exciting as I thought it would be and it's in Summit. I miss you, Mr. Monk, and this house."

"You'll get over it," she said. "The murder of Cleve Dobbs is all over the newspapers, the television, the Internet. You'd think he was president of the United States."

"His products had a big impact on popular culture," I said. "It's no surprise that his death has one, too."

"They don't mention anything about how his murder might be connected to the deaths of Grossman, Zuzelo, and Branham."

"That's because the only people who could leak it to the media are Devlin, Stottlemeyer, and Jenna Dobbs, and they're certainly not going to do that."

"Amy has her work cut out for her," Julie said.

"So does Monk," I said.

"Don't forget we've got the wedding rehearsal tonight."

"There're only eight of us," I said. "What's to rehearse?"

"Fire drills, earthquake drills, tsunami warnings, possible alien invasion, and who knows what other emergencies," Julie said.

"Knowing the Monk brothers, that might actually be the ceremony," I said.

"I bet when the judge gets to the part about 'in sickness and in health,' Ambrose will have a list that he will want read into the official record."

"There aren't stenographers at weddings," I said.

"There will be at this one," she said.

We both laughed and probably could have continued riffing on the subject of a Monk wedding for a couple more hours, but my cell phone rang. It was in a charger on the kitchen counter. I snatched the phone and answered it.

It was Amy Devlin.

"You might want to pick up Monk and come down to the station right away," she said. "Unless you want to stay at home, in which case, you can hear all about it in the news."

"Has there been a break in the search for Dale Biederback?"

"Nope, not a thing," she said. "It's like the bastard just evaporated."

"So you've developed some new leads in the Dobbs homicide?"

"Nope," she said. "We've made an arrest."

"Who?"

"Come to the station and you'll see."

I picked up Monk at his apartment and told him that Devlin arrested someone for the murder of Cleve Dobbs.

"But I haven't told her who the killer is yet," Monk said.

"She figured it out herself."

"How did she do it?"

"She's a trained homicide detective," I said, and I noticed an odd expression on his face, like he was laughing at a private joke. "Do you know who did it?"

"Of course I do," he said and turned his back to me to get his coat from the closet. "I was going to tell Devlin this morning."

"You *have* changed," I said.

"I thought I told you that," he said, his back still to me as he put his jacket on.

"You lied to me. You've never lied to me before. You wouldn't have even tried. That's why your back is still turned, because you're afraid to show me your face. You didn't solve the murder this morning—you solved it last night, at the scene, and kept the solution to yourself."

He rolled his shoulders. "Perhaps."

How had I missed his tell? I'd clearly been away from him for too long. Or maybe it was jet lag. Either way, I'd have to up my game and up it fast.

"You wanted to give Devlin a chance to solve it herself," I said. "But why?"

He turned around to face me but kept his head low.

"Penance," he said.

"You haven't done anything wrong," I said.

"Dobbs is dead and Dale is gone," Monk said. "That proves otherwise."

"So you thought letting Devlin best you was the way to make up for what you see as your recent shortcomings, your inability to predict the future."

"Something like that," he said. "It seems important to her to solve a crime before I do."

"Very perceptive of you," I said.

"I don't miss much," he said. "Except how and when Dale was going to escape and that Dobbs was going to be murdered."

"How did you figure out who killed him?"

"I considered the time of death, the fury of the attack, where the attack occurred, and the pattern of injuries on Dobbs' body and the blood spatter on the walls."

I sighed. "His wife killed him."

Monk raised his head and looked at me. "How did you know?"

"I guessed," I said. "It's not like there's a huge pool of suspects."

"There's everybody he's ever known and worked with."

"Yes, but she's the only woman in his life that I knew about."

"Here's what happened," he said, and he told me as I drove us down to police headquarters.

# CHAPTER TWENTY-ONE

# Mr. Monk and the Interrogation

Although Devlin was acting captain, she hadn't moved herself into Stottlemeyer's office. She sat at her desk outside his door. I don't know whether it was out of respect, or whether she believed he'd be coming back.

She rose from her seat when she saw us arrive and seemed quite pleased with herself.

"We've arrested Cleve Dobbs' killer," Devlin said.

"Who is it?" Monk asked in a very wooden way. That's because he already knew who it was and was acting as if he didn't. And Monk doesn't know how to act.

But if Devlin picked up on his stilted delivery, she probably took it as a sign of his discomfort at finally being bested by her solving the crime before he could.

"It's Jenna Dobbs," she said. "I've got her sitting in the interrogation room right now."

"That's a surprise," Monk said, although it wasn't for him at all.

"We kept her under surveillance last night and this morning we served a search warrant on her car," Devlin said. "We found a Hefty trash bag under her spare tire. The bag contained her bloody blouse, wrapped around a bloody knife that had her prints all over it. The ME is doing a DNA match, but I'm certain the blood will be from her husband."

"I'm sure you're right," Monk said. "What made you think to search her car?"

"Well, I have to admit you deserve some of the credit for that."

"I do?" That time, his surprise was genuine.

I was surprised, too, that she would think to credit Monk for her work. Then again, it made sense, since she'd undoubtedly felt slighted numerous times when her work wasn't recognized as being key to his solutions.

"Your harping at the crime scene on the lousy alibi she gave her husband got me wondering why she did it and where she really was while he was possibly out killing people."

"He definitely was," Monk said.

"Jenna wasn't shopping last night. She was with her personal trainer at his place in Marin County and she was with him at the Belmont Hotel when Grossman was thrown off a cliff," Devlin said. "She's been having an affair."

"She lied and gave her husband an alibi because of her own guilty conscience," I said.

"I think that's part of it," Devlin said, then looked at Monk. "I believe Jenna began to have doubts about him after the scant evidence that she'd heard from you."

"Scant?" Monk said.

"Maybe he'd lied to her for years about his tattoo. Maybe he'd lied to her about where he'd been when those three people were killed," Devlin said. "Whatever it was, you struck a nerve. You raised doubts that ate away at her. She became convinced that her husband was a liar and a serial killer—"

"He was," Monk interrupted.

"—and that she was going to lose everything they had because of it," Devlin continued. "And it enraged her."

"Now we know how the killer got into the house with ease and why Dobbs' guard was down," I said, playing along, as if I was discovering it all for myself, as if Monk hadn't already told me everything. He didn't know about the affair, but he had deduced the rest.

"Jenna came home, took the knife from the kitchen, and then went upstairs, confronted her husband and killed him," Devlin said.

"That explains why Dobbs only sustained injuries to the front of his body," Monk said. "He was facing his wife. He was pleading his case."

"And probably pleading for his life," Devlin said. "After she killed him, she changed her blouse, wrapped the knife with it, and stashed them both in a Hefty bag in her car before calling 911."

"Why didn't she try to get rid of the knife somewhere far from home?" I asked.

"She didn't have time," Devlin said. "She was afraid that she'd be seen coming home by neighbors and that we'd discover the call that her husband made to her at six thirty. And she knew the ME would determine the time of death was around seven p.m., so she had no choice but to call 911, stash the knife temporarily in her car, and get rid of it later."

"But you were on to her before she got the chance," I said. "You've solved his murder. But the problem is now you're going to have a very hard time proving Dobbs killed those three people or why he did it."

"I'm hoping he told his wife, and that she will tell us," Devlin said. "Care to watch?"

We did.

Jenna sat by herself in the interrogation room, staring into the mirror. Her eyes were bloodshot from crying but her expression was resolute and determined. She was girding herself for battle and I can only imagine the pep talk she was giving herself.

But, of course, she wasn't really alone. Monk and I were on the other side of the glass, hidden from her view in the observation room and staring right back at her, and she undoubtedly knew that.

Devlin came in with a file and took a seat on the other side of the table, her back to us.

"You've been advised of your rights," Devlin said. "Are you sure you wouldn't like to call your lawyer?"

"Positive," Jenna said. "I want to talk you out of this madness so you can concentrate on catching my husband's killer before it's too late."

"I think we already have," Devlin said.

"Now you're sounding like that awful man Captain Stottlemeyer had you drag off of our property."

"Adrian Monk. Let's talk about that, shall we?"

"No, let's not," she said. "Let's talk about how you failed to protect my husband from the monster who killed those other people."

Devlin leaned forward. "You said your husband was with you when Bruce Grossman, David Zuzelo, and Carin Branham were killed."

"He was," Jenna said, crossing her arms over her chest. "But why are you harping on that when he's dead? Why aren't you out there hunting the killer down?"

"So you're telling me that Cleve was with you in bed with your personal trainer, Teddy Rudin, at the Belmont and again at Rudin's apartment in Sausalito where, incidentally, you were yesterday evening," Devlin said. "Don't bother lying to me again. We know you parked at the Belmont and that Rudin had a room. We've got your Golden Gate Bridge Fas-Trak data and we've got detectives getting a statement from your boy toy right now. He's gladly telling all."

Jenna glowered at Devlin for what seemed like a good thirty seconds before she finally spoke. "Having an affair is not a crime."

"Lying to protect a murderer is."

"Cleve didn't kill anyone," Jenna said. "That's why I lied, to save him from false charges."

"That may be what you thought at the time, but you changed your mind later, didn't you? You started to think about all of his lies and it made you furious."

"No, that's not true," Jenna said.

"There you were, feeling guilty about your affair, while he was out killing people. That had to hurt. Your husband was a serial killer and, if that wasn't bad enough, he'd suckered you into defending him. It was one last betrayal and sickening indignity on top of all the others."

Jenna gave Devlin another death stare. "You couldn't be more wrong or incompetent. I didn't feel the least bit guilty about my affair and I don't now. The sex between Teddy and me was an extension of my workouts, nothing more. As for

Cleve, he could be a ruthless bastard, but he wasn't a killer. That's just laughable. Why would he do such a thing?"

"Here's what I think: You knew he'd killed those people, and that your alibi wouldn't hold, and that when he got caught, you'd lose everything. So you murdered him, out of rage and in the dim, desperate hope that if he was dead, nobody would ever be able to pin those killings on him."

"Listen to me, and listen carefully," Jenna said. "Take notes if you find it too complex for your feeble mind to comprehend. Yes, I wasn't shopping yesterday. I was in Sausalito, screwing my trainer, though I certainly don't need any training where that is concerned."

"Glad we cleared that up," Devlin said.

"I left his place at six. I was on my way home when Cleve called me about a half hour later and asked about dinner. You can check that out for yourself, I'm sure. When I came home, I looked out the window of the great room and saw him dead on the patio. I immediately called 911. The police were there in minutes. That's it. I never, for one second, believed that my husband killed anyone and I certainly didn't murder him."

"The evidence says otherwise," Devlin said.

"What evidence?"

"We found this hidden in the trunk of your car this morning." Devlin opened the file and passed a photograph to Jenna. "That's your blouse, and a knife from your kitchen, both covered in your husband's blood."

Jenna's eyes went wide as she regarded the photo. "That proves nothing."

"Your fingerprints are on the knife, which the ME has

positively identified as the murder weapon, and we found strands of your hair on the blouse."

Jenna tossed the photo back at Devlin. "It's obviously a setup."

"Okay, then tell me how your blouse and bloody murder weapon got in your car."

"It was planted by the murderer," she said.

"How?"

She shrugged. "He must have crept in during the night and put it in the car."

"But you set your alarm last night and we've had your house under constant surveillance," Devlin said. "And so has the media. So how did the killer get in to plant it and out again without setting off your alarm or being seen?"

She thought for a moment. "The killer must have still been in the house when I got there, planted it, and slipped out before the police arrived."

"You talked to your husband at six thirty, you got into the house at seven fifteen, called 911 at seven twenty-four, and the first police officer arrived at seven twenty-eight," Devlin said. "That's a four-minute window. Where were you when you called the police?"

"The kitchen," she said.

"Then anybody walking in or out of the garage would have had to walk past you, and you didn't see anyone or hear the garage door open, or you would have told us. The garage door was closed when the police arrived at the scene. So how did the killer plant the bloody blouse and knife in your car and get away?"

"Maybe he hid in the house and slipped out in all the excitement, dressed as a cop."

"Or maybe he called Scotty and asked to be beamed up to the *Enterprise*," Devlin said.

"I'm not the detective, you are. Do some damn detecting. I was framed. You figure it out."

"If I were you, Mrs. Dobbs, I'd make a deal. Leniency from the court in exchange for telling us whatever your husband confessed to you about the killings while he was pleading for his life."

Jenna gave Devlin another death stare. "I want to talk to my lawyer now."

"I think that's a good idea," Devlin said. Then she got up and walked out.

She joined us in the observation room and looked at Jenna through the glass. Jenna stared back at us defiantly. It was almost as if she could see us.

"So," Devlin asked, "what do you think?"

Monk rolled his shoulders. "For the most part, I thought you did the best job possible."

"For the most part? What part didn't impress you?"

"You missed a golden opportunity to answer one of the key questions," Monk said. "Whether they were planning to have dinner at home or go out."

"What do you care?"

"It's an unanswered question," Monk said.

"It's irrelevant," Devlin said.

I spoke up before the conversation went completely off the rails. "Did Cleve Dobbs' autopsy turn up anything that could help you?"

"It hasn't been done yet. They're real backed up down there," Devlin said. "But I got them to scrape under his fingernails, in case his wife killed him in self-defense. But all we got was potting soil."

"Makes sense," Monk said. "He'd been gardening when I saw him yesterday."

"You saw him?" Devlin said. "You didn't tell me that."

Monk shifted his weight. "What does it matter now?"

"Everything matters," she said.

Monk winced. He deserved that. And she obviously took great pleasure in rubbing his own words in his face.

"He wanted to hire me to prove that he was innocent," Monk said.

"And you don't think that's relevant?" Devlin asked, rhetorically, I'm sure.

"He was guilty," Monk said.

"We don't know that," Devlin said. "It's possible that Jenna killed him for the wrong reasons."

"Is there a right reason?" I asked.

"How would you feel if you'd discovered your spouse was a serial killer?" Devlin said. "I can see why she'd hack him up with a knife. But what if all his lies weren't because he was out killing people? What if he had some other, non-homicidal secret? That would mean she was consumed by her own demons and they drove her to kill an innocent man."

"That's not likely," Monk said.

"But we'll never be sure, will we?" Devlin said. "Because even if she tells us that he confessed, how will we know if she's telling the truth or just lying to get a lighter sentence?"

"She won't ever admit to guilt," Monk said, looking at Jenna, who was staring defiantly at the glass. "She'll go to prison, her husband's reputation will remain intact, and three murders will remain open and unsolved forever."

"What do you care? You're certain Dobbs did it," Devlin said. "So the cases will be closed as far as you're concerned. That would be enough for me."

"But they won't actually *be* closed," Monk said. "The account won't be balanced in the official record. I can't live with an imbalance."

"Well, you'd better learn to," she said.

# CHAPTER TWENTY-TWO

## Mr. Monk Is Less Sad

I dropped Monk off at home and we settled on a time when Julie and I would pick up him and Ellen and take them to Ambrose's house for the wedding rehearsal later that day.

I had some time to kill, so I gave Stottlemeyer a call and invited him out for coffee at a dive diner I knew he liked on a side street on the waterfront east of Potrero Hill, not far from the pier where the hearse that Dale escaped in was found.

The place was called Dora's. The booths and bar stools were upholstered in worn and cracked red vinyl, the tears patched with layers of some kind of red-colored tape. The walls were yellowed by decades of grease, the tablecloths were red and white checkered, the floor was linoleum, and the waitresses wore powder blue uniforms, little hats, and white aprons. There was a selection of pies, most with slices missing, turning in a display case behind the cash register.

There were restaurants that spent a fortune trying to replicate the fifties look that came naturally to Dora's, which didn't exactly attract a trendy crowd. Just about everybody who ate and worked there had calluses on their hands and their spirits.

Stottlemeyer was in a booth in the back, nursing a cup of

coffee and picking at a slice of banana cream pie when I came in. He wore a polo shirt and jeans and his right arm was in a sling. He looked pretty good, all things considered.

He grinned when he saw me and got up to give me a one-armed hug and a peck on the cheek.

"It's good to see you, Officer Teeger."

"You, too, Captain," I said.

"Ex-captain," he said.

"Suspended captain," I said as I slid into the booth across from him. "And that's only temporary."

"Not if Fellows has his way," Stottlemeyer said.

"He won't," I said. "We both know that. The case against you isn't going to stick."

The waitress came over. She was probably my age but looked as weathered as a merchant seaman. I ordered what Stottlemeyer had and she went off to get it.

"Fellows is right about one thing," Stottlemeyer said. "It's my fault that Dale escaped."

"No, it's not."

"I was in charge, so yes, it definitely is. I underestimated the guy and in my eagerness to make up for that blunder, I almost got Monk and your daughter killed. I want you to know how sorry I am for putting Julie in danger."

"No one is blaming you for that."

"I am," he said.

"You and Mr. Monk are both blaming yourselves and it's ridiculous. Julie made the choice to work for Mr. Monk and we all let her. We all forgot that what we do is dangerous because we do it every day. And she didn't realize how risky the job is because we take it so casually. If anyone is to blame, it's me. As her mother, I should have known better. So let's drop the blame game, okay?"

The waitress brought my pie and coffee. I put enough sugar into the coffee to make it a dessert, too.

I filled him in on what was going on in Summit, how the pressure had eased up on Randy now that he was no longer juggling two jobs—acting mayor and police chief—in the wake of a city hall corruption scandal that broke shortly after he was hired.

He and Sharona were even talking about marriage, so I warned Stottlemeyer that he might soon be making a trip back east for a wedding.

"What about you?" Stottlemeyer said. "Randy tells me you're a great officer, the community loves you, and that you're doing a fantastic job."

"I'm flattered, but what I handle is mostly petty crime and parking tickets," I said, taking a bite of the pie. It was delicious. "It doesn't take a whole lot of skill."

"You're selling yourself short," Stottlemeyer said. "You'd be a good cop on any police department. You've certainly had the best training possible."

"Are you fishing for a compliment now?"

"No, I'm stating a fact. The police academy does a good job preparing people, but you've spent years working homicides, getting the kind of experience that simply can't be taught. And let's face it, as irritating as Monk is, he's the best damn detective I've ever come across and probably ever will. We all can learn from his powers of observation. What you're doing in Summit seems easy because you've been working at a higher level here for so long."

"That's kind of my problem," I said. "I'm bored."

"Not enough dead bodies for you?"

"It's not the corpses," I said. "It's the cases. I need more of a challenge, higher stakes, a faster pace."

"Like a triple murder case and hunting down an escaped convict?"

"Yeah," I said. "Something like that."

"Be careful what you wish for," he said, lifting his arm in its sling. "You could find yourself blown out of a house on a fireball."

"You're going to think I'm crazy, but I'd prefer that to chasing Tide bandits."

"Tide bandits?"

"It's a long story and, frankly, not that interesting, though Randy assures me I've won the everlasting gratitude of the New Jersey Grocers Association."

"Don't worry, I'm sure there's bound to be a murder or a robbery or a bloody home invasion out there one of these days."

"You know what I mean. I like that Summit is a safe, pleasant, and nearly crime-free place to live," I said. "But I don't think I'm ready for safe and pleasant yet."

"But you love being a cop," Stottlemeyer said.

"I do," I said. "Besides working for Mr. Monk, it's the best job I've ever had."

"I can certainly understand that. I've put in nearly thirty years on the force and am in no hurry to get out. And yet here I am." Stottlemeyer took a sip of his coffee. "But enough about me. How is Monk holding up?"

"I take it you heard about Jenna Dobbs' arrest."

"Amy couldn't wait to tell me," Stottlemeyer said. "She closed the case fast, which impressed the brass. But what matters more to her is that she beat Monk to it. That's not something even I've been able to do."

"Actually, Mr. Monk says he solved the case last night but kept the solution to himself so Amy could have this win."

"Baloney," Stottlemeyer said. "He might have had a hunch it was the wife, but he didn't have enough evidence, even by his loose standards, to make an accusation stick, so he kept his mouth shut. Meanwhile, Amy built a case the old-fashioned way, not on deductions and observing tiny details but by checking the facts and collecting strong evidence. Her case is airtight and will put Jenna Dobbs in prison for life."

I couldn't argue with that, so I didn't.

"But Cleve Dobbs could get away with murder," I said.

"The bastard is dead, so he's not getting away with anything."

"You know what I mean."

He waved to the waitress and held up his empty mug of coffee. "You shoot for a win, but sometimes you've got to live with a tie. Okay, so maybe we're the only ones who'll ever know that Dobbs killed three people, and maybe it will stay that way, but I figure everything balanced out."

"I wish Mr. Monk could see it that way."

"He might surprise you," Stottlemeyer said. "Monk has changed."

"I know, and he's not very happy about that."

The waitress came over, refilled our cups, and walked away.

"He's never very happy about anything," Stottlemeyer said. "Only now he's a little less sad than he used to be."

"He thinks that having less sadness is costing him some of his detecting skill."

"So what if it has?" Stottlemeyer said. "Nothing in this world is free."

"You could make up for what he thinks he's lost," I said.

"What do you mean?"

"Julie has quit and I go back to Summit on Monday," I said. "Mr. Monk is going to need someone to help him out until he finds someone."

Stottlemeyer laughed. "You want me to be his assistant?"

"His partner, just until you get your old job back," I said. "That's something that could happen real fast if the two of you are working together."

"How do you figure that?"

"Because you two will find Dale," I said. "Between his genius and your investigative skills, Dale doesn't stand a chance."

"I don't think Fellows, or the brass, would appreciate me tagging along with Monk to crime scenes, or investigating Dale's escape, especially while I'm under investigation by IA for being in Dale's pocket and leaving the back door open so he could flee."

"So don't go to crime scenes with Mr. Monk," I said. "You could still help him out in a big way and help yourself at the same time."

"I'll think about it," Stottlemeyer said and took a sip of his coffee. "Okay, I'm done thinking. The answer is no."

"He's your best friend," I said.

"And if I'm his assistant or partner or whatever else you want to call it, I'll kill him. What kind of friend would I be then? I don't have your patience, your heart, or whatever it is that allows you to tolerate him day after day. I can walk away, you can't."

"I have, remember?" I said. "All the way to the other side of the country."

"Yeah, but here you are, assisting him again."

"Temporarily," I said.

Stottlemeyer smiled and took another sip of coffee.

"What?" I said.

"We'll see," he said.

# CHAPTER TWENTY-THREE

## Mr. Monk Rehearses

When I got home I found Julie at the kitchen table, her laptop open in front of her, looking at articles about Deputy Chief Fellows.

"I thought you hated the guy," I said.

"I'm trying to figure out how he rose to such lofty heights in the department when he's so dumb."

"Don't forget, he's a trained criminologist."

"How can I forget? I wonder what two-bit college gave him that degree."

"I think it was John Jay," I said. "Or Harvard. Someplace like that."

"You got to be kidding me," Julie said. "I would have figured he got it mail-order from Hungary or something. He doesn't seem smart enough to lick a stamp."

"It's not stamps you've got to lick to get where he is."

"That's just gross," she said.

"I'm talking about boots," I said. "He got where he is with political savvy and kissing up, something we can both agree neither Captain Stottlemeyer nor Lieutenant Devlin are very good at, which is why they'll probably never become chiefs and will always be braves."

"How is Leland handling his suspension?"

"He seems surprisingly relaxed about it all," I said.

"Is he investigating Dale's escape on his own and trying to clear his name?"

"Nope, I don't think so. But it's only been a day or so, and I think he's taking a little time to recuperate. He did just break his arm. It wouldn't surprise me if he got restless and impatient soon and started poking around."

"Think he'll come to Monk for help?"

"He will if he's smart," I said. "How goes the job hunt?"

"Lousy. It's much more fun cyber-stalking Fellows."

"Does that pay?"

"Not yet," she said.

"C'mon, let's get going, or we'll be late to the rehearsal."

She closed her laptop and grabbed her coat, and we went out to the car. I drove us over to Monk's place, where he and Ellen were standing out on the curb like schoolkids waiting for a bus.

They got into the backseat and I headed for Tewksbury. I turned on the radio and the news of Jenna Dobbs' arrest for the murder of her husband was the big story on National Public Radio. She was in jail awaiting arraignment on the charges and bail was likely to be equal to the U.S. gross domestic product, if they allowed her out at all.

Speaking of big money, sales of Cleve Dobbs' memoir were soaring in the wake of his murder and his wife's arrest. Perhaps readers were hoping to find some clues to what presaged the crime within the pages of the book. Perhaps Devlin was doing the same thing. In fact, I offered that opinion after the NPR report was over.

"Can you please turn that off?" Monk asked.

"Sure," I said and did as he asked. "What was it that they reported that got under your skin?"

"They're talking about Dobbs like he was some kind of hero," Monk said, "celebrating his technological achievements when what they should be doing is mourning and honoring the three people that he killed."

"Dobbs was never arrested or even charged for the killings," Ellen said.

"But he committed them," Monk said.

"A man is innocent until proven guilty."

"I proved it," Monk said.

"To yourself," Ellen said.

"And to his wife," I said, maybe a bit too defensively. "She killed him for it."

"No offense, but you don't actually know why she killed him yet," Ellen said. "Nobody has any idea what abuse she suffered or what that marriage was like."

"It couldn't have been very good if she hooked up with her trainer and hacked her husband into bite-size pieces," Julie said.

"It just goes to prove that even great fame and enormous financial success can't protect you from unhappiness," Ellen said.

"That's because it's our natural state," Monk said. "We're born miserable."

"That's an uplifting thought," Ellen said.

"I think it is," he said.

"You do?" Ellen asked.

"If misery is our natural, born state, then things can only get better," Monk said.

"Well, at least you're optimistic," Ellen said.

"That's a first," I said. "I've never heard Mr. Monk described as optimistic before."

"I bring it out in him," she said.

I waited, but Monk didn't deny it. I took that as a good sign and, from the smile I saw on Ellen's face, so did she.

Ellen had never been to Monk's family home before nor had she met Ambrose, who greeted us at the door in his usual attire, except this time he was wearing latex gloves.

"Welcome to my home and thank you for arriving so promptly for the rehearsal," he said to us all. "I hope that it was also rehearsal for your arrival tomorrow."

"Absolutely," I said, stepping forward. "We drove the whole way here with a stopwatch." I gave him a kiss on the cheek. "Congratulations, Ambrose."

"I'm so glad that you came back for this joyous event," he said. "I assume this means there are no hard feelings."

For some reason, he always felt I had the same romantic feelings for him that he'd had for me. But I didn't, and I knew that he'd only had feelings for me because I was the only woman in his life, at least until we stumbled across Yuki.

"It's taken time, but I've finally managed to get over the loss," I said and stepped inside.

Julie followed me in and gave Ambrose a hug. "I'm very happy for you, Ambrose. I hope I can still come over and watch movies and play checkers with you once you're a married man."

"Anytime," he said. "I would be hurt if you didn't."

Ambrose now faced Monk and Ellen, who stood side by side on the porch in front of him. "Hello, I'm Ambrose Monk, Adrian's brother."

Ellen smiled. "It's a pleasure to finally meet you."

"Likewise. I'm sorry it took a wedding invitation to get Adrian to bring you over to see us." Ambrose held out a gloved hand to her. She looked at it.

"I see Adrian has told you what I do for a living," she said, but more with amusement than anything else.

"Oh, no, this is nothing personal," Ambrose said. "I wear these gloves all the time, especially to open my mail and to read the morning paper, anything that passes through a lot of hands before showing up here."

"I can assure you that I wasn't handling excrement before coming over and that I have thoroughly washed my hands," she said. "And I certainly haven't been passed through a lot of hands before showing up here."

"Even so, I—," Ambrose began to say, but he stopped when Monk did something extraordinary.

He held her hand.

Ambrose stared at their clasped hands, and at his brother, then peeled off his gloves. He held out his hand to her. She shook it.

"Thank you for inviting me to be part of this very special occasion," she said. She let go of Monk's hand and came inside.

Monk faced his brother. "I thought this day would never come."

"You were hoping it wouldn't," Ambrose said.

"That, too," Monk said and came inside.

Ambrose closed the door and turned to face us. By this time, I'd noticed that the living room had been cleaned out and that all that was in there now were two rows of two white folding chairs facing a white podium. The furniture was centered in the room. There were little name tags, like those you might find on a table setting, on the seat of each chair.

Yuki came out of the kitchen carrying a platter of snacks and set it on the dining room table, which was laid out with eight plates, eight napkins, and eight bottles of Fiji water.

The platter contained a selection of little square pieces of toasted bread with a variety of toppings, like shrimp, roast beef, olives, and cheese, and little miniature sandwiches like they serve at teatime at the St. Francis Hotel.

"Welcome, everyone," she said. "I've got some finger foods to nosh on." Monk and Ambrose both cringed at the phrase. Yuki laughed and winked at me. "I love it when they do that."

Yuki gave me a hug, we exchanged pleasantries, and then she turned to Ellen.

"Well, hello," Yuki said. "You must be the crap lady."

"And you must be the tattooed ex-con biker chick," Ellen said.

They both broke into big smiles.

"I think we're going to get along just fine," Yuki said.

Monk turned to Ambrose. "What would Mother think of the two of us now?"

"Who cares, Adrian," Ambrose said. Monk's eyes widened in shock. "We're grown men and our mother is long dead. What she would have thought is completely irrelevant to our lives. All that matters is what makes us happy."

"I'm not sure I know you anymore," Monk said.

"You don't," Ambrose said. "I'm a new man and, from what I can see, so are you."

"Is that a good thing?" Monk asked.

There was a knock at the door. Ambrose opened it to reveal two uniformed mailmen, both in their late forties, one shaped like a pear and the other like a banana, as if he'd spent his whole life hunched over.

"Hello, Andy," Ambrose said to the pear. "I appreciate your coming."

Andy gestured to the banana. "You asked me if I could bring someone, so I brought Florian. He works the counter at the post office."

"We've never met," Florian said to Ambrose. "But I am familiar with your mail. I help sort it."

"Thank you for attending on such short notice," Ambrose said and gestured them inside. He turned to us. "Shall we get the rehearsal over with? Then we can be convivial."

Julie leaned against me. "Did he just say convivial?"

"He did," I said.

"He's really loosening up," she said.

We went into the living room. Ambrose went to the podium.

"Florian? Would you mind standing here? You're taking the place of our justice of the peace, who couldn't be here tonight."

"No offense to Florian," Julie said, "but couldn't we have

just pictured the justice there without you having to recruit a stranger to stand at the podium?"

"But then there would only have been seven of us present for the rehearsal," Ambrose said. "It wouldn't have been very accurate preparation."

"And an odd number of guests," Monk said. "That's not acceptable. We aren't barbarians."

I looked at Yuki. "You sure you're ready for this?"

"We all have our eccentricities," she said. "And relationships are all about compromises."

"I couldn't agree more," Ellen said.

Ambrose quickly walked us through the choreography of the ceremony.

The judge would enter first, taking his place behind the podium. Then Monk and Ellen would come in and sit in the two front seats. Then Julie and I would come in and sit in the two seats behind them.

Ambrose would then lead Yuki in, arm in arm, to the front of the podium.

Finally, Andy would come in and stand in the back of the room, on a mark placed on the floor, so that he would be even with the judge. At that point, with everyone and everything in the room symmetrical and in perfect balance, the ceremony would begin.

The judge would say a few words, then Ambrose and Yuki would say a few words of their own preparation, and then the judge would pronounce them man and wife.

"At which point," Ambrose said, "we will retire to the dining room for the joyous reception, followed by Yuki and I embarking on our honeymoon in our motor home."

"Where are you going?" I asked.

Yuki waved her arm toward the wall. "That way."

"You don't have a destination?" Monk said. It was more of a protest than a question.

"Nope," Ambrose said. "Exciting, isn't it?"

"You might as well be skydiving," Monk said. "Without a parachute."

"That may be the best description of marriage I've ever heard," Florian said.

# CHAPTER TWENTY-FOUR

# Mr. Monk and the Floater

The next morning I slept in and basically lazed around the house until lunchtime. I wasn't actually working for Monk, so I felt no obligation to rush over to his place first thing in the morning, especially since he wasn't actively investigating any mysteries.

Technically, I suppose he was still investigating Dale's escape from the hospital, but he had nothing to go on and was basically waiting by the phone for Devlin to call with a lead, and that's presuming she'd bring him in to help if she had one.

I was getting the sense that Devlin was finally beginning to appreciate Monk's skills. On the other hand, she was also beginning to understand his limitations. The truth is, she was probably a lot better at chasing down fugitives than Monk was.

The serial-killing case was a dead end, too. Although the murders of Bruce Grossman, David Zuzelo, and Carin Branham were still officially unsolved, Monk knew who killed them. But he couldn't prove it and, unless Jenna Dobbs offered new information, he had nothing more to go on.

So Monk had nothing to do, which meant he was probably cleaning his apartment down to the foundation and studs, and I didn't want to be around for that.

At about noon, I set out for a leisurely stroll down 24th Street, where all the best shopping in Noe Valley is, but ended up dodging hordes of women pushing babies in Peg Perego strollers and walking their dogs. I felt like a spaceship trying to navigate a meteor storm and took refuge, bruised but unbowed, in a patio seat at Martha & Brothers coffeehouse.

I ordered a San Francisco blend coffee, treated myself to a blueberry muffin, and browsed through the morning edition of the *Chronicle* that someone had left behind on the next table. Naturally, the Dobbs story was explored in the paper from every possible angle. It was too juicy and salacious not to be. But unless Stottlemeyer, Devlin, Monk, or Jenna talked, I doubted if any enterprising reporter would manage to dig up that Cleve Dobbs was suspected of multiple murders or that the three seemingly accidental deaths were even connected.

Buried in the back pages, at the bottom of an inside column, was a small story on the continuing search for Dale Biederback. It included an artist's rendering barely larger than a postage stamp of what the fugitive might look like now.

I would have studied the photo closely, and committed it to memory, but I forgot to bring my electron microscope with me. I'd ask Devlin for a copy of the sketch the next time I saw her.

My cell phone rang and, lo and behold, it was Devlin.

"I was just thinking about you," I said. "Could you get me a copy of the police sketch of the new, thin Dale?"

"Sure, I'll e-mail it to you," she said. "In the meantime, I could use Monk's help on a case."

"You're kidding," I said. "You're actually inviting him to a crime scene?"

"We've got a floater down at Marina Green," she said. "He's naked and has no ID. We might be able to figure out who he is from dental records, and maybe fingerprints if we can recover any. But the body is in very bad shape, so, if it's possible at all, it will take time. I'm not even sure it's a murder. I'm overwhelmed right now trying to run homicide. I'm hoping Monk can pull a lead out of nowhere and get us something to go on."

"I'm sure he will be glad to try."

He was more than glad. He was ecstatic and, I think, truly thankful to have a new mystery to occupy his mind and distract him from what he perceived as his recent, and humiliating, failures.

I picked him up in front of his house and we drove down to Marina Green, an eight-block-long flat expanse of grass right on the bay, offering spectacular views of the Golden Gate Bridge and Alcatraz and built atop the ruins of disaster.

The area was a marsh until the 1906 earthquake, when the rubble of old San Francisco was dumped there, creating a very unstable landfill that, despite the threat of another temblor, became the site of the 1915 World's Fair.

After the fair, the structures were removed and the area

became a park, where people picnic, fly kites, play games, jog, toss Frisbees for their dogs, take pictures of the Golden Gate, and find dead bodies.

Actually, that's not entirely accurate or fair. The body was found floating between slips of the St. Francis Yacht Club, adjacent to the park.

By the time we got there, the body had been pulled out of the water and brought inside a white tent erected by the medical examiner and forensic team on the western edge of the Marina Green parking lot.

We met Devlin outside the tent.

"Thanks for coming down," she said.

"I appreciate being asked," Monk said.

"You may not after you see what we've got here," she said. "I hate floaters, and this is a bad one. He's been in the salt water for a couple of days, so he's very ripe, and it looks like he's been hit by a couple of boat propellers and nibbled on by fish and crabs. He's just eviscerated. His eyeballs are gone and he's missing teeth. Getting fingerprints from him is going to be a real challenge. I'm really not sure there's anything you can do for us, but I figured it was worth a try."

I was tempted to ask if I could sit this one out, but I didn't want to look like a sissy.

"Any signs of foul play?" I asked.

Devlin shrugged. "With all the damage to the body, it's hard to say at this point. At first glance, and that's about all you'll want to take, there are no apparent bullet holes or stab wounds. Could be a suicide, or maybe a sailing accident, or maybe a murder. We don't know."

Monk nodded, lifted the tent flap, and stepped inside. I took a deep breath to steel myself and followed him in. Devlin remained outside.

Here's one of the fascinating contradictions about Monk. He won't look at a naked woman sitting across from him, and he's repulsed by someone with crooked teeth, but he has no problem whatsoever scrutinizing a putrid, hacked-up, water-swollen, fish-chewed naked body pulled out of the ocean.

I grew up in Monterey, around the ocean, the beach, and the fishing industry. I've come across dead seals and dolphins on the beach. I've smelled a lot of rot.

But I've smelled nothing that compares to a human body that's been decomposing in the sea. The odor was overpowering. Even holding my breath, the odor seemed to seep into my skin. Every instinct I had made me want to leave that tent and retch.

And I haven't even told you what the corpse looked like. I won't go into too much detail, except to say the body was extremely bloated and disgusting. It was laid out on a blue plastic sheet and all kinds of fluid was seeping out of it.

I couldn't look at it, but Monk squatted down right next to the body, peering at it closely and examining it from head to toe, his hands out in front of him, framing his perspective.

"He didn't take very good care of his teeth," Monk said.

He wasn't holding his breath or averting his gaze but was taking it all in, without flinching, without the slightest hint of revulsion.

In fact, he even poked at one of the wounds with his gloved fingers. That was too much for me.

"I'm sorry, Mr. Monk, I can't take it. I have to step outside," I said and didn't wait for his answer.

I got the hell out of the tent and walked over to the park before risking a breath. But there still must have been molecules of rot from the tent in my nose, because the stench was lingering and I nearly retched.

I took a few quick, deep breaths to try to clear my nose. Devlin came up beside me and handed me a Kleenex and a tiny bottle of Scope.

"Blowing my nose and swishing around some Scope in my mouth usually does the trick for me," she said.

I followed her advice. I blew my nose. Then I took a mouthful of Scope, swirled it around, and spit it out on the street.

My mouth tasted minty fresh and all I smelled was the fresh air.

"Thanks," I said.

"No problem," she said. "What does Monk know?"

"All he's told me is that the guy had bad teeth," I said. "How are things going with Jenna Dobbs?"

"She hasn't said a word since lawyering up. She's got one of the best law firms in San Francisco on her case, though it's not going to do her any good," Devlin said. "The judge is going to deny bail. Maybe after she's marinated a while in a cell she'll be more willing to make a deal and tell us what her husband might have admitted to her."

"Maybe he didn't admit anything," I said.

"You'd be surprised what stabbing a guy will do to loosen his tongue."

"I wouldn't know," I said. "But I'm worried about why you do."

She was about to reply when something behind me caught her eye.

"Is he smiling?"

I turned around and saw Monk standing outside the tent. He appeared relaxed and entirely at peace.

And he was smiling, no doubt about it.

"He's solved it," I said.

"Solved what?" she said.

"Whatever happened to the guy," I said.

"He seems happier than that to me."

"To me, too," I said.

We went over to Monk, who seemed positively giddy—not exactly the reaction you'd expect from any normal person who'd just been scrutinizing a decomposing body.

"Do you know who the dead man is?" Devlin said.

"Yes and no," Monk said.

"Was he murdered?"

"Yes," Monk said.

"Do you know who did it?"

It seemed like an absurd question to ask based on how little Monk had to go on.

"I do," Monk said.

Even I was stunned by that. At least it explained why he was so upbeat. He'd got his mojo back.

"How can you possibly know that?" Devlin asked.

Monk turned to her and his smile got even bigger. "I also know that Dale Biederback didn't escape the way we thought he did, and I can tell you where he is right now."

I gestured to the tent. "Is that him in there?"

"Call Julie and Captain Stottlemeyer, ask them to meet us

at the hospital," Monk said, clearly ignoring my question. "They deserve to know what actually happened when Dale got away from us."

"Can't that wait until we've apprehended him?" Devlin asked.

"There's no hurry," Monk said. "He isn't going anywhere."

That last comment only reinforced my suspicion that the corpse in the tent was Dale. But Monk wouldn't say anything more.

That was frustrating, of course, but I was used to it. He always kept the solution to himself until he could present what he knew and how he'd figured it out in his own way, in his own time, and on his own terms. It was always best for him if he could do it at the scene of the crime, which in this case was the hospital.

He cherished that final moment, when he explained how everything fit together, because that was when he felt certain that the world was in perfect balance, that he'd restored order out of chaos.

I wouldn't begrudge him that pleasure. The truth was, the frustration I felt was familiar, exciting, and something I actually welcomed. It was like waiting to go on a new thrill ride at your favorite amusement park. Yes, you wish the line would move faster, but the expectation of the excitement in store for you only makes the ride better once you're on it.

It had been way, way too long since I'd felt this wonderful frustration. I didn't appreciate it before, not until it wasn't part of my life anymore.

Monk was silent as I drove him to the hospital, but he had a look of pure contentment on his face.

We parked at the hospital and went up to the second-floor lobby to wait for Devlin, Stottlemeyer, and Julie to arrive.

"Can you give me a hint?" I asked Monk.

"About what?"

"How Dale got away or where he is now, and how seeing that floater solved it all for you."

"Okay," Monk said.

That took me completely off guard, because I honestly didn't expect him to give in. He'd always refused to offer me anything ahead of time.

Monk really had changed.

"You will?" I said.

"Dr. Wiss, the plastic surgeon who operated on Dale, won a trip to Hawaii and left the morning after the operation."

"Okay, and . . ." I rolled my hand, like I was turning a wheel.

"And what?" he asked.

"What's the hint?

"That's your hint," Monk said.

"That's not a hint," I said. "That's just restating a fact."

"A fact that's a hint."

"How is that a hint? We know Dr. Wiss was in Hawaii. He left before Dale escaped and has been there ever since."

"That's true," Monk said.

"And we know it's Dr. Wiss, not someone else pretending to be him, because Devlin saw his picture and positively identified him."

"I agree. That is absolutely, irrefutably, Dr. Wiss in Hawaii and not an imposter."

"Then how is that a hint?"

"It's not just a hint," Monk said. "It's the solution."

"How can that possibly be the solution?" I said. "The solution to what?"

"Everything," he said and smiled.

# CHAPTER TWENTY-FIVE

# Mr. Monk and the Musical Chairs

**M**onk remained silent until Devlin, Stottlemeyer, and Julie arrived at the hospital. When they came out of the elevator, it was clear how each of them felt. Devlin was impatient, Julie was excited, and the captain was delighted.

"I knew you'd do it, Monk," Stottlemeyer said.

"Me, too," Julie said.

"I'm glad you two did," Monk said, "because I certainly didn't."

"He hasn't done anything yet," Devlin said and looked at him expectantly.

We all did.

But he didn't say or do anything. A long, awkward silence followed. Awkward for us, maybe, but not for Monk. He seemed completely at ease.

"Well, are you going to tell us what's going on or not?" Devlin snapped, tapping her foot with anxiety.

Monk held up his hand in a halting gesture and glanced at the clock on the wall.

"It will only be a few more minutes," Monk said.

"What is he waiting for?" Devlin asked me.

I shrugged. Stottlemeyer sighed and took a seat on one of

the chairs in the waiting area. Julie and I sat down on either side of him. Devlin remained standing beside Monk.

"Do you have to be so damn dramatic?" Devlin said. "Why can't you just get to it?"

But Monk didn't answer. He just watched the clock.

"This is going to be good," Stottlemeyer whispered to us.

"How do you know?" I whispered back.

"Look at him," Stottlemeyer said. "He's like a conductor in front of an orchestra, getting ready to play."

"I have a present for you, Leland." Julie took a sealed envelope out of her purse and tucked it into the captain's sling.

"What is it?" he asked.

"Take a look after Mr. Monk has finished," she said. "I'm sure you'll put it to good use."

At that moment, a doctor emerged from the elevator and seemed startled to see all of us there.

"Detectives," he said. "May I help you with something?"

Julie leaned across Stottlemeyer to whisper to me. "That's Dr. Auerbach, the plastic surgeon who works with Dr. Wiss."

I nodded, wondering where this was all going.

"No, we're just revisiting the events surrounding Dale Biederback's escape," Monk said. "You're right on time for your rounds. How are Jason McCabe and Frank Cannon doing?"

"You have a good memory for names," Dr. Auerbach said. "They are recovering nicely."

"Good," Monk said. "You may carry on."

"Thank you for granting me permission to see my patients," Dr. Auerbach said sarcastically and went into the ward where the two patients were recovering.

Monk turned to us and it was clear he was ready to begin his summation.

"As you will recall, Dale's operation was the third of the day for Dr. Wiss and involved gastric bypass and extensive liposuction and excision of the excess flesh left over from the removal of all that fat," Monk said.

"Yes, yes, we know," Devlin said impatiently. "Can we please move this along?"

"You weren't here for this," Monk said. "The risks of that surgery, as we were informed by Dr. Wiss, included dehydration, blood loss, heart attack, and infection from wound dehiscence."

"Dehiscence?" I asked.

"He could burst like a piñata," Monk said.

"I'm feeling déjà vu," Julie said.

"Wholly intentional," Monk said. "I want you to relive the past and pay close attention, because the answers are there. Dale emerged from the operation wrapped in bandages from head to toe and relieved of perhaps half his previous weight. Dr. Wiss told us that Dale would go into the ICU and then require constant medical supervision during his recovery. However, Dr. Wiss informed us that his wife had won a vacation to Hawaii and that his partner, Dr. Auerbach, would be handling the post-op care of his three patients, beginning the following morning."

"What does all of that have to do with anything?" Devlin said.

"The next day, Dale's girlfriend, Stella Chaze, sent a runaway truck down Powell Street," Monk said. "The truck collided with a cable car and a bus, killing four people and flooding this hospital with patients."

"Yes, we know," Devlin said. "Dale and Dr. Wiss' two other patients were moved out of the ICU into another ward, freeing up the ICU to handle the critically injured victims from the accident. Chaze snuck in as one of the victims, and in the chaos that ensued, she wheeled Dale down to the morgue and slipped him out of here as a corpse in a hearse that she'd stolen from a mortuary. She took him to the waterfront and that's where the trail went cold."

"Because we were following the wrong trail," Monk said.

"What do you mean?" Devlin said.

I thought about the hint Monk gave me and, in that second, it all came together. I saw the whole thing. For the first time, I felt a giddy sense of balance, of everything fitting together as it should. Myself, included. I was exactly where I was supposed to be, in my place, at the right time. I felt connected to the world, and the family and friends around me, in a way I never had before.

It was a wonderful feeling.

I must have a tell, too, because I suddenly realized that Monk was looking at my face and seeing right through me.

"You've figured it out," he said.

Stottlemeyer looked at me. "You have?"

I nodded. "You'll discover, once you do a little digging, that the trip Dr. Wiss won to Hawaii wasn't a contest at all but a sham, a gift from Dale."

"Dr. Wiss was in on the escape?" Stottlemeyer asked.

"No, he's entirely innocent," I said. "He has no idea that he didn't actually win anything."

"So Dr. Auerbach is the other accomplice," Devlin said, "the one with medical training that we've been looking for."

"No, he's entirely innocent, too," I said. "But a vital part of Dale's escape plot."

Monk smiled. "You really have figured it out. I'm proud of you."

"I've been with you a long time, Mr. Monk."

"I wish you'd never left," Monk said.

I almost said, *Me, too*, before I caught myself.

"Some of us still don't know what the hell is going on," Devlin said.

"You can include me in that," Stottlemeyer said.

"A naked corpse was found floating in the bay today. He was all ripped up, presumably by boat propellers," Monk said. "But that's not what happened. He burst apart as a result of the bloating that is a natural stage of decomposition."

"Bodies don't just explode when they decompose," Devlin said.

"They do when they are all cut up and held together with stitches," Monk said. "The bloating caused his large surgical incisions to split wide open, making it appear as if his corpse had been hit by a propeller while at sea."

"Wound dehiscence!" Julie said.

"Exactly," Monk said. "You pick up on this stuff very fast."

"So the dead guy is Dale Biederback," Devlin said. "He fell off into the bay during his escape. You're saying we've been searching all this time for a dead man."

"No, I'm not," Monk said and then noticed Dr. Auerbach emerging from the ward. "Excuse me, Doctor. May I ask you a few questions?"

"Sure, if you make it quick," Dr. Auerbach said. "I'm running a little behind."

"Before Dr. Wiss left on his vacation, and you took over his rounds, had you met Jason McCabe, Frank Cannon, or Dale Biederback?"

"Nope," Dr. Auerbach said.

Stottlemeyer smiled. Now he got it, too.

"I'll be damned," the captain said.

"How are Mr. McCabe and Mr. Cannon doing?" Monk asked the doctor.

"Fine, no complications, not that it's any of your business," Dr. Auerbach said. "They should be released in a few days."

"Have Mr. McCabe or Mr. Cannon had any visitors?" Monk asked.

"Cannon's wife has come by, and I think his son, too," Dr. Auerbach said. "But as far as I know, no one has visited McCabe."

"That's about to change," Monk said and walked into the ward. We got up and crowded in after him.

There was a man who looked like a mummy sitting up in one of the two beds, reading a book on a Kindle. The other patient's bed was surrounded by a curtain.

Monk gestured to the curtain. "I have never met Jason McCabe. But I can tell you that he was single, homeless, morbidly obese, and had no family. An anonymous, extraordinarily generous benefactor paid for him to have liposuction. That donor was Dale the Whale, and he's right here."

He whipped back the curtain to reveal another bandaged man sitting up in bed. The man's eyes blazed with fury.

"I told you it would be good," Stottlemeyer said to me.

"Adrian Monk," Dale said, each word dripping with dis-

gust. "You're like a disease that keeps mutating to avoid erad-
ication."

"You knew you couldn't escape without proper medical
care, so you arranged an escape that didn't involve escaping,"
Monk said. "You took McCabe's place and since Dr. Auerbach
didn't perform your surgery, and hadn't met you before, he
never suspected a thing. If everything had gone according to
plan, you would have walked out of here in a few days with a
new face and, presumably, a prearranged new identity."

"It's a pity you weren't killed with my little acolyte in that
explosion," Dale said. "It would have been so fitting for you
to die like your wretched wife."

If Dale was hoping to strike a nerve, he failed. Monk
stepped up to the bed.

"Trudy caught you first, and it was easy. And every time
you've tried any scheme since, I've always caught you, too.
Some genius you've turned out to be." Monk leaned in
close. "Tell me, Dale, do you ever get tired of failing so spec-
tacularly?"

"This isn't over," Dale said.

"So the answer is no," Monk said, straightening up again.
"Oh well. I guess with your unbroken record of abject fail-
ure, I don't have much reason to worry about what you come
up with next." Monk stepped away from the bed and looked
at Devlin. "He's all yours."

Devlin handed Stottlemeyer a pair of handcuffs. "Would
you like to do the honors, sir?"

Stottlemeyer took the cuffs, clamped one end on Dale's
wrist, the other to the bed railing. "Dale Biederback, aka
Dale the Fail, you're under arrest."

Frank Cannon, the patient in the next bed, spoke up. "Does this mean I'll be getting my own room? That man snores like a pregnant walrus."

Monk turned and walked out. His job was done. That's when I noticed Dr. Auerbach standing by the door, stunned by what he'd heard.

"I was Dale's puppet and I didn't even know it," he said. "How could I have been so easily duped?"

"Don't be too hard on yourself," I said. "We all feel that way after Monk does one of his reveals."

Julie and I went into the lobby and joined Monk, who was busy organizing the magazines on the waiting area coffee table by name and date.

"Congratulations, Mr. Monk," I said. "That was quite a show."

"It wasn't a show," Monk said. "I discovered the correct order of events and conveyed those facts to you."

"In as dramatic a fashion as possible," I said. "You're a performer at heart."

"Let me make sure I understand what happened," Julie said. "During the confusion in the hospital, Stella put Dale in McCabe's place, killed McCabe, slipped his body out of the hospital, and tossed him in the ocean."

"Yes," Monk said. "That's correct. She killed five people and then herself out of twisted love for a monster."

"Okay, but there's still one thing I don't get," she said. "How did you know all that stuff about McCabe being single and homeless if you never met him?"

"From his teeth and skin when I examined his corpse," Monk said. "The rest I deduced."

"How?" Julie asked.

"Simple logic. The only way the switch could possibly have worked was if the person whose place Dale took had no relatives who would show up to visit or who would miss him if he disappeared."

Stottlemeyer came out of the room. "Devlin is going to stay with Dale until we get some officers down here. He's not going anywhere this time."

"He never went anywhere last time," Monk said.

"I stand corrected," Stottlemeyer said. "And grateful."

Julie gestured to Stottlemeyer's sling. "You can open my present now."

The captain took out the envelope, opened it, and read the sheet of paper that was inside. He glanced at Julie. "Is this true?"

"It's the only thing that is," she said.

"Unbelievable," Stottlemeyer said.

"What's this all about?" I asked.

"Your daughter has great instincts." Stottlemeyer gave Julie a kiss on the cheek. "Are you sure you aren't interested in being a detective?"

"Positive," she said.

"Our loss," he said and waved the piece of paper. "Would you like to see me cash this in?"

"I'd love to," she said.

**D**eputy Chief Fellows liked dogs. His office at police head-quarters was filled with pictures of his three golden re-trievers at play. The pictures of his dogs outnumbered the pictures of his wife and two sons by three to one. He also had a dog bed and a basket of chew toys in one corner of his office in case one of them ever came to the office for a visit. He didn't have anything around for his family to chew on.

Stottlemeyer and Julie showed up unannounced and found Fellows at his desk going through some files. Fellows looked up from his work and wasn't pleased to see who was at his door.

"How did you two get in the building?" Fellows demanded.

"We're Lieutenant Devlin's guests," Stottlemeyer said, then gestured to Julie. "She's my driver."

"You have been suspended, Stottlemeyer, so unless you have come to cut a deal, you are not welcome here," Fellows said.

"That's exactly why I'm here," he said.

"That's a wise move. Take a seat and have the girl wait outside," Fellows said and reached for the phone. "I'll get the IA detective handling your case down here."

"I'd hold off on that if I were you," Stottlemeyer said. "There have been some developments in the Dale Biederback case you need to know about first."

Fellows put the receiver back in the cradle. "Do you know where he is?"

"I do," Stottlemeyer said. "He's in police custody, handcuffed to a bed at San Francisco General."

"Did Devlin find him or did you give up his location in exchange for leniency?"

"Neither. Adrian Monk found him. He figured out that Dale never left the hospital, that the whole escape was an elaborate ruse."

"So Dale was right under your nose," Fellows said, shaking his head. "I knew you were incompetent, but not to this extreme. No wonder you brought in Monk as a consultant and fought so hard for that lunatic all these years. Without him covering your back, your stupidity would have been obvious to everyone. You haven't been riding his coattails, you've been hiding behind him!"

"You're missing the point," Julie said. "I told you that Mr. Monk would find Dale. I also warned you what would happen when he did. There's going to be a press conference soon, and you're not going to like what he has to say about you."

Fellows stood up. "Don't threaten me, little lady. Perhaps you have forgotten who you are talking to. I am a deputy chief of the San Francisco Police Department. I have the power to immediately cancel Monk's consulting contract. So if Monk is smart, he'll watch his mouth and not bite the hand that feeds him. And although Monk may have assisted the police in apprehending Dale Biederback, that doesn't clear Stottlemeyer of bribery or his breathtaking incompetence. I could make life very unpleasant for Lieutenant Devlin as well, if Monk says the wrong things. Do I make myself clear?"

"Immediately following Monk's press conference," Stottlemeyer said, "I am going to be making an announcement of my own."

"Your resignation, I presume," Fellows said. "Don't expect a letter of recommendation."

"I'm going to reveal that I got a tip from a private citizen about one of our deputy chiefs, whose entire career is based on a lie," Stottlemeyer said. "That deputy chief is you."

"And that private citizen would be me," Julie said. "I couldn't figure out how someone as arrogant and stupid as you could have possibility earned a degree in criminology, so I checked with your university. You got a degree in business administration in 1980, but the closest you got to a criminology degree was a sophomore English class on contemporary detective fiction. The criminology degree wasn't even offered until a year after you graduated."

Fellows sat down slowly in his seat and wouldn't look at either Stottlemeyer or Julie. Instead, he focused his gaze on a picture of one of his golden retrievers on his desk.

"You said you came to cut a deal," he said, his voice barely above a whisper. It was as if he couldn't summon the air to speak. "What do you want?"

"All charges against me dropped and expunged from my record, a written apology, official commendations for Monk and my detectives, and your immediate resignation," Stottlemeyer said. "Use whatever excuse you want for quitting, but be out of here by Monday morning or I'll go public."

Fellows nodded. Julie stepped up to the desk and wagged her finger at him the way he had at her.

"I warned you," she said, and then she and Stottlemeyer walked out.

Monk didn't hold a press conference, of course. But Captain Stottlemeyer did. No mention was made of his suspension. It was as if it never happened (and, officially, it never did). He announced that Dale had been captured as a result of exemplary work by police consultant Adrian Monk and homicide lieutenant Amy Devlin, both of whom were being rewarded with commendations from a grateful department for their efforts.

He reported that Dale Biederback was now recuperating from his surgery in his cell at San Quentin, where he was already serving two life sentences in connection with previous murders. But he would soon be standing trial for the murder of Jason McCabe and the murders of the four people killed by the crash he engineered in Union Square.

Monk had defeated his archenemy yet again, but his happiness didn't last.

It never did.

He was still troubled by the three open murders on his unbalanced balance sheet. He looked at the murders from a dozen angles, but with Cleve Dobbs dead, the only hope he had of closure, of balance, was if Jenna Dobbs talked.

And so far, she was keeping her mouth shut.

What Monk needed was a distraction. There wasn't another murder to occupy his mind, so I got him thinking about his brother's wedding and his speech.

"What speech?" Monk asked when I stopped by his place for a visit on Friday morning.

"You're his brother and his best man," I said. "You need to make a toast at the reception."

"I can't do that," he said.

"You have to," I said. "That's the tradition."

I knew he'd fret about that and I left him to do it. At least it would take his mind off the three solved but officially unsolved murders.

The last few days had been a whirlwind. Cleve Dobbs was murdered, Jenna Dobbs was arrested, and Monk solved the mystery of Dale Biederback's apparent escape.

It was an addictive pace and it was easy to get caught up in it again. And when it was over, there was a definite crash, like the kind that follows too much sugar and caffeine.

I spent the day like a tourist, walking all over the city and revisiting my favorite haunts in a melancholy, nostalgic daze. It was as if I'd been away for years instead of months.

But my new life in Summit was never far from my thoughts, not with my badge and gun in my purse. I liked the weight, what they represented, and how they made me feel. In a way, I felt like someone with a secret identity.

Or somebody living two lives.

There was the life I had led in San Francisco, and had revisited over the last three days, and the life I led in Summit.

The contrast between them was so distinct that it was hard not to keep comparing the two in my mind, and to wonder whether there was a way to bring them together, if not geo-graphically, then perhaps in some other way.

It took me all day to realize I was wrestling with some big decisions that, just one week ago, I didn't know I'd have to make.

Sunday came fast and Ambrose's wedding day was upon us. It was a day I certainly thought would never come and, if it was unbelievable to me, it must have been utterly inconceivable to Monk.

What were the odds that someone who'd only left his house three times in thirty years would meet a woman and fall in love? And that woman would agree to marry him?

It was improbable and also incredibly romantic.

The wedding was scheduled for noon. At about nine forty-five, Julie and I put on our fanciest dresses and drove over to pick up Monk and Ellen, arriving at Monk's door at ten sharp.

Yes, I know it was a full two hours in advance, but Monk wanted to be absolutely sure there was no way we could arrive late to his brother's wedding.

I resisted the urge to let myself in with my key and knocked on the door instead. I didn't work for him anymore and it wasn't my home. What made me think I could just breeze in like Kramer on *Seinfeld*? What if Monk was finally in a romantic clinch with Ellen?

I know that seems improbable, but stranger things have happened, like an agoraphobic, middle-aged writer of instruction manuals marrying a tattooed ex-con biker chick.

Monk opened the door and stood in front of us, wearing

his tuxedo. I'd never seen him dressed in anything but his usual clothes and a hazmat suit, so it took a moment for the sight to sink in. I stepped inside and walked around him, my hands in front of me, Monk-style.

The tuxedo was simple, black, and a perfect fit.

"The name is Monk," I said. "Adrian Monk."

"Yes, of course it is," he said. "Are you feeling all right?"

I knew explaining the James Bond reference to him would be more effort than it was worth, so I just let it go.

"You look great, Mr. Monk," I said.

He tugged at his sleeves. "I'm not very comfortable."

"You're never comfortable," I said.

"I'm more uncomfortable than usual."

"That's because the tuxedo is something new," Julie said.

"I don't like new."

"Look at the bright side," Julie said. "It's only new once. Tomorrow it will be old and familiar."

"I won't be wearing this tomorrow," he said.

"Why not?" Ellen said, coming out of the living room in an elegant black dress. "Now that you have a black-tie outfit, we can paint the town."

"I've always wanted to paint the town," Monk said. "But with actual paint."

She laughed, though I know Monk didn't mean it as a joke. "We can go to parties, the theater, and the finest restaurants."

"Those are places I try to avoid."

"Now you won't have to because you finally have the right clothes for the occasion."

"The right outfit for those occasions is a hazmat suit," Monk said. "And I have two."

"This is a much better look for you," Julie said. "Like Mr. Clean in a black tux."

"I tried to put a flower in his lapel but he wouldn't let me," Ellen said.

"I am not going to show up at my brother's wedding covered with yard trimmings," Monk said.

"It's one flower," Ellen said.

"It would have to be two," Monk said. "One on each lapel. I'd look like a compost heap with a bow tie."

"How are you feeling?" I asked.

"I wish I could wear my regular clothes," he said.

"I meant about the wedding," I said. "Don't dodge the question."

"It's a big change," he said.

"For Ambrose," Julie said. "Not for you."

"He's always been my rock," he said. "I knew that my home would always be there and that he would always be in it. Now he's leaving and when he comes back, it will be *their* home, and when I show up, I will be a guest. It will be the same physical structure, but everything inside will be different. I could say the same about Ambrose. I'm not sure I know him anymore."

"So now you can look forward to getting to know him again," I said. "And Yuki, too."

"There's another way to look at this," Ellen said. "If Ambrose can change so much and find happiness, so can you."

Monk rolled his shoulders and checked his watch. "We should go."

"It's ten oh five," I said. "We'll be way too early."

"I want to get there before the crowd," he said.

"We are the crowd," I said. "Have you come up with your toast?"

"Yes, I wrote it down." He patted his chest with both hands. "I have it right here."

"Which pocket is it in?" Julie said.

"Both," Monk said.

"You tore the paper in half?"

"I made two copies," he said. "One for each pocket. This way I won't be off balance and will have a spare in case of an emergency."

My cell phone rang. I dug it out of my purse. The caller ID said it was Stottlemeyer. I was tempted not to answer it. But on second thought, I realized that Stottlemeyer knew it was Ambrose's wedding day and wouldn't be calling to drag Monk into a case. So I answered it.

"Good morning, Captain. What are you doing working on a Sunday?"

"Crime doesn't rest on Sundays."

"But you usually do," I said.

"I have to catch up on the paperwork that accumulated while I was on my little vacation," he said. "I came across something ironic that I thought Monk would appreciate."

"I'm not sure he understands irony," I said.

"I'm sure he'll get this," Stottlemeyer said. "Put me on speaker."

I did and held the phone up. "It's Captain Stottlemeyer."

"Hey, Monk, congratulations on Ambrose's wedding. I hope you'll give him my best."

"I will," Monk said.

"I thought you'd like to know that you were right about

the trip Dr. Wiss won to Hawaii. The contest was a sham sponsored through a dummy company that Dale set up. Dr. Wiss was told that his wife won the contest for being the one millionth customer to purchase a particular brand of shoes online. And Jason McCabe's lipo operation was bankrolled by a fake charity called Freedom from Despair, which was supposedly dedicated to easing the medical burdens of the homeless. They reached out to McCabe through a homeless shelter in the Tenderloin. The counselors there identified the Freedom from Despair rep as Stella Chaze."

"I know you take comfort in confirming in detail the conclusions I have already reached, but it really isn't necessary to share that process with me for my peace of mind," Monk said. "I have absolute faith in my own deductions."

"That was just the warm-up for the best bit of news," Stottlemeyer said. "I got the autopsy report on Cleve Dobbs."

"We know how he died," Monk said.

"What you don't know is that he was killed for nothing," Stottlemeyer said.

"We know why he was killed, too," Monk said.

"The irony is that Cleve would have been dead in a year anyway," Stottlemeyer said. "He had an extremely aggressive form of amyotrophic lateral sclerosis, also known as Lou Gehrig's disease."

"What a horrible way to die, your whole body slowly becoming paralyzed while your mind remains sharp," Ellen said. "You become a prisoner of your own body until you no longer have the ability to breathe. Jenna did her husband a favor."

"I'm sure that was the last thing she had in mind," I said.

Monk tilted his head from side to side. "Captain, I need you and Devlin to meet us at the Dobbs estate right away. Be sure to bring the house key."

"Why?" Stottlemeyer said. "We know what happened. The case is closed."

"There are still three murders that haven't been solved," Monk said.

"Have you forgotten about your brother's wedding?" I said. "Can't this wait until afterward?"

"Absolutely not," Monk said.

"We're going to be late," I said.

"I'll make it fast," he said. "As long as those murders are unsolved, the universe is not in balance. I don't want that for my brother. I want everything even. For him and for me."

"Why can't you just tell us now what you know?" Stottlemeyer said. "Why do we have to go to the Dobbs estate to hear it?"

"Because that's where the answers are," Monk said. "And that's when I will actually know what I know."

# CHAPTER TWENTY-SEVEN

# Mr. Monk Gets Even

The media circus had long since decamped and moved on from the front of the Dobbs estate. It had been five days since the murder, a lifetime in the network news cycle, so there were no cameras and no reporters to see us drive up in our finest clothes.

We'd been there only a minute or two when Stottlemeyer and Devlin arrived in the captain's Crown Vic. We got out of my car and waited for them at the gate.

"This is exciting," Ellen said to Julie. "I've never seen Adrian at work."

"It's much better when there's someone to catch," she said. "This feels kind of anticlimactic to me. The killer is dead."

Stottlemeyer and Devlin strode up.

"Wow," Devlin said. "You clean up nice."

"I'm always clean," Monk said. "When have you ever seen me dirty?"

"The name is Monk," the captain said. "Adrian Monk."

"Yes, I know that," Monk said. "What is wrong with you and Natalie today? Why do you feel the need to tell me my own name? We don't have time for this nonsense. Did you bring the key?"

"And the code for the gate," Devlin said and went to the keypad.

I cleared my throat. "Are you forgetting something, Mr. Monk?"

He patted his chest and his pockets. "I don't think so."

I gestured to Ellen and suddenly it occurred to him.

"Oh yes, forgive me," Monk said. "Captain Stottlemeyer, Lieutenant Devlin, I'd like you to meet my friend Ellen Morse. She sells crap."

"One man's crap is another man's art," Stottlemeyer said and offered her his hand. "Pleased to meet you."

"It's actual crap," Monk said.

"Likewise," she said to Stottlemeyer. "I know you've been a great friend to Adrian."

"It's not easy," Stottlemeyer said.

Devlin opened the gate. "We're in."

We all filed past her and Monk led us to the backyard. The blood, bone, and brain matter had been hosed off the patio, and the flowers that Cleve Dobbs planted seemed to be thriving. His gloves and shovel were still where he'd left them, though, which was kind of creepy.

Monk held forth in front of the new flower bed.

"When Julie and I last saw Cleve Dobbs alive, he was standing here, working on his garden. He wanted to hire me to find whoever had killed Bruce Grossman, David Zuzelo, and Carin Branham." Monk glanced at Ellen. "Grossman was the CEO who replaced Dobbs at Peach. Zuzelo was the high school math teacher who told Dobbs he'd amount to nothing. And Carin was his first love, who dumped him."

"There's no need to explain things to me that the others already know," Ellen said. "I appreciate the courtesy, but please press on. Don't let me slow you down."

It was good advice, since we had only an hour left before the wedding and we still had to get clear across the bay.

"Very well, let's go inside," Monk said. "Julie, would you please bring those garden gloves with you?"

I couldn't imagine why Monk wanted the gloves, but I didn't ask. I wanted to keep things moving along.

Devlin led us to the house, unlocked the back door, and let us in. The house smelled strongly of cleansers, Pine-Sol on steroids, which indicated to me that the crime scene cleaning crew had come and gone. That was a good thing. Nobody wants to see a room splattered with blood before a wedding.

Now Monk took the lead, taking us upstairs to the office where Dobbs was killed. It was now as clean, white, and sparkling as a Peach store. All that was missing were the salespeople and all the products to try. The white walls made Monk really pop in his black tuxedo. He'd never looked so cool. I was tempted to take a picture.

"We found this room covered with blood that was spattered and spilled in the midst of a horrific attack. The blood was a storyteller, revealing Cleve Dobbs' entire struggle with his knife-wielding wife, who backed him out onto the deck. Dobbs fell over the railing to his death on the patio below," Monk said. "Lieutenant Devlin later found the bloody knife, part of a set in their kitchen, hidden in the trunk of Jenna's car and wrapped in her bloody blouse."

"I thought you weren't going to tell us what we already know," Devlin said.

"It's what we thought we knew," Monk said. "But that's not what happened at all."

"You aren't making any sense," Stottlemeyer said.

"Jenna Dobbs is innocent," Monk said. "She's not the one who killed her husband."

"But her fingerprints were all over the knife," Stottle-meyer said. "The DNA confirms that it was Cleve Dobbs' blood on the knife and the blouse."

"I'm sure that it was," Monk said.

"You know how tight all the timing was," Devlin said. "Based on the times of Dobbs' call to his wife, his death, her call to 911, and the arrival of the first officers on scene, there's no way another person could have been in the house when she got here and escaped being seen."

"You're right," Monk said. "There wasn't anybody else."

"And the house was under surveillance after we left," Devlin said. "So nobody could have planted the evidence later."

"It wasn't planted later," Monk said. "It was planted in her trunk before."

"Before what?" Julie asked.

"Before Cleve Dobbs was killed," Monk said.

"But that's impossible," Julie said. "How could the murder weapon and the blouse, with her fingerprints on the knife and his blood over everything, have been put in her car before he was killed?"

"Here's what happened," Monk said.

I leaned toward Ellen and whispered, "I love it when he says that."

"You will recall that Cleve Dobbs had a limp. He thought he'd sprained his ankle and that it wouldn't go away. So he went to the doctor, who ran some tests and told him some very bad news. Cleve had an aggressive form of Lou Gehrig's disease, which is an awful way to die. Knowing that the end was coming, Cleve finished his memoir and decided to die with his life balanced."

"He killed the people he felt had wronged him," Devlin said, "knowing he'd never have to pay for it."

"That's right," Monk said. "He was going to get even with everyone, going all the way back to high school. But then we caught on to him, which he hadn't planned, so he had to go right to the end of his list: his wife, who was cheating on him."

"But he didn't kill his wife," Stottlemeyer said.

"No, he had something worse in mind for her," Monk said. "He framed her for his murder instead."

"How?" Ellen asked. She was completely caught up in the drama now.

Monk smiled. "Before Jenna left the house to see her lover, Cleve planted the bloody knife, which he knew she'd handled many times in their kitchen, and her blouse in her car."

"But we saw him that afternoon, in his backyard, and he was fine," Julie said. "There wasn't a scratch on him."

"He was establishing his alibi," Monk said.

Devlin rubbed her forehead. "You're saying the victim

called you to establish an alibi for himself for his own murder."

"Yes," Monk said.

"That makes no sense," Devlin said.

"It was a suicide made to look like a murder," Monk said. "It was very important to him that we see him in the garden planting flowers and see that he wasn't hurt."

Ellen was staring at Monk with unabashed love and admiration. This was a side of him she'd never seen before and she liked it.

"So how did he do it, Adrian?" she asked.

"Two identical knives," he said. "With the first knife, he cut himself and bled all over her blouse, then hid it all in her trunk before she went off to see her lover. After she was gone, he called us to visit him."

"Where did he cut himself?" Julie asked.

"See for yourself," Monk said and gestured to the garden gloves in Julie's hands, which, until that moment, she'd forgotten that she was holding.

Julie looked at the gloves, then turned them inside out. The lining in both gloves was stained with blood.

"He cut his palms," Julie said. "That's why he didn't take his gloves off when we saw him. You even accused him of plotting his own suicide when we were there. You meant it as a joke, but I'm sure he crapped himself thinking you might already be on to him."

"I wish I had been," Monk said. "The rest of his plot came down to precise timing. He called his wife around six thirty to find out when she was coming home. He then took the second knife and reopened the wounds on his palms so the medical examiner wouldn't know they'd been slashed before and would appear to be defensive wounds. He then stabbed himself, playing out an imaginary scenario of pleading with his wife, spreading blood all over the room. Then he jumped off the deck."

"You're brilliant," Ellen said.

"That's a great theory, Monk," Stottlemeyer said. "There's just one big, glaring problem. Where's the second knife?"

"Dobbs was a very smart man," Monk said, then looked at Julie. "The two times that we met him, where was he?"

"Gardening," Julie said.

"That's right. In fact, the second time, he made sure we knew he was using potting soil in his flower bed, just so we wouldn't suspect anything when we found the same dirt under his fingernails in the autopsy." Monk walked out onto the deck and pointed to the potted plant. "That's because he buried the knife in this plant before throwing himself over the rail."

Devlin glanced at Stottlemeyer. He nodded his consent. She put on a pair of rubber gloves from her pocket, crouched in front of the potted plant, and carefully dug around in the loose soil.

"Damn," she said, then slowly pulled the bloody knife out of the dirt.

Ellen actually gasped. I thought she might even applaud. Instead, she went over to Monk and kissed him right on the lips.

"Adrian, you are incredible," she said.

And most amazing of all, Monk kissed Ellen right back.

Julie snapped a picture with her iPhone, capturing the moment forever.

I guess things had evened out for Monk, in more ways than one.

I glanced at my watch. His happiness wasn't going to last long.

"It's eleven thirty. Ambrose is going to be furious. There's no way we're going to make it to the wedding on time."

Stottlemeyer smiled. "Don't be so sure about that."

# CHAPTER TWENTY-EIGHT

# Mr. Monk Goes to a Wedding

It was five minutes before noon, and Ambrose was contemplating whether to go forward with the wedding without us rather than start late, when the whole house shook.

He looked outside and saw an SFPD helicopter landing in the street in front of his house. Even more remarkable, he saw Julie and Ellen emerge, followed by me, carefully guiding out Monk, who was handcuffed and blindfolded with a black scarf.

Monk was terrified of helicopters. Restraining him was the only way we could get him into the chopper and it was a testament to his devotion to his brother that he consented to our taking him against his will.

I guess it wasn't against his will if he gave us permission to do it, but he knew there was no way he'd be able to get in the helicopter unless he was bound, and no way he could endure the flight if he could see what has happening.

Even so, he screamed the whole way. Luckily, it was a very short trip and the rotors were very loud.

As soon as we were clear of the chopper, it rose up again and streaked back across the bay. I uncuffed Monk and removed his improvised blindfold. It wasn't the most dignified way to arrive at a wedding, but at least we got there on time.

Monk went up to Ellen. "I know I squealed like a baby. Have you lost all respect for me?"

"On the contrary," she said. "I've never seen anything more brave or met a brother who was more loving."

Julie had a huge smile on her face. "This is the best wedding I've ever been to and it hasn't even started yet."

We straightened ourselves out and went to Ambrose's door, where he was waiting for us in his tuxedo, a stern look on his face.

"Nice of you to make it, Adrian," Ambrose said and opened the door.

The judge and the mailman were milling around in the living room. The judge was in his robes and easily in his sixties, his hair gray and his face sagging with wrinkles. He looked very judgelike to me. Andy the mailman had pressed his uniform to military crispness.

"Where's Yuki?" I asked.

"Upstairs," Ambrose said. "She doesn't want us to see each other until the ceremony."

"Let's get this show on the road," the judge said. "I have two more weddings today."

As the maid of honor, I went upstairs to see how she was doing. I knocked on the bedroom door and announced myself. She told me to come in.

Yuki stood in front of a full-length mirror in her wedding dress. It was a strapless, silk-satin dress and tight above the waist, accentuating her curves. There were no frills or embroidery or other embellishments. Only a hint of the snake tattoo that wrapped around her spine peeked out from the back of her dress. It was a sleek, smooth, clean look, something I knew Ambrose would appreciate.

She looked at herself as if it were the first time she'd ever seen her own reflection.

"You're beautiful," I said.

"I've never looked so feminine in my life," she said.

"You picked the right occasion for it," I said.

She took a deep breath, ran a hand down her stomach, and turned to face me.

"You made quite a grand entrance," she said with a smile. "Very impressive. Trying to show us up?"

"It was entirely unplanned," I said. "Mr. Monk decided to solve a few murders on our way here."

"If you were talking about anybody else, I'd say you were joking."

"It's better he solved the murders before arriving," I said. "The last time I went to a wedding with him, there was a murder during the ceremony. I'm hoping he's had his cosmic quota for the day."

"Me, too," she said. "Are you ready?"

"I'm the one who should be asking that question."

"I am," she said and handed me Ambrose's wedding band.

I opened the door and announced that the bride was ready. I went downstairs.

The mailman went to an iPod docked in a tiny speaker system on the floor in the living room and hit PLAY. The wedding march began.

The judge took his position at the podium, Monk and

Ellen walked hand in hand to their seats, and then Julie and I took our seats behind them, just as we'd been instructed. We all turned around so we could see Yuki come down the stairs to meet her groom.

Ambrose jerked when he saw her, and for a moment I was afraid he might be having a heart attack.

He held out his hand to her. It was shaking.

"You are the most beautiful woman I've ever seen," Ambrose said. "I can't believe this is really happening to me."

Tears streamed down Yuki's cheeks. "Let's do this before you change your mind."

"I was thinking the same thing," he said.

He led her into the living room, down the short aisle between us, and to the podium. Andy the mailman took his place on his mark in the back of the room.

The judge cleared his throat. "We are gathered here today to join Ambrose and Yuki in holy matrimony. They have prepared some thoughts of their own to share with you before they declare their vows. Ambrose, you may begin."

Ambrose turned and took Yuki's hands in his own. "I have waited all of my life for you and it was worth the wait. I promise to love you with all of my heart and that I will always be here for you, and not just because I am afraid to leave the house."

Yuki took one of her hands from Ambrose to wipe the tears from her eyes, then she held his hand again.

"I've always known that something was missing from my life," she began, "and now I know what it was. While you were waiting for me, I was searching for you. Now that I've found you, I will never let you go."

The two of them turned to face the judge, who then recited the typical wedding vows you've heard a thousand times, so I won't repeat them here. But I will say that when he got to the part about "in sickness and in health," Julie and I had to fight back giggles.

Monk got up and gave Ambrose Yuki's wedding ring at the appropriate time and returned to his seat, and I did the same when it was Yuki's turn.

"By the power invested in me by the state of California," the judge concluded, "I now pronounce you man and wife."

Ambrose and Yuki kissed, soft and sweet.

Andy the mailman went to the iPod and switched to the next track, the typical after-vow wedding fanfare, which played loud and clear in the small room.

The couple turned to us and we all stood up and applauded. Ambrose and Yuki hugged Monk and Ellen, then gave us hugs, too.

"It was a wonderful ceremony," I said to the happy couple.

"I filmed it all with my iPhone," Julie said.

"I forgot all about photographs and videos," Ambrose said. "I'm so glad it occurred to you."

Ambrose and Yuki posed for photographs with all of us, and then the judge left and the mailman—wisely sensing that he was now truly the odd man out—found an excuse to depart as well.

The six of us went to the living room for the modest reception.

Ambrose and Yuki would not let go of each other.

"She told you she will never let you go," I said to Ambrose.

"And he promised he would always be here for you," I said to her. "You can let go of each other."

"Holding on is the only way I am certain that what's happening is real," Ambrose said.

"And I love being held," Yuki said.

Monk poured everyone cold Fiji water in crystal glasses and cleared his throat.

"I have a toast, which I am told is customary and required by brothers in situations such as this."

"You don't have to if you don't want to, Adrian," Ambrose said.

"I want to," Monk said. "I just want to apologize now if I am not very good at it."

"Think of it as a summation and you will do fine," I said.

Monk held up his glass. First very high, then very low, then right in front of him. Then high again. Then low. He finally set his glass on the table in frustration.

"This just isn't working for me," he said.

"It's not supposed to work for you," I said and gestured to the happy couple. "It's supposed to be about them."

"I think we all need to agree on an appropriate height for the glasses before I continue," Monk said. "Can someone get a tape measure?"

"We don't need a tape measure," Ellen said and held the glass straight out in front of her. "Everyone just hold out your glasses so they are even with mine."

"But don't touch hers," Monk said. "That would be unsanitary."

"Thank you very much," she said.

"I would have said the same thing if it was Natalie," Monk said.

"In a toast, you're supposed to touch your glasses together," Julie said.

"Don't worry, Adrian," Ambrose said. "The glasses have been thoroughly cleaned and no one has had a sip yet, so the rims have no germs on them."

"Okay, in that case, we may proceed," Monk said.

Everyone held out their glasses so they were the same height as Ellen's and then kept them in place.

Monk cleared his throat again to signal that he was about to begin. "I used to think that it was wrong, unnatural in fact, that people only wore a wedding ring on one hand and not matching ones on both of their hands. One ring on one hand was uneven, unbalanced. How could that be right? I wrestled with this for years."

"You did?" Julie said. "Really?"

I nudged her with my elbow.

"And then I met Trudy," Monk continued, "and I realized why we each wore one ring on one hand. It's because it was the two of us together that made us whole, that made us one. Now I can see that the same is true for both of you. You are two pieces that fit together and were always meant to. You can leave the house now, Ambrose, because this isn't your home anymore. Yuki is your home. That is the end of my toast."

"That was perfect, Adrian," Yuki said.

"My sentiments exactly," Ambrose said.

We all touched our glasses together. Ambrose and Monk

did so with absolute precision and the least amount of contact possible with everyone else's glasses. Laser targeting devices couldn't have done a better job.

After sipping their water, the couple sliced the wedding cake, which Ambrose cut into six perfectly square pieces. He proceeded to sort and distribute the crumbs that were left on the platter to us in equal measure.

We spent forty minutes chatting about some of the places Ambrose and Yuki hoped to visit on their honeymoon road trip.

"I would like to see Pocatello, Idaho," Ambrose said.

"What's there?" Ellen asked.

Monk and his brother stared at Ellen as if she'd asked what there was to see in Washington, D.C.

"The Museum of Clean, of course," Ambrose said.

"There's a museum for cleaning?" Julie said. "Really?"

"It's right up there with the Smithsonian," Monk said. "Only better."

"A six-story monument to cleanliness that contains six thousand historical cleaning devices," Ambrose said.

"Note the even numbers," Monk said to me.

"Duly noted," I replied.

"The collection includes a two-thousand-year-old terracotta Roman bath, hundreds of antique mops and brooms, a sixteen-hundred-year-old bronze toothpick, and two hundred fifty preelectric vacuums," Ambrose said. "The key attraction is a horse-drawn vacuum from 1902."

"They even have interactive displays that teach kids how to clean their rooms, properly make beds, and sweep floors,"

Monk said. "The museum was built as a labor of love by a millionaire janitor."

"There are millionaire janitors?" Julie said.

"His name is Don Aslett, and he believes that *clean* is the answer to all the world's problems," Ambrose said. "Clean air, clean water, clean mind. Clean is always great—it's the one thing everyone can agree on."

"Don Aslett should be on Mount Rushmore," Monk said.

"That's for presidents," Julie said.

"He should be president," Monk said.

Ambrose nodded. "I'd vote for him."

"I've seen him clean a window on TV," Monk said. "He's an artist with a squeegee."

"They should invite him to clean the windows of the Sistine Chapel," Ambrose said.

"We ought to go there," Ellen said.

"The Sistine Chapel?" Monk said.

"To the Museum of Clean," Ellen said. "It sounds terrific."

"We can't just go to the Museum of Clean."

"Why not?" Ellen said. "I'm sure you can visit it without being on a honeymoon."

"Yes," Monk said, "but it's worth saving for the occasion."

"Why?" Yuki asked with a mischievous grin and a wink at Ellen. "Are you planning on getting married soon?"

"I didn't say that," Monk said.

"You realize, Ambrose, that you'll have to get out of the motor home to visit the museum," I said.

"I think that's one of the few places on earth besides this house where I would feel entirely safe and secure," he said.

"Who wouldn't?" Monk said.

Yuki squeezed Ambrose's hand. "It's one forty."

"Oh my, already?" Ambrose said. "I can't believe how fast time flies when you're swept up in wedded bliss. "We need to change. We want to be on the road by two p.m."

Monk nodded in agreement. "That's a good time to go."

Ambrose and Yuki excused themselves and went upstairs to change, and we began cleaning up the dishes. They came down a few minutes later.

"No suitcases?" Monk asked.

"We've got the RV all loaded up," Ambrose said, then looked at me. "Do you mind if I borrow that black scarf that you put over Adrian's eyes for the helicopter ride?"

"It belongs to Amy Devlin, but I'm sure she won't mind," I said and went to dig it out of my purse. It was under my badge, gun, and handcuffs. If the badge weren't there, someone going through my purse might think I was very kinky. "What do you need it for?"

"In case I chicken out on walking outside from the back door to the motor home in the driveway," he said and passed the blindfold to Yuki.

"You won't need it." She handed the scarf back to me. "Keep your eyes on me and you'll be fine."

"Okay, then I guess we'll be going now," Ambrose said. "Feel free to continue the festivities as long as you like. But be sure to lock the house up tight, Adrian, before you go. And leave the light switches on. I've set up the lights on timers to fool and befuddle potential burglars."

"I will," Monk said. "If you give me a few days' advance notice of your return, I will come in and dust."

"That would be very nice," Ambrose said and took a deep breath. "Here we go."

Ambrose took Yuki's hand and she led him to the back door. I opened it and held it for them.

"Bon voyage," I said.

Yuki walked outside and Ambrose followed, his head held straight, his eyes locked on her back all the way into the motor home. Once he reached it, he practically dove inside and then slammed the door tight behind him.

The four of us went outside and waved farewell to them as Yuki drove the RV out of the driveway.

Someone had written "Just Married" in white on the rear window and tied a string of six empty Lysol disinfectant spray cans to the back bumper that bounced along the pavement with a nice *clickety-clack* as the RV disappeared down the street.

"Who did that?" Monk asked.

"You're the detective," I said. "I'm sure you'll figure it out."

# CHAPTER TWENTY-NINE

## Mr. Monk and the End

**Y**ou couldn't turn on a television or surf the Web that
Monday morning without coming across the news
that the charges had been dropped against Jenna Dobbs
and that her husband, Cleve, had killed himself to frame
her for his murder.

It was a clever crime, one worthy of a man who'd become
famous for his ingenuity in designing the Peach, and that
alone would have captivated the world.

But with the added revelation that the San Francisco police also believed that Cleve Dobbs murdered three people,
the Dobbs story became a global phenomenon.

Everybody was talking about it, from San Francisco to
Tarawa. And Adrian Monk was right in the center of it, because Captain Stottlemeyer gave him full credit for solving
the case.

The bizarre story of Cleve Dobbs, his murders and his
foiled attempt to frame his wife from beyond the grave, in-
stantly became the most famous case of Monk's career. Reporters from all over the world wanted to interview him.

He refused their interview requests and unplugged his

phone, but that didn't stop them from converging on his apartment building and setting up their satellite trucks.

Monk plugged his phone in just long enough to call me and ask if Julie and I could pick him up and take him to Ellen's house on our way to the airport for my flight back to Summit.

Ellen had agreed to let him hide out at her place until the media frenzy died down. Big surprise there. Monk was too busy trying to elude the media to think about the ulterior motives at work behind Ellen's offer. And I certainly wasn't about to tell him.

He didn't want Ellen to pick him up since it might tip off the media about where he was holed up, so that's why he asked Julie and me for a ride.

"I'll have to slip out of my house in disguise, so you probably won't recognize me," Monk said. "I'll be the hippie beatnik on the corner of Alta Park on Jackson and Steiner."

I took a long, scenic route.

It was a bright, sunny day and there was a slight breeze, pushing whipped-cream clouds across vibrant blue skies and creating a cheerful backdrop for the new single-tower eastern span of the Bay Bridge, which I could see stretching from Yerba Buena Island to Oakland as I topped Nob Hill.

The old eastern span, deemed seismically unsafe, was still there, awaiting demolition. Old and new, side by side.

The new span was wide and graceful, two parallel viaducts curving toward a single-tower suspension bridge. The old span was narrow, blunt, and double-decked.

There was something comforting and familiar about the new span. It was undeniably more modern and sleek, but it followed the same path as the old one, and even evoked the iconic suspension span of the western section of the bridge that connected Yerba Buena Island to the city.

I looked at the view until an impatient driver honked at me and I turned left, heading west toward Alta Park.

I found Monk standing at the appointed spot wearing a baseball cap and sunglasses, his pressed shirt unbuttoned at the collar. His sleeves were carefully rolled up so the cuffs were in the same place on both arms. I'm sure he measured them to be sure. The cuffs were so smooth, there was no doubt that he'd ironed the sleeves after he rolled them up.

He was snapping his fingers and bopping to some imaginary tune as I pulled up to the curb. I rolled down the passenger window.

"That is a brilliant disguise," I said.

Monk opened the door and got in. "The trick to a successful disguise isn't clothes or makeup—it's attitude. You have to embody the character you are portraying."

"What song were you thinking about as you were snapping your fingers?"

"The theme to *Sesame Street*."

"Is that what hippie beatniks listen to?"

"They listen to anything with a beat," Monk said. "That's how they get their niks."

"Kicks," I said.

"I am pretty sure it's niks," he said. "Hence their name."

"You would know," I said. "You're much more plugged into the hippie beatnik scene than I am."

"To be honest, most of what I know about hippie beatniks I got from *Dragnet*." He buttoned his collar. "Do you have any evidence gloves in your purse?"

"There's a box in the glove compartment, of course," I said. "Why do you need them?"

"I want to tuck in my shirt," he said.

I decided not to pursue that line of questioning any further. He got a pair of gloves and slipped them on as I drove.

"Where's Julie?" he asked.

"She's at home," I said. "Looking for a job."

"I hope I'm not going to make you late for your flight by asking you to take me to Ellen's," he said.

I shifted a bit in my seat. "I think I've found a woman who can replace Julie as your assistant."

"You didn't have to do that," Monk said, tucking in his shirt.

"I wanted to be sure you're well taken care of," I said.

"Have you met her?"

"I have," I said.

"Is she clean and presentable?"

"She is," I said.

"What are her qualifications?"

"Considering that your first two assistants were a nurse and a bartender, this one is a real step up," I said. "She's got experience in law enforcement."

"Sounds intriguing," Monk said, carefully peeling off his gloves. "Tell me more."

"She's an ex-cop," I said.

"From here?"

"From back east," I said. "And here's the best part: Before she joined the force, she spent ten years working for a famous detective."

Monk turned his head and looked at me. "Are you sure she wants to work for me?"

"She doesn't want to work for you," I said.

"Now I'm confused," Monk said.

"She wants to be your partner," I said. "If you agree to work with her, she'll apply for a gun permit and get a PI license."

"Would she still drive me to crime scenes, take me to the grocery store, and pick up my dry cleaning?"

"I think she would," I said.

"Would she answer my phone and maintain my schedule?"

"Most likely," I said.

"Would she help me organize my silverware and label the items in my refrigerator?"

"Hell no," I said.

"Would she take me to see my psychiatrist?"

"She will, but the relationship that you'll have with her is going to be different from those with your past assistants, mainly because she won't be your assistant. She will be your partner."

Monk nodded, found a small evidence baggie in the glove compartment, and put his used gloves into them. "Does she have any references?"

"She comes highly recommended by the chief of police of Summit, New Jersey."

"He's a good man," Monk said.

"But I wouldn't call him just yet," I said. "He's a little upset with her right now."

"I can imagine," Monk said. "When can she start?"

"Immediately," I said.

We drove for a while in silence. And when Monk spoke again, he sounded a little choked up. I know that I was.

"I've missed you, Natalie."

"I've missed you, too, Mr. Monk."

"It didn't feel like home here anymore without you."

"You've lived in that apartment for decades," I said. "It hasn't changed one bit."

"But I have," he said. "I've learned that home isn't the place where you live—it's the people that you have in your life."

I nodded. "I need you in mine."

"Very true," he said. "You were a mess until I came along."

"Hey, I'm not the one who desperately needed help," I said. "You hired me as your full-time assistant, remember?"

"Only to rescue you from the squalid life you were leading," he said.

*"Squalid?"*

"It means dirty, wretched, and poverty stricken," he said.

"I know what it means," I said. "If you were so worried about my living in poverty, you would have paid me more."

"I was your employer, not your sugar daddy."

*"Sugar daddy?"*

"It's a man who—," he began.

"I know what it means," I said, interrupting him. "You do know I carry a gun now, right?"

"I hope you know how to clean it," Monk said. "Because if you treat it anything like your house, there's probably a filthy sock stuck in the barrel."

God, it was good to be home.